RESIDUUM

GHOSTS OF SOUTHAMPTON BOOK 2

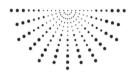

ID JOHNSON

Copyright © 2018 by ID Johnson

All rights reserved.

No part of this book may be reproduced in any form or by any electronic or mechanical means, including information storage and retrieval systems, without written permission from the author, except for the use of brief quotations in a book review.

Cover by The Graphics Shed

✿ Created with Vellum

For all the survivors, those who have overcome the odds and made their way in the world despite any obstacle that comes their way.

PROLOGUE

"The water was so cold, little crystals of ice immediately formed atop anything and everything that crested the surface. The sensations below weren't any better, however. It was as if a thousand tiny pins were plunged into my flesh all at the same time. Even through my leather shoes, my coat. It didn't matter; so I took them off. The entire Atlantic Ocean was already pulling me down. I didn't need anything else hastening my journey to the abyss."

The man in the brown leather chair cleared his throat and adjusted his spectacles. "And then what do you remember next?"

There was a long pause of consideration as thoughts fought to both spring to the surface and hide deep in the recesses of his mind. At last, a sentence was formulated. "I didn't have a lot of time to decide what to do. There'd been plenty of chances, mind you, to climb into one of the lifeboats. I'd declined. Even though I'd been below deck and had seen what it was like down there, had seen the water crawling up the walls, lapping up the staircase, one concrete step at a time, I suppose even then it was difficult to wrap my mind around what was actually happening. But I was determined not to take the seat of another, particularly a mother or child. And though I had given great consideration to what I might do when I inevitably found myself in the Atlantic, my plan wasn't as developed as I would've liked."

"You say you had a plan though?"

"Not really. I suppose I'd like to think I had one, that I would come up with something spectacular at the last moment to save myself. That's what I'd reassured everyone else, all those who beckoned me aboard the lifeboats with them. In retrospect, it wouldn't have mattered to the hundreds of women and children who ended up in the ocean if I had climbed inside a lifeboat. No one else filled those seats. Hundreds of empty seats. Did you see that? In the papers?"

He glanced up from his notes. "I did. I read it later, after the reports were filed."

"Right. So, here I was trying to be... heroic or chivalrous, I suppose. It turned out my efforts were wasted, and I ended up dying because of it. Momentarily, anyhow." He remembered what it had been like to slip away and then come crashing back to his own existence and pushed those thoughts aside, returning to his previous trajectory. "I believe there's another word one might use to describe my actions in turning down a perfectly good lifeboat."

He scratched his balding head beside a thin line of light brown hair touched with gray. "And what word might that be?"

"Foolish."

There was a "hmmm" sound in response, which was neither an agreement nor a disagreement. "So once you were in the water, what happened then? Do you remember exactly?"

The words were having difficulty placing themselves in the correct order again. It took a moment of forced introspection. "I had intended to find something that would float. I assumed a ship with that much lumber aboard—deck chairs, tables, doors, what have you— would have enough debris to easily find something I could mount and wait. I was under the impression that the lifeboats would come back —the half-empty ones for certain. It made little sense to me to think that those people, the thousand or so who had made it safely aboard a life vessel--would sit idly by. I assumed it would only be a matter of moments before there was a rescue party, if you will. I also remembered seeing a light on the horizon before we went under. I thought this other ship would be our salvation. It turns out I was mistaken in all of my optimistic assumptions.

"In answer to your inquiry, however, there really is no order of things, no chronological account I can replicate for you. There was no time. Curious souls often ask me how long it took for the rescue boat—that's what they like to call it, which I find quite ironic—the rescue boat to come back and begin to check to see who was still alive. I can't answer that question, honestly. It was an eternity. It was the blink of an eye. I can't precisely tell you what happened after I found myself completely submerged in the Atlantic. Nothing happened. Everything happened. All at the same time."

There was a long pause as the thin man in the upright leather chair seemed to ponder how to proceed. "Can you describe how you felt?"

He pushed the palm of his hand into one eye socket, pressing hard enough to feel an ache before running his hand through his brown hair and straightening the hem of his jacket. He cleared his throat. "I felt like I was going to die. My body was both on fire and frozen solid at the same time. It's hard to describe, but at some point, the human body becomes so cold it burns. I had the fleeting thought that there were three choices that lay before me, and I didn't truly have any options because there was no time to weigh the potential outcomes. I only had time to react."

"What were the choices?"

"The first one was to fight—to swim as fast as I could in any direction; it really didn't seem to matter which. Thrash about, try to make a headway in one bearing or another. I couldn't see any of the lifeboats, so there was no sense in attempting to reach one, but swimming would be action, and action seemed to be an option.

"The next was to do nothing. To stay perfectly still and allow the ocean to take me, as she so clearly wanted to do. As I said, I could feel her pulling me. It wasn't the suction created by the ship or some such rubbish would-be scientists will try to explain in their overly-wordy, overly-educated statements. It was the ocean itself. She wanted me, wanted all of us, and her lapping waves were an invitation to let go of everything I'd ever known before and simply cease to exist."

He went quiet again, and the man across the room seemed perplexed as to whether or not he should issue another prompt or simply wait. He tried the latter for a lengthy while, and then, just as his thin lips parted to probe, the story was continued.

"The third option never really existed. I just thought it might. I thought there was a chance that I could employ the same tactic I had every other time I'd been in such a precarious situation, sure of nothing but certain death. It didn't work this time, however."

"What tactic is that?" he asked, squinting behind his thin-rimmed glasses.

The answer came more quickly than expected. "Wake up."

The inquisitor absorbed the answer and then gave one short nod of the head. "I see," he said quietly, as if it had never occurred to him that a person might even think that was an option. "I suppose it makes sense one might assume, under the circumstances, they must be having a dream."

"A nightmare," he corrected.

"Indeed."

"Once I realized that my preferred escape method was not a true possibility, a parade of familiar faces skirted through my mind, people I wished to see again, and I began to look around for an alternative. That's when I saw the collapsible lifeboat."

"About how far away do you think it was?"

"In truth, not far at all. At that point, it didn't matter, however. Any sort of movement whatsoever was excruciating. All of my joints had frozen stiff after just a few minutes in the water. It could've been a hand's breadth away and reaching it would've been nearly impossible. I'd say, it was less than ten yards' distance. It may as well have been floating up next to the mocking moon which didn't even bother to show its face."

"And yet, you were able to reach the collapsible, eventually."

"I was. I'm sure I don't know how. When I started out on my journey, there was quite a commotion surrounding the upturned vessel as those nearby struggled to gain traction and buoyancy. By the time of my arrival, everyone was much more... still. Some were grasping hold with all their might. Others slipped below the surface and were not strong enough to recover from the siren call of the abyss. There was no helping them, no matter how badly the others wished they could assist. At that point, it truly was every man for himself."

"You were able to find a spot somehow, and to grab hold?"

"Somehow," he agreed. He began to strum his fingers on the arm of the couch intermittently, as if typing out a message using Morse Code.

"And you've no idea how long you were there, you say?"

"No." The answer came quickly, unlike all of the other words that refused to form coherent sentences.

"Do you remember being plucked from the water, then? When the lifeboats finally returned?"

"No." Equally as easily accessible. "I don't remember anything again until after I awoke on *Carpathia*." He was quiet for a very long time again, before he reconsidered his statement. "That's not true. I do remember something else." His voice was soft now, just above a whisper, and the man across the room leaned forward in his chair, straining to hear. "It's the true reason I'm here."

"What's that?"

The strumming stopped, and he looked up, a shift in his countenance. "The photographs in my mind are one thing. I see their faces. That's... troubling. It's not the worst of it. But every time I close my eyes, I distinctly see each of them. A woman with short, curly hair. A man with some sort of wrap on his head, his face frozen in anguish. Literally frozen. A little boy, maybe six, clinging to a woman I presumed to be his mother. A baby wrapped in layers of blankets and nestled between an arm stiff with frost and a bosom that would never feed the child again. Their faces are haunting, and they are everywhere. Despite that daily terror, it isn't the worst."

"It isn't? What is it then? What could possibly be worse than seeing the faces of the dead everywhere you look?"

"Dr. Morgan, have you ever considered the different definitions for the word 'drown'?"

The question seemed to take him aback, and he scooted his shoulders into the chair. "No, I can't honestly say that I have."

"I looked it up in the dictionary because I was curious as to precisely what it might say. It's such an interesting word. It doesn't quite roll off the tongue, does it? Drown. *Drown. Drowning.* It sounds almost as morbid as the meaning behind it. The latter definition is almost as unsettling as the first, though, when you think about it. You can't just stick to the first definition, mind you, doctor. You have to read them all. 'To die under water of liquid or other suffocation.' Yes, of course, we all know that one. We were all trying so hard to avoid it that night, though I'm not sure any of us thought of the true cause of death—freezing. Nevertheless, the Atlantic that night was full of over two thousand persons trying hard not to succumb to the first definition of the word drown.

"If you'll read further, however, my good man, you'll come up with another definition. 'To overwhelm as if to render inaudible, as by a louder sound.' Dr. Morgan, since I've arrived back in New York City, I've heard all sorts of loud sounds. Whistles, horns, people shouting, doors slamming, music playing. Some of them startle me because I now have a new association with each of them. I can't describe what happened the time I heard the loud popping sound of a firecracker exploding, much like the distress signal that was fired off that night. But one thing that still eludes me, Dr. Morgan, is the second part of that definition—a *louder* sound, one that renders the original sound inaudible."

"I'm not sure I know exactly what you mean."

"It's quite simple, really, Dr. Morgan. I've come here, I continue to come here, because I'm hoping that you can help me extinguish, or otherwise drown out the constant noise I'm hearing, not with my ears, but with my mind. Not just while I'm sleeping but even when I'm awake. It never stops. It's there all the time. And, Dr. Morgan, while I'm quite certain that a psychiatrist of your caliber is just as capable as anyone in the world at helping me with this problem, I must admit I'm afraid it might be a lost cause."

"Why do you say that, Mr. Ashton?"

"Because, Dr. Morgan, it's been nearly six months since *Titanic* sank, and I still hear them. I still hear the screams, the wails, the cries for help. I still hear the thrashing sound of two thousand people desperately trying to survive, trying to accept option one and fight for their lives, for the ones they loved, many of which were right there with them, freezing to death, being dragged under by the pull of the Atlantic. I'm afraid, Dr. Morgan, that I've reached the startling conclusion that, despite the irony of the word itself, there's no helping my situation. Quite frankly, kind sir, I'm of the opinion that nothing drowns out the sound of drowning."

Dr. Laurie Morgan was silent for some time, taking in the statement his patient had so decidedly declared, not sure how to respond. Eventually, he cleared his throat, and taking off his spectacles, he picked up a cleaning cloth from his desk beside him and began to carefully clean the lenses. "Mr. Ashton..." he began.

"I've told you, doctor. Please, call me Charlie."

"Right. Charlie, I do think there is an answer, that we will find a way to make the noises stop, or at least lessen. I understand you've been through the sort of traumatic experience only a few people can identify with. However, I believe if we continue to work together, we will eventually see results, and you'll begin to feel much better, particularly now that I have this information."

Charlie ran a hand through his hair and let out a deep sigh. He wanted to believe the doctor. He'd already made some progress in the few months they had been working together, but he didn't know for sure if there was any solution. Today had been a bit of a breakthrough

ID JOHNSON

in that he was able to tell the doctor precisely what it was that was still troubling him. Choosing to be optimistic, he nodded, and reaching over next to him on the lounger he refused to lie on, he grabbed his hat before standing. Dr. Morgan rose out of his chair and stepped forward, and Charlie had to tip his head and peer down at the much shorter man. "Thank you for your time, doctor." He extended his hand, and the doctor shook it. "I will see you next week."

"Thank you, Charlie," Dr. Morgan replied. "Yes, next week. I hope to work on finding some answers then."

Charlie nodded and forced a smile, thinking that might be all but impossible. He headed for the office door, and waving goodbye, he let himself out. The receptionist, an older woman with graying hair, smiled at him, and Charlie wished her a good day before making his way down and out of the office building into the busy streets of New York where, amidst a crowd of thousands, he felt just as alone as he had when he'd been floating in a sea of faces in the frigid Atlantic.

CHAPTER ONE

April 18, 1912

The silence was deafening. There had to be over a thousand people on the deck surrounding Meg as she peered off into the distance at New York City as it grew larger, but no one seemed to be saying a word. Only the gentle pitter patter of raindrops as they hit the metal railings and the sodden wooden planking broke the torturous sound of nothing ringing in her ears.

She still wore the same white shirtwaist and plaid skirt the stewardess, the one who had been so helpful when they'd first come aboard three days ago, was able to find for her, but she wasn't much worried about how she looked. Her hair was pinned up more to keep it out of her way, but she had noticed it was starting to fall out, and she tried not to touch it for fear her hand would pull away a fresh clump.

For three days, she and Jonathan had taken turns sitting alongside Charlie's bed. He was lucid at times, very much aware of where he was, of who he was. Other times, he had no idea. He could hardly recognize his own name. The doctors had been giving him something

—what it was she couldn't be certain—but it was supposed to help him stay calm. It worked to a degree, but there were instances when he awoke from a restless sleep screaming, and Meg would do her best to try to calm him, though it was impossible as those were the times when he was least likely to know who she was. The nurses would come and give him another dose of whatever it was, and the cycle would repeat itself. Though Meg was assured this was the case with many of the passengers who'd been plucked from the water, knowing the despair was shared did not make it any easier.

When he'd first returned from the dead, she thought everything would be fine. The doctor had said he might have some frostbite and could potentially lose a toe or the tip of a finger. She didn't expect him to be so mentally altered. Jonathan assured her it was due to the trauma of being in the water for so long, and he was quite confident the old Charlie would be back soon. Meg believed that at first, but three days seemed like forever, and now she didn't know what to think.

Jonathan had sent a wire to Mr. and Mrs. Ashton to let them know Charlie was alive, but he wasn't specific. There were so many messages going in and out, it was difficult to get anything sent at all. Rumor had it that part of the reason *Titanic* had hit the iceberg in the first place was because the wireless officers had disregarded dozens of warnings from other ships as they sent out messages from passengers. Clearly, this group of entitled individuals each felt the message they needed to send was more important than anyone else's, and it made Meg angry to think of the lives that were lost at least partially due to this privilege.

Meg had wondered if Charlie's parents had even known he was aboard *Titanic*. Jonathan said he didn't think so, but they still might wonder if they hadn't heard from him for several days. Word of the disaster would've reached them by now, and Jonathan wasn't sure if Charlie had sent them a message earlier in the trip to let them know he was on his way back. Meg was well aware that Charlie's stay in

Southampton was initially supposed to be much longer, but then, she'd gone and ruined all that.

Her own mother and uncle would have no way of knowing she was aboard *Titanic* unless Madeline Astor told them, and since she had heard that the young woman's husband did not make it off *Titanic*, she doubted Madeline would concern herself with Meg. Therefore, Mildred and Bertram Westmoreland would still be wondering what had happened to their respective daughter and niece. It might cross their minds that she had boarded *Titanic*, but they probably wouldn't think it too likely unless they happened to see Kelly and Daniel O'Connell's names aboard the list of rescued. She wondered if her mother would even bother to look for their names. For that matter, she wondered if her mother would even bother to look for her daughter's name. At any rate, she wouldn't be sending any messages to her family to let them know she had survived.

Her name was listed as Meg West, Third Class Passenger, and in many ways, that's who she felt she was at this point. Her clothing matched the description. Her family now consisted of the woman who'd been her servant in Southampton but also been her best friend, along with her husband and their two small girls. Charlie was another matter entirely; if he didn't come around to himself, would he even be compelled to honor the arrangement he had to marry Mary Margaret Westmoreland? He had proclaimed to Meg that he loved her and wanted to marry her, but once he had some time to decide which Charlie he wanted to be, perhaps he might change his mind. Or perhaps he would have little choice in the matter, and the Charlie who had loved her would be just as lost once they landed in New York as he had been when he slipped away from her for those few minutes right after they'd been reunited aboard *Carpathia*.

There were so many possibilities, and she'd spent the better part of three days attempting to sort them all out in her mind. Now, with the shoreline looming in the distance and the certainty that they would soon dock, she needed to consider what her next step would be. Perhaps it was the arguing of her own thoughts that made the silence amongst her shipmates so overwhelmingly loud.

"Meg," a quiet voice said behind her, and she turned to see Jonathan Lane standing there, a concerned expression on his face. He almost always wore a black bowler hat, which covered all but patches of his dark hair, graying at his temples. He was still wearing the same suit he'd had on when they'd boarded the lifeboats three days ago. Spending countless hours sitting next to Charlie, wandering the decks looking for any sort of mental release, and sleeping in it had left the suit wrinkled, and Meg likened her own emotions to a crumpled black suit that no longer fit properly or served its original purpose.

"Is Charlie all right?" It was the first thing that came to her mind when she saw him standing out here, away from his employer's bed. One of them had been with Charlie the entire time. Now, neither of them was there, which sent waves of panic through her insides.

"He's fine," Jonathan assured her. "They're getting him ready to transfer. The doctor wants him taken straight to the hospital as soon as we arrive. They thought it best that we all step out while they do so."

Meg nodded and took a deep breath. Worry that something might happen to Charlie was a constant state of mind for her now, with these spikes in panic each time something else presented itself as evidence that he might not be all right, and her heart would be happy when there was no more reason to suspect the worst. "Was he awake when you left?"

"He was," Jonathan confirmed, stepping up to lean against the wet railing beside her. There was no sense in attempting to stay dry at this point, and Meg had given up hours ago, though she did have a shawl wrapped around her shoulders. "He asked about you. He wanted to know if you were planning to go to the hospital with him, and I said I'd ask."

She swallowed a lump in her throat. "He didn't even know who I was when he awoke this morning. I had to remind him. Again."

"I know," Jonathan said, adjusting his hat. "I believe his memory loss is due to the medication, Meg. They've been sedating him heav-ily. I think, once he sees his family again, once he's home, his own doctor won't press such high doses of medication on him, then his memory will start to come around again."

Wanting to believe his words and knowing they were true were different matters, and Meg began to slowly shake her head. "All we can do is try, I suppose," she said, her voice just a hoarse whisper.

"Will you go with him then? I'm not certain where we might find his parents, and I thought it might be best if I attempt to track them down while you accompany him to the hospital. There's bound to be hundreds, if not thousands, of people waiting when we get off at the pier. Reporters, photographers, family members who've yet to hear anything, people who simply want to gawk at us, as if our pain is nothing but a sideshow at a circus."

Meg stared at him in wonder; none of those things had occurred to her, except for the bereaved families, of course. "Do you think so?" she asked, pursing her lips together.

Jonathan nodded. "I heard Ismay sent a message to the White Star Line to let them know what transpired. That alone would be enough to alert the newspapers. Who knows what others are sending over the wire. There will be plenty of people awaiting our arrival."

They were nearly at the docks now. Meg could see the Statue of Liberty, but she didn't stare at it. So many times she had imagined what it would be like to approach New York Harbor by boat, having gained her freedom from her abusive mother and uncle. She had envisioned that lady with the torch symbolizing a new life for her, but now, with Charlie injured possibly beyond repair, and so many widowed women, fatherless children, and lost souls standing around her, looking up at the statue and dreaming of renewal seemed scur-rilous. Averting her eyes and choosing not to acknowledge it at all seemed like a more respectable thing to do.

"He wants you with him, Meg," Jonathan repeated, drawing her attention back to his face. "You'll go, won't you?"

"Yes, of course," Meg replied. She didn't want to. She wanted to blend in with the throng of people exiting the boat, to put her head down and melt into them, disappearing into the New York night. Where she might go after that, she wasn't sure. Perhaps a boarding house or a shelter of some sort. Would White Star even provide these people who had nowhere to go a place to sleep tonight? It was nearly 10:00 PM. What about the children who had no parents? She realized Jonathan was speaking and tried to concentrate on the reality of what was about to happen to her, not the Meg in her mind who was bold and carefree—perhaps careless—who would be willing to step off of a ship and into a world she'd only dreamt of as if she hadn't a care in the world.

"They said you could wait outside of his door, and they'd let you walk out with them. It might be a while. They're going to let all of the *Carpathia* passengers off first."

Meg only nodded, her mind still darting between scenarios.

"I believe we've passed the pier we should've docked at, though," Jonathan muttered, reaching up on his tiptoes to look out over the water, as if that might somehow help. "I'm going to go and see what might be happening. I'll come find you when I know more."

"All right," she managed.

"Do you know where Kelly and Daniel are?" he asked.

"No. Daniel said you gave him an address?"

"I did. It's a boarding house where many of our workers live until they can find more suitable accommodations. I told him to go there and let them know I sent them. They'll be safe for the night, and then once I speak to Mr. Ashton, we can decide where to place them permanently."

She wasn't exactly sure what that meant—permanently—but she nodded in agreement. At least Kelly and the girls would be safe. Daniel's arm would be in a cast for another couple of months, but Charlie had assured the Irishman he would find him work at the factory. At least Jonathan would be able to guarantee that promise even if Charlie was in the hospital for weeks... or longer.

"Meg," Jonathan said, taking her gently by the arms and peering into her eyes. "Everything will be all right. I promise you."

She nodded again, thinking she was acting like she was the one who'd been given some sort of magic elixir.

"I'll see you in a bit." He smiled at her reassuringly and then let her go, blending into the crowd and disappearing.

Meg took another deep breath then turned in the direction that would take her to Charlie's makeshift hospital room. She had no idea where she'd lay her head that night, but she was hopeful that, wherever it was, when she awoke, she'd see things much more clearly.

Jonathan Lane made his way through the crowds to find a porter or an officer who looked like he might know what was going on. There was one in particular who had been a constant force of good information, and he knew if he was able to find Briggins he'd know precisely why *Carpathia* had passed the Cunard piers.

He found the officer where he expected to, over near where the lifeboats from *Titanic* were being stored. He was giving directions as the lifeboats were being shifted about on the deck. The man saw Jonathan coming and offered a small smile of recognition. Jonathan was a master at finding out what he needed without troubling anyone or making his existence exhausting. "Briggins," he called out as he approached. "Do you happen to know where we are headed?"

"New York Harbor," the older man said with a chuckle. He looked tired and the laugh was forced. The entire crew of *Carpathia* had been worked to the bone these past three days, and Jonathan hoped White Star would find a way to compensate them for their work.

"I know that," Jonathan replied. "Where about?"

He shouted a direction to one of the crewmen before he turned back to Jonathan. "We're going to drop these lifeboats at White Star first, pier 59. Then, we'll go back to 54."

Jonathan's forehead crinkled. "Really?" he asked, as if he might have misunderstood. "Seems peculiar."

"Not sure the thinking," Briggins replied. "But we're getting them ready to unload as quickly as possible. We know there are a lot of people ready for this voyage to be over."

The phrase made Jonathan's gut tighten. It had ended abruptly for two-thirds of *Titanic's* passengers. He knew Briggins hadn't meant it that way. "Thanks for letting me know," he said. "Your crew has been nothing but accommodating."

"It's the least we could do," Briggins said, his smile morphing from good-natured to sympathetic. "How's Charlie?"

Briggins knew that Jonathan had a friend who was ill; he didn't know it was the millionaire Charles Ashton and that Jonathan was actually his liegeman. There seemed no reason for an elaborate explanation when all Jonathan needed at the time was information. "He's doing better," Jonathan said. "They're taking him straight to the hospital once we arrive."

"I believe they intend to get the *Carpathia* passengers off first," Briggins explained. "The captain thinks it will be less of a spectacle that way. Not sure what the plan is for transporting the sick and injured after that."

Jonathan had already heard that the original *Carpathia* passengers would be getting off first, but he was glad for the confirmation. "I'm sure they'll take care of them. So far, the doctors and nurses have done an excellent job of caring for Charlie and the others."

Briggins nodded in agreement. "Well, if I don't see you again, Jonathan ol' boy, it was nice to meet you," the officer said, offering his hand.

Jonathan shook it. "It was nice to meet you as well. Thanks again for your help." Briggins nodded, and Jonathan turned to get out of the way as they neared the pier. Why they thought the lifeboats needed to be removed first was beyond him, but he knew there must be a reason. He made his way back toward the hospital room, hoping Meg would be there. She'd been acting peculiar the last two days, and he was beginning to grow suspicious of her again. There was more going on with Miss Westmoreland than met the eye.

She was standing about where he expected her to be. Her hair looked more like a contained bird's nest than the beautiful blonde tresses she'd worn the other night when she'd accompanied Charlie to dinner in the First Class dining hall—a million years ago, five days ago. The outfit she had on fit her even more poorly than the clothes she'd been wearing that belonged to Kelly, who was taller and a bit shapelier. She stood wringing her hands, crossing and uncrossing her arms, taking two steps one way and then two steps the other way, leaning against the wall, standing. Clearly, the young girl had a lot on her mind.

Jonathan did as well, but he continued to push it aside and compartmentalize it, as he had always done. He knew eventually he would have to face his own fear and regret, the realization that he had lived while others had died, that he had occupied a seat one of those frozen women or children could have sat in. The rationalization that there hadn't been anyone else around to take that spot was neither here nor there. Now wasn't the time to ponder such possibilities, however. He had a job to do—the same one he'd been doing for years. Charlie needed him, and even though at that particular moment it meant leaving him, he'd still do his best to facilitate a safe transition for Charlie back to solid ground.

"Meg?" he said, waiting for her to acknowledge his presence. It took her a moment as her back was to him, as it had been earlier. Eventually she turned, and he could see recognition in her eyes, though they were having trouble focusing on his face. She reminded him a bit of a skittish rabbit, and he wondered if she was about to bound off in the opposite direction in an attempt to flee for her life. "Are you all right?"

"Yes," she said. "They haven't opened the door. You said to wait here, didn't you?"

"I did," he assured her. "I found out we're going to unload the lifeboats from *Titanic* first, and then we'll return to the Cunard pier."

She nodded, that distant look in her eyes starting to narrow so that she appeared to be with him again. "That seems... peculiar."

"I agree. But that is what we are doing. And then, you'll get off with Charlie, and I'll get off and go find Mr. and Mrs. Ashton."

Another nod, this one more forceful. "And Kelly and Daniel will take the little girls and go to the address you gave them?"

"Precisely."

"Have they any money? Do you know?"

"I gave Daniel a few bills. He said he had managed to grab a little of what they had before he got off of the boat."

Meg nodded again. "I don't suppose I'll need anything."

The thought hadn't crossed his mind. He assumed Charlie had his wallet with the rest of the few belongings that had come out of the water with him, which would mean he had money, but there was a chance Meg might need something, and she had absolutely nothing of her own with her. Not a thing. Reaching for his own wallet, he said, "Here, let me give you a few dollars, just in case."

"Oh, no, that's all right," she said gesturing with her hands as if to push the money he held out away from her. "I don't think I'll need it for anything."

"It's only twenty. I don't have much more than that on me. Take it, Meg."

She looked at the money and up at his face before taking a step back. "I don't think that's a good idea, Jonathan," she said.

His eyebrows arched. "Why ever not? You might need to buy something to eat or pay for a cab."

She shook her head again. "No. If I do, I'll just... I don't know what I'll do, but I don't want to take it."

"Meg, it's not anything to worry about. This is less than pocket change to Charlie."

"I know," she said. "It's not that."

"What is it, then?"

She looked at the money, at him, and then off in the distance before returning her blue eyes to his face. "I'm afraid... if I take it... I might... run away."

He was shocked. He had no idea what to say. It made sense, though. She truly was a frightened rabbit. He managed a weak smile. "Meg, you're not going to run away. You've already done that." He winked at her, but she didn't seem to think it was a joking matter. Pressing the money into her hand, he said, "Take it in case you need it, Meg. You're not going to abandon Charlie. You are a brave and industrious soul. You would never leave Charlie while he's in the hospital. I know it's frightening. You're in a new place surrounded by strangers with nothing of your own. But I'll be there as quickly as I can."

She took the money and shoved it into her pocket, as if she wanted to forget it was there. "What do you think Charlie's parents will say when they meet me? Do they know... what I did?"

"No, they don't know anything, as far as I know. Frankly, they won't even know you're you, unless you tell them. I have no idea what Charlie's plan is as far as letting them know the pair of you have chosen to stay together. For that matter, I don't even know if you are planning to stay Mary Margaret Westmoreland once you reach New York City. Or will you be Meg West?"

Her eyes were darting around again, and it took her a moment to answer. Finally, with a gulp, she said, "I guess that makes two of us. Jonathan, I have no idea who I am either."

Taking a step forward, he pulled her against his chest and patted her back. "It will be all right, Meg. The important thing is that we are all alive and together. We will help each other figure out what comes next. For now, we'll see if Charlie is up to explaining things to them. If not, I'll just tell them you're Meg and leave it at that. If you decide you want to explain, you can, and if not, be Meg West for as long as you need to be."

She pulled away, nodding. "I don't want my mother to know. I already reminded Kelly. If anyone should happen to ask her about me, she's to tell them she doesn't know if I was on *Titanic* or not, and that for all she knows, I'm somewhere in Southampton. I don't think anyone will realize she was my lady in waiting, but should they ask, she won't give away any clues to my mother that I'm alive."

Jonathan nodded. "That makes sense to me, Meg." The boat wasn't moving anymore, and he realized they'd reached the first port, pier 59. He tried not to think about the alternate reality where *Titanic* was pulling into port instead of *Carpathia*, or that John Jacob Astor, Ben Guggenheim, and so many others should be finishing up their brandies preparing to escort their wives and lovers off of the ship. It would do no good to dwell on those thoughts.

Meg seemed to notice the stop as well. Her eyes widened. "We've arrived."

"I hope so," Jonathan muttered. "I hope so."

CHAPTER TWO

Every time Charlie opened his eyes, he had to stop and think about where he was supposed to be. It never quite added up to him. Occasionally, a face he did not know would be next to his bed. Sometimes it was a nurse or doctor. Sometimes it was someone he was meant to know. This time, he knew he was aboard *Carpathia*. He was aware that he had died, but now he was alive. He did not see anyone he knew, and the people scurrying about in his room were all dressed as if they were medical professionals. If any of them noticed he was awake, they didn't acknowledge him as they shouted orders to each other about preparing the gurney, whatever that meant.

Eventually, an older woman with her brown hair done up underneath a cap said, "Oh, Mr. Ashton, you're back with us. Good. Are you in any pain?"

"No," he replied. "A sip of water would be nice, though." Sometimes he felt capable of moving his arms and other times he knew any such sort of requirement could be a disaster.

"We are in New York," she explained. "You will be transferred to a local hospital. An ambulance will meet us at the pier."

All of that made perfect sense to him, but it did not help the scratchiness in his throat or the fact that his tongue felt thick and sticky. "Might I have a drink before we go?" he asked.

She looked a bit annoyed, as if she was in the middle of something quite important and couldn't pause for a few seconds to raise the glass he could still see next to the bed to his lips. With a sigh, she did it, however, and though he didn't quite get enough down to make the sandpaper feeling go away, it was better than nothing.

Once she'd set the glass back down and returned to her important task, he asked, "Where's Meg?"

"She's waiting in the hall," the woman replied. "She'll accompany you."

Charlie nodded. He wondered what was so complicated that it was taking them so much work to get him ready for an ambulance, but he didn't ask. A few minutes into the ordeal, a man he didn't recognize wheeled in a gurney, which the nurses went about preparing with sheets, and he decided watching them was only making his head hurt, so he closed his eyes.

When he opened his eyes again, he knew he was on dry land. The rocking sensation he'd been feeling for more days than he could count had declined substantially, though from time to time he still felt as if he were swaying just a bit. He was staring up at a stark white ceiling. At first he heard absolutely nothing—not the ticking of a clock, the pounding of feet in the hallway, the labored breathing of a restless soul nearby, nothing. The silence was calming for the few moments that it lasted. But then, he began to hear screaming, thrashing, clawing, begging, and he shot up in the bed, looking around for the source of the torment.

"Charlie? Are you all right?" A petite woman with blonde, wavy hair and blue eyes rose from a chair just a foot or so away from his bedside. She was dressed in the simple clothes of an immigrant from the European mainland, the same type of outfit he'd seen crossing the Atlantic many times, but her accent sounded English. She was beautiful, but her eyes showed concern. Somehow, clearly, she knew his name, but he couldn't place her.

The woman took another step forward. "Do you need the doctor?" she asked, her voice quivering a bit. "Or some water?"

Attempting to calm his racing heart, Charlie glanced around the room again and saw that the source of the screaming must not be nearby. Perhaps, if he was in a hospital as he suspected, it was coming from another room. "What's that noise?" he asked, trying to keep his voice even.

She let out a small sigh. "There is no noise, Charlie, darling. It's in your head. You're still hearing the people in the water. Take some deep breaths, and it will go away. I promise."

At first he thought she must be mad. Of course there was a noise, plenty of noises. But when she mentioned people in the water, then it came back to him. Pressing the heels of his palms into his eyes, Charlie took several deep breaths.

"Here, take a sip of this water," she suggested, lifting the glass from beside the bed to him. "It usually helps as well."

He did as she recommended. The water was lukewarm, but it did help the dryness in his throat. She was holding the glass for him, but he soon took it out of her hand and drained it. Once it was empty, she took it back and set it down on the table, looking at him expectantly.

"Thank you," he said, readjusting the blankets and leaning back. The noises faded, though he could still hear them if he let his mind focus on them. He tried not to do that.

Returning his attention to the woman, he thought perhaps they'd had a shortage of nurses with so many people being injured. Possibly this woman had volunteered. Maybe she had been a nurse in her home country. She looked nice, though worried. She continued to stand by the side of his bed, that same expectant look on her face, and he wondered if there was something else he was forgetting to say.

Before he had a chance to ask, the door to the small room opened, and another woman, this one much plumper and older, dressed completely in white came in. "Aw, Mr. Ashton. I see that you're awake. How are you feeling?"

"I'm all right," he managed, glancing from one woman to the

other. He wasn't sure what to make of the situation. Why would he need two nurses?

"That's good to hear," she replied, though her no-nonsense expression didn't change. She went about checking the room and bed to make sure nothing was out of line and then looked at a piece of paper he assumed was his medical information. "Do you need the bedpan?" she asked.

Charlie felt his face flush. "No, thank you," he replied, and since she'd asked, he did distinctly remember having had to use one of those recently, which wasn't the most dignified experience of his life.

"Well, Dr. Hunt examined you while you were sleeping, but I will let him know that you're awake, and he'll make his way in shortly." She cut her eyes at the other woman. "You know you'll have to go when the doctor comes in?"

"Yes, I know," the blonde woman replied, her voice indicating she didn't need the reminder. She crossed her arms. "He's hearing them again."

The nurse's eyes went back to Charlie. "Are you hearing them now, Charlie? The screams?"

Her face indicated that the wrong answer might land him in Belleview. "No, I don't hear anything right now," Charlie replied, ignoring the wails that seemed to whisper to him in the distance.

"Good," she said, and the first smile she'd managed since she came in the room briefly shadowed her face as she gave the blonde another look of annoyance. "The doctor will be in soon." She turned on her heel and made her way the few steps to the door.

The blonde shook her head in disgust. Still looking at the door, she said quietly, "They don't know who I am." She turned her head so that she was looking at Charlie. "I told the stewards who brought you over from *Carpathia* not to tell them but to let them know I am to stay with you until your parents arrive or Jonathan catches up to us."

She looked familiar now, he realized. Asking who she was seemed rude, especially if she knew Jonathan. There must be a way to discover her name and significance without admitting he couldn't remember ever seeing her before. "Are we in New York then?" Charlie asked, thinking perhaps he might gather a clue that way.

"Yes, we disembarked about an hour ago. You're in hospital. I'm not sure the name of it. I know Jonathan will be able to tell you when he arrives. I believe it's the closest one to the port, but he said something earlier about making sure you had the best medical care available, so it's possible he'd already arranged to have you taken elsewhere. I've never been to New York before so I haven't any idea if we went across town or not. It didn't seem far."

She was looking at the small window across the room by the end of her statement, as if she was trying to see New York through the panes, but it was near the ceiling and it was very dark out. Eventually, she dropped her head and unfolded her arms so that her hands were clasped in front of her. Even though he still couldn't place her, he realized, even in this disheveled state, she was quite lovely. Obviously, she was worried about him as well.

"I'm happy to be back in New York," he said quietly. "It really is the most amazing place on Earth. If you've never been here before, you'll want to see everything. Perhaps when I'm feeling better, I can take you to Central Park. There's a zoo there, you know?"

Her blue eyes flittered over to him, and he could see they were glistening. "I know," she said quietly. "Charlie," she took a step in his direction, "have you forgotten who I am again?"

He felt his face flush a bit, though not as deeply as when the other nurse had mentioned the bed pan. What had given him away? "I'm sorry," he admitted, watching her face fall. "I remember very little, actually. I do remember the water." He didn't feel the need to elaborate—to add that the water was freezing, that it was sucking him down into an abyss, that it was alive with screaming souls.

She nodded and swallowed hard enough for him to see it in her elegant neck. "Do you remember what ship you were on? What the ship was called that sank?"

Sank. He hadn't considered that word, but it made sense. Why else would so many people be in the water all at once? And then he remembered—he was aboard a ship that wasn't supposed to be capable of sinking. *"Titanic."* He said the word as if it were a curse, and then looked up at her face. Her nod let him know that he was correct. "It hit an iceberg."

"Yes," the woman replied. "And you decided not to get on a lifeboat because you wanted other people, women and children, to have a chance."

He remembered that as well, now that she mentioned it. Except, they hadn't had a chance. There were plenty of them thrashing around in the water as well. Plenty who stopped thrashing rather quickly.

Before he could elaborate on the thought, she asked another question. "Do you remember where you had been? Before you boarded *Titanic?*"

It wasn't a difficult question. Surely, he knew where he had been. And yet, it took him a moment of consideration. He knew he'd gone to England for... something... and that he was coming home sooner than expected. Why would he need to go to England? Suddenly, he remembered. Flickers of images from a ball crossed his mind, and then a house, an older woman crying. He was angry, embarrassed, about something. He'd told Jonathan he was done and to book passage on the next ship to depart... Southampton.

"Mary Margaret!" The words flew out of his mouth before he had any context for them. A look of relief spread across her face, like he knew everything, though he'd still have to admit all of it was coming back together very slowly, as if he were doing a jigsaw puzzle without benefit of seeing a picture of the completed work beforehand.

"Yes, that's right. You were in Southampton. To see me." A cautious smile adorned her pretty face. "Do you remember me now?"

Something about what she was saying did not quite seem right. He began to slowly shake his head. "No, Mary Margaret Westmoreland. She... we were supposed to meet at a ball, but she didn't show up. She ran away with one of the house boys. I boarded *Titanic* swearing never to have anything to do with her again."

The woman let out a deep sigh and clutched her hair at the roots with both hands. It took her a moment before she let go and turned to face him. "Charlie, I am Mary Margaret. I didn't meet you at the ball, but I explained everything to you while we were aboard *Titanic*. I told you why I didn't go. You understood. We danced together." She took a step toward him. "You kissed me. We fell in love."

He was still shaking his head. There was no question that if what she was saying was true, he would remember it. "No, that's not possible. I will never forgive Mary Margaret Westmoreland."

This time, her exhale was so audible her entire upper body seemed to vibrate. "Charlie, please? We've been over this so many times in the last few days. I am Mary Margaret—Meg. I'm Meg. You do love me. We are getting married." She dropped her eyes to the floor. "Damn, why do they have to insist on giving him that same stupid medicine." She looked back up at him. "Every time they give you that medicine, you forget who I am."

He wasn't quite sure what she was talking about, although his brain did still feel a bit foggy, as if he had recently taken some sort of medication. He had no way of knowing. He did know, for certain, he would never forgive Mary Margaret Westmoreland for what she did. "I'm sorry, miss, but whatever it is you want, I'm afraid I won't be able to help you. If it's money you're after...."

"Charlie!" Her eyes were pleading with him more than her voice. "I don't want your money. I want you." She shook her head. "I know when Jonathan gets here, he will explain all of this to you again, but dammit...."

Before she could complete her sentence, there was a brisk knock at the door, and then it opened without anyone having the opportunity to call out that it was okay for the older gentleman dressed in a white coat to come in. "Aw, Mr. Ashton, you're awake."

That seemed to be the greeting of the day, and Charlie said, "Yes, I believe I am."

He chuckled and scratched the top of his bald head, short tufts of gray hair jutting out around his ears the only evidence that he'd ever had anything at all atop his crown. "I'm Dr. Stephen Hunt. I'll be taking care of you while you're here with us." He looked at Meg. "I'm afraid you'll need to step out now, miss."

"Yes, I know," she replied tartly. She looked at Charlie and shook her head slowly, as if she was exasperated. Returning her attention to the doctor, she continued, "Every time he takes whatever medicine it was they were giving him aboard *Carpathia*, he awakens having no recollection of anything that happened on the boat. If it is at all possible, will you see if there's something else he can take instead—if he still needs a sedative at all?"

"A sedative?" Charlie echoed. "Why would I need a sedative?"

"You've been through quite the traumatic experience, Mr. Ashton," the doctor replied. He had Charlie's paperwork in his hand. He read through a bit and then nodded his head. "Yes, that sort of medication could do that."

"I don't want to be sedated," Charlie said, looking the doctor squarely in the eye.

He forced a smile. "Mr. Ashton, I assume you had some... emotional outbursts while aboard *Carpathia*. It's difficult for people to adjust after such intense experiences."

"Emotional outbursts?" Charlie repeated. Surely, if that had been the case, he would remember.

"It wasn't that so much as... the voices," the woman, Meg, as she called herself, explained, looking at Charlie out of the corner of her eye. "He was hearing screams from people in the water, long after everything was over."

"I'm not hearing anything now, I assure you," Charlie spoke up, looking at her as if she were a classmate who just told the entire class he'd wet his pants. It didn't matter that he actually was hearing screams at that very moment. If the doctor knew, he might well lock Charlie up in an asylum.

"I'm glad to hear that you are feeling better," Dr. Hunt said, smiling at Charlie and then looking at this Meg person again. "It is normal, I assure you," he replied.

She didn't look as if she was willing to accept his definition of normal. "Well, forgetting someone you've known most of your life isn't normal," she muttered. "Dr. Hunt, please do whatever you can to help Charlie, but please don't give him anything else that might alter his memory."

The doctor rested his hand on her arm. "If Mr. Ashton is no longer hearing voices, and he feels well, I don't believe any more of that sort of medication should be in order. Now, if you'll excuse us, miss, I need to examine him in private."

"Of course," she said, glancing back over her shoulder. "I'll see you soon."

The words came out of her mouth as if she was asking a question, and Charlie almost felt compelled to answer. While he didn't know who she was, Jonathan must, and therefore, he assumed he would see her again, so he nodded, and then she walked out the door. He was fairly certain she was wiping tears from her cheeks as she went, though he couldn't tell for sure. Whoever she was, she was pretty and seemed to care about him; he hated to make her cry.

MEG WAS SITTING in a small waiting area near Charlie's private hospital room, attempting to take deep breaths and calm herself when she heard multiple sets of urgent footsteps and looked up to see Jonathan leading an older, well dressed couple, followed by a younger, equally as nicely outfitted couple, and a few servants down the hall. She knew this must be Charlie's family, and her anxiety over Charlie not remembering her morphed into nervousness at the thought of meeting them. She had no idea if they even knew who she was.

As they drew closer, she realized the men had their arms around their wives, as if they wouldn't believe Charlie was alive until they saw him for themselves, and she pushed her own selfish thoughts away. She was certain they had more important matters on their minds than who she was and why she was here.

"How is he?" Jonathan asked as he stopped a few feet away. "Is the doctor in?"

Meg stood, her legs a bit shaky. "Yes. Dr. Hunt is in with him now. He's awake. He's... fairly lucid, though his memory is about how it has been the last several times he's awoken."

Jonathan's shoulders fell, an indication that he understood what she was saying. "It will be all right, Meg," he assured her, and she wanted to believe he was right. He had been right the last few times, after all, but she didn't know how much longer she could play this game. Charlie's emotions ebbed from thinking he hated her to knowing he loved her, and it was growing quite exhausting. She only nodded and bit her lip against saying more.

"You must be Meg." Charlie's father, John Ashton, stepped forward and offered his hand. "It's lovely to meet you. Jonathan told us how you and Charlie became friends aboard the ship."

Meg took his hand, and looked to Jonathan, who simply shrugged. "It's very nice to meet you, sir."

"You must be completely drained," Mrs. Ashton said as she took the same hand Mr. Ashton had just released. "Poor, poor dear."

The differences between Charlie's parents and Meg's own mother left her dumbfounded for a moment. While she had always suspected they must be kinder, more caring, seeing them for the first time, so very concerned not only for their son but for her as well—a complete stranger so far as they knew—it made Meg's heart ache just a bit. She was torn between envy of Charlie's good fortune at having loving parents and pity that he was, nevertheless, the one lying in a hospital bed.

"This is our daughter, Grace Buckner, and her husband, Peter," Mrs. Ashton said, gesturing in the direction of the younger couple.

From the moment Grace's eyes met hers, Meg knew Charlie's older sister was suspect of her some way or another. Though she took her hand and said, "It's nice to meet you," Meg could see that she didn't mean it, and she wondered if Grace somehow knew who she was.

Peter, on the other hand, seemed charmed, "Lovely to meet you, Meg," he said. "I just adore your accent."

"Why, thank you," Meg managed, though she wasn't sure how he could adore her accent when she'd only spoken a few words.

Meg assumed the introductions would stop there, but Mrs. Ashton introduced her to the help as well. An older woman named Kathleen, a younger woman named Carrie, and a middle-aged man named Horace, each of whom, Mrs. Ashton explained, had been in their service for years and had come to help in any way possible. "In fact," she continued, "Jonathan thought it might be a good idea for Carrie to accompany you to the hotel down the block for the evening. Our understanding is that you've had to borrow someone else's... gown. Carrie can help you find something more suitable to wear in the morning, if you'd like, Miss West."

So he had given them her fake name. Meg took a deep breath and glanced at the several faces staring at her. Now, clearly, didn't seem like the time to explain herself, though she thought sooner rather than later was probably best. Before she could respond, Dr. Hunt opened the door to Charlie's room, and all of the attention shifted in that direction.

"Oh, Mr. and Mrs. Ashton, you've arrived," the doctor said as he stepped out into the hallway. He shook Mr. Ashton's hand. "I'm Dr. Stephen Hunt. Pleasure to meet you. Charlie is doing quite well. Miraculously, the doctor aboard *Carpathia* was able to treat his frost-bite, and he won't need to lose any digits."

"That's wonderful to hear," Mrs. Ashton exclaimed.

Meg took a step back toward the chair she'd been sitting in, toward the wall, toward the door at the end of the hallway.

"He is having a bit of trouble remembering everything, but that is to be expected. I've given him some medicine for his head, but it shouldn't cause him to be sleepy or agitated."

He glanced at Meg with that remark, as if he was letting her know Charlie would need no more sedatives for now, and yet she still took another step back as soon as his eyes returned to Charlie's parents.

"While I expect he may have some trouble sleeping for the next few weeks, I think he will be back to his usual self in no time."

"That's such a relief to hear," Mr. Ashton said, smiling at his wife.

Meg took another step toward the door.

"I would like to keep him here for at least tonight, possibly the next few days, just for observation. If you'd like for your family doctor to visit him here, as well, that can be arranged. For now, just try not to excite him too much. Don't ask questions about what's happened, though it's fine to ask him how he's feeling. I would like to limit it to no more than two guests at a time, however. We don't want to over-whelm him."

She took another step back. She was closer to the door now than she was to the family—the family huddled together concerned about their son, their brother, their pride and joy. The family she'd only just met who had been kind and considerate but to which she didn't belong. The family that would likely toss her out as soon as they knew who she was, what she'd done. All the doubts and fears she'd thought she'd worked through while on *Titanic*, while in Charlie's arms just before she boarded the lifeboat, all came rushing back to her, so Meg took another step back, her hand resting on the door.

Mr. and Mrs. Ashton stepped around the doctor into the hospital room and Peter directed his wife to the same chair Meg had been sitting in. There were other seats nearby. They'd fill them and begin to chat, ask Jonathan how he was feeling after his harrowing adven-ture. Eventually, he might look around and realize she was gone, but by then, she'd be wherever twenty dollars in cab fare could get you.

"Meg," Jonathan said, stepping over toward her, "where are you going?"

His voice was quiet and calm. She'd known he wouldn't let her slip away, that he'd notice before she could even get through the door. "I... I was trying to get out of the way."

He knew it wasn't the truth, yet he said nothing to contradict her. "I think it would be best if you did as Mrs. Ashton suggested and went with Carrie to the hotel. She's been a lady-in-waiting for years. She'll be able to attend to your needs and can help you find proper attire tomorrow. When you are dressed like yourself again, I'm sure you'll feel much better."

She felt no need to attempt an explanation regarding the fact that she was currently unsure whether she was Mary Margaret Westmoreland, wealthy heir to the Westmoreland Textile Factory, or Meg West, Third Class Passenger. It was late. They were exhausted. She nodded.

"Do you want me to tell them who you are?" It was a whisper in her ear so close she could smell the mint on his breath.

"No," she said quickly. "I want you to tell Charlie who I am, though."

He let out a short sigh, and she wondered if he was exasperated at her, at Charlie, or at having to rehash the entire situation once again. "I will," he promised, and she believed him.

"I think Charlie and I should tell them ourselves, but not until he remembers... obviously."

"That makes sense."

"Do you think that will make them angry?"

"No Nothing makes them angry."

"What are you two whispering about over there?"

It was Grace, Charlie's older sister, the one who looked at Meg as if she wasn't sure if she should use one dagger or two. "Nothing," Jonathan called with a smile. "I was only explaining to Meg that Carrie would be taking her over to the hotel now. She's a bit apprehensive, as you can imagine, this being her first trip to New York City and having absolutely nothing of her own with her."

Grace pursed her lips together. "That does sound dreadful. It's a shame you lost all of your gowns and jewels aboard the ship."

For a moment, Meg thought of the dress she'd borrowed from Lucy Duff-Gordon, just a few nights ago, to wear to dinner. It had been exquisite, as had been the jewels she'd borrowed from Molly Brown. Both women had been aboard *Carpathia*, but she hadn't had much of a chance to speak to Molly, and Lucy knew who she really was, so only a fleeting glance had passed between them. Meg brought herself back to the hospital. "There were many others who lost so much more than I," she said, her voice low and calm.

Grace nodded, and Meg felt as if perhaps she had just passed some sort of a test.

"Carrie, if you would," Jonathan said, gesturing in Meg's direction as he gave her a slight push in the back, enough to start her feet moving. "Meg, I will be by tomorrow to check on you and bring you back to the hospital if Charlie is still here."

She nodded at him over her shoulder. "Thank you, Jonathan." Carrie looked kind enough and was smiling at her, so Meg decided to go with her, even though part of her still wanted to try for the exit unaccompanied again. "It was lovely meeting you," she said to Grace and Peter as she approached.

Grace nodded and said, "Likewise," without much of a smile, but Peter climbed to his feet and took her hand again. For a moment, Meg thought he might kiss it, but he didn't, and he mentioned he felt charmed to make her acquaintance. Meg wondered how starved for attention he might act when she didn't have a bird's nest for hair.

Meg had never been to a hospital before, so she tried not to stare as nurses and doctors made their way past. The lower levels seemed particularly busy, and when they neared a pool of blood on the floor, some poor soul in an orderly uniform attempting to clean it up, she felt her stomach tighten a bit. "Sorry you had to see that, miss," Carrie said as she steered Meg toward the exit. "You've already been through so much."

She said nothing, only followed behind, and once she was standing outside on the large steps leading to the hospital, the fresh April air hitting her in the face, Meg felt relief. Even though it was still city air, it smelled a thousand times better than the stench of the hospital, the stagnant Third Class air, or even the fog she was used to at home.

Despite the fact that it was late, there were still lots of people milling about, and Meg realized she could quickly become lost in the crowd if she wanted to. She didn't dart off, though. She followed Carrie through the throng. Pieces of overheard conversation let her know that some of these people had come to this hospital thinking their loved ones might somehow be inside. Meg hoped they were but knew they likely were not. A surviving passenger list had been posted and printed, and unless there were others such as herself who were trying not to be discovered, the chances were if loved ones had not caught up with each other at the pier, they would never meet on this plane again.

"The hotel is just this way," Carrie said as she paused for Meg to keep up. She was maybe three or four years older than Meg, with kind brown eyes and a splay of freckles across her nose. Her hair was also dark, and though it was pinned up tightly, Meg assumed it would be curly if it was ever let down. Her nose was a bit crooked, but her smile was kind, and Meg felt at ease, as if they were old friends, almost at once. "It's quite a town, isn't it?" she asked gesturing with her head. "I remember when I first arrived. I had no idea what to think of all the... busyness."

"Yes, it is something else," Meg agreed. She couldn't even imagine what it must be like to go downtown where the real action was. "I always knew I'd come here someday, I just didn't think it'd be so soon."

"Where are you from?" Carrie asked, and then added, "If you don't mind me asking?"

Meg hesitated. Surely a servant in the Ashton home would know about his engagement. "I'm from... Southampton," she finally admitted, deciding the less lies she told now, the better off it would be when she had to tell the truth. A quick change of the subject couldn't hurt. "What about you?"

"I'm from Wisconsin." Carrie said it like she was admitting she had arrived straight from the underworld. "I came here to escape farm life."

Meg snickered, understanding what she meant by "escape." She could see a hotel just in front of them and wondered if that was where they were headed. "And do you like it?"

"Oh, yes," she exclaimed immediately, without hesitation. "The Ashton's are wonderful to work for. I love being in the city where there's always something to do, some place to go. And Mr. and Mrs. Ashton give me plenty of free time."

While Meg was happy to hear it, she felt a little sad for the servants back home who scarcely ever got time to themselves. "They seem quite generous," she agreed.

"This is it." Carrie gestured at a grand-looking establishment with large front steps and a doorman. "Mr. Lane said we shouldn't have any trouble getting a room so long as we speak to Harold and explain that you are a friend of the Ashtons."

Meg took her word for it and followed Carrie up the front steps, wondering if it was her outfit that had Jonathan concerned they might be turned away or something else. While she knew she really would feel much like her old self as soon as she was dressed in the type of clothes she was used to, she wasn't necessarily sure that was a good thing. Her old self had made some bad decisions, while her new self seemed to have more sense. As she entered the foyer of one of the nicest hotels she'd ever seen, she was hopeful she'd find a way to merge Mary Margaret Westmoreland with Meg West, taking only the bits she wanted and leaving the rest behind.

CHAPTER THREE

Meg's new gown was simple, but it felt much more elegant than anything she'd worn for weeks, except the night she'd gone to dinner with Charlie, of course. It was a royal blue color, which she knew went well with her eyes. Carrie had gotten her a charming new brush and comb set and had lovingly helped her work out all of the knots in her hair without supposing how they might have gotten there. Meg remembered there had been a crown of icicles around her head not long ago. Thoughts of the hours she'd spent in the lifeboat, soaking wet and then freezing, praying for Charlie in her mind and then aloud, made her shudder, and she pushed them away, back into a corner, into the same compartment where she kept remembrances of the awful things her uncle had done to her.

"You look absolutely stunning, Miss West," Carrie said, smiling at Meg's reflection in the mirror.

"Thank you, Carrie, but please do call me Meg," she insisted, not for the first time that day. "If you keep calling me Miss West, I'm afraid I might not answer."

The servant giggled, as if she assumed Meg was implying she just wasn't used to being called by her surname, not that it wasn't even her name at all. "I'll try to remember."

There was a knock at the door, and the girl moved in that direction. "That might be your room service," she said over her shoulder. She went out of the bedchamber, and once the door was opened, Meg recognized the voice and knew it wasn't breakfast. Standing, she made her way out into the living area to see Jonathan there.

He looked tired, as if he had spent another night sitting next to a hospital bed. But his clothing was fresh, a new un-wrinkled suit, a new hat, new shoes. He smiled at her, and Meg went to meet him at the door. "You look radiant, Meg," he said as he embraced her.

"Thank you," she said. "Please do come in. Did you spend another night at the hospital?"

"I did," he admitted as he took a seat next to her on the plush, velvet sofa. "Charlie is doing well though. He is being dismissed this morning. The family physician, Dr. Shaw, came by first thing this morning and said he could be released into his care."

"That's wonderful news," Meg said, though she wasn't sure she even believed her own words. There were more questions she needed answered before she would trust all was well with the younger Mr. Ashton.

"He asked about you first thing this morning, Meg," Jonathan said, glancing around to see that Carrie had gone back into the bedroom. "His very first words were, 'Where's Meg?'"

She swallowed hard. This was not the first time he remembered her only to forget her a few hours later. "And what did he remember?"

"Everything," Jonathan assured her. "I asked him several questions about who you are and how he came to know you. He remembers every detail now, Meg."

She wanted to believe him, but she'd need to see it for herself today. And tomorrow. And the next day. "Do you think it will last?"

"I do. I think it has just been that sedative, Meg, that has made him forget. He couldn't remember Mrs. Brown the other day when I asked him about her either. It's as if everything in his recent memory has been wiped out by the drugs. But then, as soon as they leave his system, he's his old self again."

She had to disagree with that. "No, Jonathan. He's not his old self. Even when he remembers me, he's still hearing the screams—still hearing the voices in his head."

Jonathan let out a sigh and took off his hat, running his hand through his hair and replacing it. Meg hadn't seen him without it often at all, and she'd assumed at first it must be due to a receding hairline, but it wasn't. She absently wondered if he slept in it. "Meg," Jonathan continued, "I can understand why you are concerned, but can't you remember the voices, too, when you think on it? We've all been through a jarring experience. It's natural to think some of the sensations from that night will stay with us for a while."

"Of course, I remember them, Jonathan," Meg replied, leaning toward him. "I remember everything that happened. The screams from the people in the water, though we were far away, were haunting, and I distinctly remember listening to see if I could hear Charlie, to see if maybe I would know where he was, so I could instruct the boatmen to go back. So... yes, I *remember* them. But that's not the same as what Charlie is experiencing, and we both know that."

The liegeman took a deep breath, as if he wasn't sure exactly how to respond. "I think... Charlie may be experiencing a more traumatic effect due to his actually being in the water with the people who were... expiring. But I'm sure he'll be back to his old self completely soon enough. If he's not, then there are plenty of doctors who can help him."

"Doctors? Like psychiatrists?" Meg asked the question with knots in her stomach. She didn't know much about psychiatric help, but she was familiar with asylums as she'd often wondered if her mother or uncle belonged in one of those places.

Jonathan swallowed hard. "Let's not worry about that right now, all right, Meg?" he asked. "Charlie is going home today, and that's good news. I'll take you over to his house in a few hours, once he's settled in. He's asked to see you, but I think it might be best if we let him get situated first. Also, his parents will be there, along with his sister and Peter. I asked Charlie if he was ready to tell them the truth about you, and he said whatever you wanted to do was fine with him."

Meg realized she was pulling on a lose thread on the sofa and stopped abruptly, thinking she might somehow unravel the entire piece of furniture and end up in a heap on the floor. "What if we tell them, and he forgets again, and when they ask if my story is true—if Charlie and I really do love each other and plan to marry—he says he doesn't know who I am?"

He was shaking his head before she even finished the sentence. "I don't believe that will happen, Meg. He knows you now. He hasn't taken any more of that medication. It will be fine."

"But does he know me, Jonathan?" she asked, turning her body so that she was facing him even more. "What I mean to say is, the last time we spoke aboard *Titanic*, he was still quite angry at me. Then, we parted, not knowing if we would both survive. What happened aboard *Carpathia* could easily be dismissed as a cathartic dream. Clinging to each other made sense when that's all we had. Now, here we are, back where he belongs, with his family and friends. And I am also here, but that doesn't mean he even really knows me, let alone wants me to be part of his life."

"Meg, he has been planning to marry you since he was eight years old." The reminder was gentle, but firm. "He knows who you are. He remembers what you told him—about your uncle."

"You asked if he remembered?"

"No, I didn't have to. He said you'd already been through so much at home, it was a shame you had to add the sinking of *Titanic* to your experiences as well. I could tell by his expression that he remembered precisely what you'd said. He also mentioned being well enough to travel back to Southampton so he could clear a few things up with 'that bastard.'"

Meg was certain he must have remembered then. Bertram Westmoreland was the only bastard he could've been speaking of. She dropped her eyes to the floor for a moment in concentration before returning them to his face. "If I tell the Ashtons who I really am, do you think they will be angry?"

"No, and certainly not if you tell them why you've kept it a secret."

"Do you suppose they will keep my secret? I'm still not certain what I plan to do."

"Do you mean as far as your mother is concerned?"

Meg nodded. There was a knock at the door, and a male voice shouted, "Room service." Carrie entered the room and smiled as if she was apologizing for intruding. The conversation froze in place as Carrie and the gentlemen set up Meg's breakfast on a table across the room, and then he left, Carrie returning to the bedroom.

Jonathan had scarcely even blinked the whole time they had company. "They will keep your secret, Meg, but there are some things we need to consider."

She felt her stomach tighten again. "Consider? Like what?"

For the first time, he looked away from her. "You do know about the contract, correct?"

Meg nodded. She was aware that her father, Henry Westmoreland, had arranged with Mr. Ashton for her to marry Charlie before Henry mysteriously died when Meg was only six.

"You know there is a substantial amount of money involved?"

She didn't know the details, but she assumed there had to be something of that nature. "What's substantial?" she asked.

"Fifty thousand dollars," Jonathan replied, inhaling deeply and then letting it go.

Meg's eyes widened. Suddenly, she felt very nauseous. "Fifty thousand dollars?" she repeated. All of the color was seeping out of her face, and she felt her head begin to spin. "Well, no wonder then," she managed to utter. She leaned back on the sofa, resting her head back so that her face was tipped to the ceiling.

"No wonder—what?" Jonathan asked, his voice indicating he was confused, but Meg couldn't see his expression to say whether or not she was correct.

"No wonder Charlie was willing to put up with me despite my antics, the way I'd ridiculed him and dragged his good name through the mud. I mean, I am shocked he's that motivated by money when he has plenty of it, but fifty thousand is an extraordinary amount of money!" She was still looking up at the ceiling, one hand clutched across her midsection, the other palm up, pressed to her forehead.

Jonathan began to laugh.

Meg looked up, thinking she might slap him across the face. "What in the world could possibly be funny about this situation?"

"I'm quite sorry," he managed to say, attempting to bring himself back together. "It's only... there's been so little to laugh about lately, and I suppose it's all gotten a bit bottled up."

"I'm afraid I don't follow," she said sharply, crossing her arms.

"Meg, darling, Charlie doesn't get the money for marrying you. Even if he did, fifty thousand pounds is nothing to him, you realize?"

She felt her cheeks fill back in, this time with red.

"Your mother and uncle get the money. But only if Charlie marries you before you turn twenty-one. Of course, Mr. Ashton agreed to the original terms, that you would marry before your twenty-first birthday, because that's what your father wanted. His hopes were that you and Charlie would marry, then your mother and uncle would leave you in peace if they had the money. But now... I'm not sure your father would want them to have it at all. Which complicates things just a smidge."

While Meg hadn't quite gotten over his laughing spell at her expense, she was very relieved to hear that Charlie was not marrying her for the money after all. It didn't make much sense to her either when Jonathan had first mentioned it, but she'd never imagined anyone would be willing to marry her so that someone else could make that sort of money. "You think my father wanted them to have the money so that they'd leave us alone?"

"That's what Mr. Ashton said."

"And what happens if I'm twenty-one and one day when we marry?"

"Then the money is yours."

Meg's eyebrows raised. Her father had already left her quite a bit of money, something she'd just come to find out recently. Having fifty thousand dollars more, would be life altering, even for her. And yet, she realized once she married Charlie—if she married Charlie—she would never even have to think about money again. She could take that money and do whatever she wanted with it. Give it to Kelly. Or Kelly's mother, Patsy. She could build a children's hospital or a school.

Her mind was wandering and she didn't realize Jonathan was talking to her until he was finished. "I'm sorry?" she said, looking at him expectantly.

"I said, we'll have to sort all of that out, but it is something to consider. I do think it's perfectly safe to go ahead and let the Ashtons know who you are."

Meg nodded. The thought of explaining everything to them seemed ominous, but she was hopeful Charlie would remember and could potentially do at least some of the talking. After all, he knew his parents better than she did.

"All right then, Meg. Why don't you eat your breakfast, and I'll be back to get you in a bit? And don't say you're not hungry because you need to eat. You've scarcely eaten a bite since... for a few days. Now, go."

He stood and walked toward the door, and she came to her feet as well. There was something about his tone that seemed to make everyone snap to attention. "Tell Charlie I said hello." She followed him to the exit.

"I will," he promised, and Meg bid Jonathan goodbye and closed the door behind him, praying that Charlie knew who she was the next time she saw him.

CHARLIE'S HOUSE was unlike anything Meg had ever seen before, and she could scarcely believe she was engaged to the man who lived here. While she could easily imagine it sitting out of town on a few hundred acres and still being imposing, it was situated between two other similar dwellings, though Charlie's was by far the most impressive. It resembled a French chateau and reached at least three stories into the air, though Meg thought the turrets might count for one more. She stood outside on the sidewalk next to Fifth Avenue trying to catch her breath.

"It's stunning, isn't it?" Jonathan asked at her elbow. "His mother picked it out. Charlie was far too busy with his work at the factory and his other interests to go house shopping."

"I don't even know what to say," Meg admitted. "It's breathtaking."

"He can explain the history to you once he's feeling up to it. At least, he likes to retell the story even though I'm quite sure he'd have managed just as well in a much smaller dwelling."

"Do you live here as well?" Meg asked as Jonathan offered his arm and led her up the ample steps.

"I have an apartment in the back, above the carriage house."

Thoughts of the carriage house made Meg's stomach queasy, but she dismissed the statement quickly. "It's nice that you live nearby."

"Less of a commute," Jonathan joked. Meg managed a giggle, but when Jonathan opened the front door without even knocking, she became serious again. She'd expected a moment to compose herself as they waited on the front stoop.

Carrie was behind them, and as soon as Jonathan led her into the opulent foyer, Carrie shut the door quite loudly, making both of them jump. "Pardon," she said with a slight bow. Meg smiled, realizing there's no way the young woman could possibly know the visions that loud noises brought up in her mind—and apparently Jonathan's as well—and rather than dwell on those memories, she returned her attention to the foyer.

A large chandelier hung overhead, adorned with crystals and

gold leaf. The floor was polished wood and appeared to be cherry. Meg knew next to nothing about architecture and décor, but she was impressed with the soaring ceiling and details in the molding.

"I thought I heard voices." Pamela Ashton, Charlie's mother, entered the room through an adjoining parlor. She was dressed in a blue gown a similar shade to Meg's, which made the younger woman finger her frock, wondering if it would be considered a fashion faux pas to wear the same color as your fiancé's mother upon a proper introduction.

Stepping forward to greet her appropriately, Mrs. Ashton took both of Meg's hands. "Meg, it's lovely to see you again. You look divine." She pressed her cheeks to each of Meg's in turn and made kissing sounds as she did so, and Meg wondered at this American greeting, which seemed oddly French or Spanish to her. "It must be so nice to be back in more proper attire."

"It's nice to see you as well, Mrs. Ashton," Meg replied.

"Please, call me Pamela. Mrs. Ashton is my mother-in-law," she joked. "Now, Charlie is in the library, and he's been asking about you all morning." The second half of the statement garnered a stern look for Jonathan, as if he'd been secretly keeping her occupied all morning for no reason. She took Meg by the arm and led her through the parlor toward an adjoining room. "Have you contacted your family yet?"

The question was a simple one which made perfect sense, and yet Meg had no way of knowing what to say. Jonathan, who was behind them, answered for her. "She hasn't contacted them yet, but the list of survivors has made it to Southampton."

"I'm sure you'll want to let your parents know you're well."

Meg turned her head to look at Jonathan, hoping he'd intervene, but he didn't. "I... well, it's rather complicated," she stammered.

Pamela looked at her with her eyebrows raised. Before she could ask more, they were standing before the library. The solid mahogany doors were open, and Peter stood from his seat next to Grace and exclaimed, "There's our Meg!" as soon as she was visible.

"Meg, you remember our son-in-law, Peter?" Pamela asked as she led her across the room.

"Yes, lovely to see you again," Meg said, acknowledging him with a nod and a smile, but she was more concerned with Charlie, who was sitting near the fireplace across from his sister and her husband in a large overstuffed chair beneath a thick blanket. His face was pale and his eyes looked glossy, not entirely different from the way he'd looked the last several days, but he was grinning at her, and Meg was hopeful this meant he knew who she was.

Peter hugged her, which Meg found to be both uncomfortable and questionable, before Grace said, "Good morning, Meg," in a snippy voice. She didn't stand, but when Peter finally let Meg go, she did offer her hand, which Meg squeezed and replied in kind.

"Meg," Mr. Ashton said, smiling, "please take my seat next to Charlie." He patted her warmly on the shoulder, and though Meg attempted to insist she couldn't take his seat, she soon found herself sitting there anyway, Mr. Ashton having found a spot on the sofa where his wife was also now seated.

Turning her attention to Charlie, Meg felt her face grow red, the sensation of a thousand people watching them, though it was only his immediate family—and Jonathan, who already knew all there was to know and then some. "Good morning," Charlie said to her with a smile. "You are absolutely stunning."

His voice was weak, and he only turned his head slightly to look at her, as if turning around completely would be too exhausting, but Meg could tell by the words he chose and the light behind his eyes that he knew who she was. "Thank you," she replied, quietly. "It's nice to see you... sitting up."

He chuckled, and Meg felt her blush meet the apples of her cheeks. While she wanted to add it was best of all to know he remembered her, she couldn't say that in front of his family.

"Charlie was just telling us about how you'd gone back into the bowels of the ship to rescue a little girl," Pamela explained. "Your lady-in-waiting's daughter?"

Meg looked at Charlie who gave her a reassuring nod. "Oh, yes," Meg said. "Ruth is more like my niece than anything else. She'd lost her doll and slipped away from her parents. So I went down to find her."

"It seems odd to me that the daughter of a First Class passenger's lady would go all the way down there to find a doll. Is that where she was being accommodated?" Grace's inquiry had even more questions behind it, and while Meg could understand why the older sibling was suspicious of her intentions, she felt her abdomen tighten and her palms grow clammy.

"Everything was chaotic that night," Charlie stated. "People were everywhere, running about, shouting. I spent at least half-an-hour trying to convince women who spoke no English to get aboard the final lifeboats. It's quite easy to understand how a child might get lost."

His voice was still raspy, but it grew stronger the more he spoke, and Meg longed to reach out and hold his hand, the way she'd held it most of the time they were aboard *Carpathia*.

"And then once you found her, what happened next?" The question came from Mr. Ashton, whose eyes reminded her of Charlie's. Twinkling and inquisitive.

Meg didn't like to think about what happened directly after that, so she skipped over the part where she was certain she and Ruth were about to drown or freeze to death in the rising water. "Then Charlie found us and led us to safety," Meg replied. She wanted to tell his parents that Jonathan had managed to procure a key that he'd given to Charlie that allowed him to unlock the gate which had prevented Meg and Ruth from going any higher in the boat, but the moments she'd stood there with Ruth clinging to her shoulders were some of the most dreadful of her entire twenty years, and she didn't intend to rehash them now.

"That's simply marvelous!" Pamela proclaimed. "How did you manage to find them?"

She was looking at Charlie, and it took him a moment to answer.

Eventually, he gave a small shrug. "I'm honestly not sure. I just kept looking until I could hear them shouting my name, and then I hurried to the source of the noise."

His eyes flickered to that haunted look Meg had seen so many times aboard *Carpathia* when he'd complained of the screaming, but then they cleared almost as quickly. She wondered if some of the voices he heard in his head were hers and Ruth's.

"How lucky is that?" Mr. Ashton said with a laugh, looking at his wife.

"Charlie makes his own luck," Peter offered, joining in on the chuckle. Grace said nothing, only forced a smile on her pretty face that looked every bit as fake as the pearl necklace Meg's doll, Lilac, had worn when she was a child.

Meg exchanged glances with Jonathan as the rest of the family continued to comment on how fortunate they all had been, and then she returned her attention to Charlie. While it was true they were all lucky to be sitting there, she certainly didn't think their experiences were as jolly as they were being made out to be, and she wondered if this was just the family's way of dealing with the pent up emotions from not knowing where Charlie had been.

After the giddiness died down a bit, Mr. Ashton turned to Meg and said, "I'm sure your parents were relieved to hear you are well."

She glanced at Charlie whose eyes told her he had not revealed anything, and then she looked at Jonathan who gave a small shrug. "Actually," Meg began, with a sigh, "my father died when I was a little girl, and I've only my mother."

"How very sad," Pamela replied, but Mr. Ashton looked at her long and hard, as if he saw something familiar in her face.

"Would it be possible for Charlie and me to speak in private for just a few moments?" Meg asked, not sure how to best explain the situation to them but seeing that their time was limited by the expression in the eyes of her father's former roommate.

"Certainly," Pamela said. "We are happy to step out for a moment."

As she and Mr. Ashton rose, Peter following, Grace lingered on the chair briefly. Peter offered his hand, and she pulled herself up, muttering, "My brother has only just returned from the dead, but why not? Take your time."

"Grace," Pamela said sharply, under her breath, as she took her daughter's arm, "give them a moment." She looked over her shoulder and offered Meg a smile, as if she was apologizing for her daughter's rudeness, but Meg honestly didn't care at the moment. She was certain Grace would hate her even more once she knew who she really was, especially if she knew what she had done to Charlie before they left Southampton.

Jonathan was the last to stand, and before he went to follow the family out the door, he said, "Now is as good a time as any."

Meg nodded in agreement, knowing fully what he meant. If they were going to be honest with Charlie's family, they needed to do so now. He went out and closed the mahogany doors behind him, careful to keep it as quiet as possible when they came together.

She wanted to see Charlie properly, but as he was mostly facing the fire, the angle of her chair was wrong, so she scooted it around, minding the legs of the chair on the wooden floor. Once she was seated as near to him as possible, her knees brushed up against the side of his leg beneath the heavy blanket, she let go a sigh of relief.

"Hello, gorgeous," he said, reaching for her hand, and Meg gave it to him. "How are you really doing this morning?"

She couldn't help but smile at him. His hand was much warmer now than it had been for days. The tips of his fingers were rough in spots where they'd suffered frostbite, but she was glad to see they were healing. "I'm managing," she admitted with a shrug. "It's nice to see you know who I am today."

Charlie's green eyes grew wide for a moment. "What does that mean?" he asked.

Meg exhaled deeply through her nose. She'd done this same song and dance more times than she could count, and since she'd brought the topic up, she knew she'd have to say more, but she was determined not to go into a lot of detail because it always upset him to learn that he didn't know who she was. "There were times, before, when we were on *Carpathia*, that you didn't remember me."

His eyebrows grew close together. "You don't say? Is that so?"

"Yes, but I suppose it doesn't matter now." She was reluctant to tell him the same thing had happened just yesterday at the hospital. She determined it would be best to leave that out altogether.

He squeezed her hand gently. "Well, I certainly know who you are now." With his free hand, he reached over and stroked her cheek, brushing one of the curls framing her face back behind her ear. "I suppose my parents should also know."

"Yes, I suppose they should," she agreed. She took his hand in hers as he brought it back down so that she was holding both of them. "But I wasn't sure what to say in order to make them understand why I did the things I did." Meg's eyes shifted from his face to the glowing fire next to them. Its flames were licking the top of the brick enclosure, and she began to notice just how warm the room was. "I'm not sure they *can* understand why I made the choices I made."

"Leave that to me," Charlie assured her. "They don't need to know everything."

Meg's eyes fell on his again. "You don't think just knowing who I am will make them angry?"

"Why would it? They have no idea you didn't attend the ball, though I can tell them any reason I like to explain why you weren't there if you prefer. They certainly don't know anything about that yard boy. I'm certain they suspect your mother and uncle were anything but loving, though they don't know about... the things that you went through."

She was happy he chose those words. There were other words he could've spoken instead that made her feel like a victim, and even though that might be the case, she hated to feel that way. And she nearly chuckled when he referred to Ezra as "that yard boy." That's truly all he ever was. Part of her wished he'd been aboard *Titanic* so she could watch him freeze to death in the water, though that was a part of her she wasn't happy to acknowledge. "All right then," she agreed. "I just wanted to make sure that you were ready to tell them and that you're certain they'll be accepting of me."

"I know they will," he assured her.

"Also, they must know they cannot tell my mother. We need to decide what to do about that. Jonathan has just informed me about the money my mother and uncle will receive if we marry before I'm twenty-one."

Charlie nodded. "Which is in September."

She smiled, glad he remembered even that small detail. "Yes, and I'm not sure I like the idea of that money going to such horrible people."

He nodded again.

"On the other hand, I'm not sure I want to wait until October to marry you."

Charlie's face brightened, and he brought both of his hands up to cup her chin and cheeks. "I'm so glad to hear you say that, Meg. I wasn't sure how you'd feel now, especially since... I'm not quite myself."

She placed her hands on the outside of his. "You will be. Soon enough. I'm sure of it." She smiled at him and brought his hands back down to her lap, still holding them. Thoughts that she was wrong— that he would never be himself again, that she would never be herself again—fought to the surface, but she kicked them back to the recesses of her mind, next to the box that housed her uncle. "Shall I go get them then?"

"Not yet," Charlie said quietly. "There's just one more thing." He let go of her hands to place his fingers on the tips of the armrests and carefully pushed himself forward so that he was leaning in toward her. Meg could see it took a considerable amount of effort, and she wished she could help him. "I love you, Meg," he said quietly.

She realized what it was that he wanted, though he couldn't let go of the chair and stay so near to her. "I love you, too," she replied, meaning it with all of her heart, despite the transformation they'd both recently undergone. She rested her hands on the sides of his handsome face and pressed her lips against his. His lips were warm, much more so than they had been the last time she'd kissed him aboard *Carpathia*, and she could've allowed herself to melt into him if there hadn't been a sound at the door that caught her attention.

Meg began to pull back, but Charlie caught her lips again with his one last time, causing them both to giggle, and the familiar clearing of a throat finally convinced her to turn her head.

Jonathan looked amused, though he stood near the door with his hands shoved deep into his trouser pockets. "Are you done with your discussion then?" he asked.

"No," Charlie replied, a smirk on his face. "We've only just begun our discussion. Tell the rest of them to come back in half an hour."

"Charlie?" Meg laughed.

"All right then, make it an hour."

She was happy to see him returning to his former self. "You can let them in," Meg said to Jonathan, and Charlie leaned back in his seat, a sigh of rejection filling the library as he did so.

"You really are a bit ridiculous, aren't you?" Meg asked as she stood to turn her chair back around just a bit.

"Are you only just now discovering this?" he asked as she found her place on the edge of the chair. "Give me back your hand."

She raised her eyebrows at the command but appreciated the voracity by which he longed to touch her, and she slipped her hand into his where it lay between them on the armrest.

The family walked in, discussing what the newspapers were saying about the sinking, and Meg tuned them out. She had no interest whatsoever in learning the misinformation being spread across the world as if it were fact.

"Charlie, you've got some color in your cheeks," Pamela noted as she returned to her spot on the sofa. A small smile played at the corners of her mouth as if she thought she could guess why that might be.

"Meg's presence always makes me feel better," Charlie assured her. Grace let out a small scoffing snicker and was met by another sharp look from her mother. Charlie either didn't notice or didn't care to acknowledge it. "We actually have some information we'd like to share with you, but first we want to caution you that what we are about to tell you cannot leave this room."

"My god! Is she carrying your child?" Grace leaned forward in her seat so far, Meg thought she might tumble to the floor.

"Heavens, no!" Charlie shot back, before Meg even had the chance to gasp or faint or be properly offended. "Grace, will you please straighten up. You're embarrassing all of us."

Grace's cheeks were bright red, and she opened her mouth as if she might say something in return, but then she snapped it shut, and Meg wondered if Charlie hadn't recently died if she might feel differently about arguing with him.

"I know that you all think you have an idea who Meg is, but you don't really know for sure, and we want to clear that up," Charlie continued once Grace seemed calm. He looked at Meg, as if he were inquiring as to whether or not he should continue or if she would like to.

As easy as it would've been to sit there and listen to him completely tell the tale, only nodding along when she felt it necessary, Meg took a deep breath, and turning to look directly at Mr. Ashton, she said, "I'm Henry's daughter. I'm Mary Margaret."

The older gentlemen's eyes grew only slightly, and he gave a little nod, as if he recognized her. He had seen her before, though it had been well over a decade, and she had been a small child. Still, Meg knew she looked at least a little like her father, and that may have been one of the reasons he suspected.

The only audible noise came from Grace, whose gasp gave away the fact that she'd had no idea.

"I didn't want anyone to know I was aboard *Titanic*. I was running away from my family. My mother and uncle have been quite abusive.... I'd prefer they didn't know where I am."

53

"And that's your reason for using an assumed name?" Pamela asked, a small smile of understanding on her kind face.

"Yes," Meg confirmed. "I went aboard *Titanic* under a false name, and when they asked for my name for the list, Daniel, my lady's husband, gave them a different assumed name, but still not my own. Only Madeline Astor, Molly Brown, and possibly Lucy Duff-Gordon know that I was aboard *Titanic*, and I'm hoping that none of them will say anything to my mother."

"Where does your mother think you are?" The question came from Peter, who was staring at her intently.

Meg wasn't sure if she could trust Peter or Grace, but she had no choice at this point. "They think that I ran away."

"They have no idea that she is with me," Charlie replied. "When I last left their home, they had called the police, thinking she had been abducted."

"That's terrible," Grace exclaimed.

Meg wondered if she meant it was terrible that her mother thought she was abducted or that she was lying to her only surviving parent. "It's better this way," Meg replied, averting her eyes to the fine oriental rug beneath her feet that stretched across the room and ended beneath the sofa.

"Did you help devise this plan?" Mr. Ashton asked his son.

"No, I didn't. But once I became aware of it, and especially when I knew what Meg had suffered, I went along with it. And I will continue to go along with it for as long as she asks me to. I would hope that all of you will also."

"Yes, of course," Pamela answered first. The rest of them nodded and verbally said that they would, though Meg still wasn't sure whether or not Grace could ever take her part.

The room was silent for a long moment before Pamela spoke again. "Well, Mary Margaret—may I call you Meg?" She nodded. "Meg, it is so very nice to meet you at last."

"Your father was a fine fellow. In fact, quite possibly the finest fellow I've ever met," Mr. Ashton assured her.

"Yes, I was always quite fond of Henry," Pamela agreed.

"Thank you," Meg replied. Tears formed in the corners of her eyes, but she did her best to hold them back. She hated for others to see her cry.

"I'm sure you miss him terribly." Grace was staring at her with only a hint of sympathy in her voice, and Meg thought perhaps she was attempting to see how far she could be pushed to make the tears come out.

"I do miss him. Every day."

Charlie cleared his throat. "We will need to speak with the lawyers to see what needs to be done now to prevent Mr. and Mrs. Westmoreland from receiving the money. If it's possible to keep Meg's identity a secret and avoid them getting the money, then that's what we want to do."

"But Charlie, I promised Henry I'd see to it that the pair of you were married before she turned twenty-one so that Mildred would get the funds he had left for her," Mr. Ashton insisted.

"I understand that, Father," Charlie nodded, straightening up just a bit in his chair, "but if you had any idea all that Meg has gone through these past several years, you wouldn't want them to receive it either. They honestly don't deserve a dime, and I wish I hadn't sent them any money the last few times they forced Meg to ask for it."

Meg glanced at him, wanting to tell him it had been that money that kept her lights on and food on the table, but now wasn't the time, and he probably assumed her mother had spent it on superfluous items. While that was certainly the case with some of it, not all of it had been used unwisely.

"We don't need to discuss any of that right now," Pamela said with a smile. She patted her husband on the knee. "Charlie, have you thought about where Meg will be staying until the wedding?"

Meg had been wondering the same thing herself, and her eyebrows arched as she turned to face her fiancé.

"I've given it plenty of thought but don't necessarily have an answer," he admitted. "There are options. We could rent an apartment nearby."

"Ooh, there's a cute townhome for lease over by the factory," Grace chimed in.

Charlie looked at her for only a moment before saying, "I don't think she wants to live by the factory."

"Is that near Kelly?" Meg asked, leaning in toward his ear.

"It is, but it isn't that close to here, and since I likely won't be back to the factory for a month or two, I'd rather have you nearer to me." His voice was quiet, as if they were sharing a secret others could hear only if they strained to, and Meg felt the heat rising in her face again, like he was sharing an intimacy with her.

"She could stay in the carriage house apartment, and I could move in here for a bit," Jonathan said with a shrug. "That way she's nearby, but your parents wouldn't have to be concerned about a lack of chaperone."

"That is awfully close," Pamela pointed out with raised eyebrows.

"You can't beat Jonathan as a chaperone," Mr. Ashton assured her.

Meg had no idea how she would feel staying so close to Charlie, but she didn't want to impose on Jonathan. "I can't take your apartment, Jonathan. That seems very improper."

"Don't be ridiculous," he said, waving her off. "I'm hardly there anyway. Most of the time I'm here or at work—with the factory being my primary location."

"It's true," Charlie agreed.

"Then it's settled," Pamela said, her shoulders relaxing a bit as if she'd just solved one of the world's greatest problems. "Meg will move into the carriage house."

Meg desperately wanted to call it something else--anything else.

"Now, will your lady be returning to your side, or will you need to keep Carrie?"

The question was another good one. "If you say Kelly's new home is far away, then it wouldn't be easy for her to attend to me here. And, I believe she was planning on staying home with the girls." She was looking at Charlie, but she would've accepted a response from anyone.

"I plan to give Daniel that foreman's position that just opened up," Charlie said to his father. "His arm is currently in a cast, but he's a fine young man, and I know he will be able to do the work."

Mr. Ashton nodded. "Of course, I trust your judgment."

"That position will come with an apartment, and he will make enough so that Kelly can stay home," Charlie explained to Meg.

"Very good then," Pamela stated. "That solves that. I'll let Carrie know."

"But wouldn't you rather I found my own help?" Meg asked. "That is, Carrie works for you, doesn't she?"

"She does, but when I hired her, I had you in mind. I thought you might need someone when you came here. I didn't know if you'd bring your own girls or not. Carrie is just right for a young woman like you, I think. Wouldn't you agree?"

It had never occurred to Meg that while she was in Southampton planning to escape her marriage to Charlie, he and his family were in New York City making arrangements and accommodations for her. "Yes, she's lovely," Meg said quietly.

"Originally, we'd assumed you'd simply stay in a hotel for a few days if the wedding were here in New York and then move straight into this home. But now that you are here, and we don't know precisely when the wedding might be, we'll make adjustments." She exhaled loudly with a smile, as if she were breathing out after stopping to smell the roses.

"I appreciate all of your assistance, and your understanding," Meg said meekly.

"Absolutely," Mr. Ashton assured her. "Henry was my greatest friend, and you were—are—his pride and joy. Anything I can do to assist you, I will do."

She knew he meant it sincerely, and it warmed her heart.

Knowing her father was looking down on her always made her feel more secure.

"We will need to find a dressmaker, of course. You can use mine if you like, though Grace might have a better one for a young woman such as yourself." Grace snorted, and her mother ignored it. "Or we can simply go down to the shopping district."

Meg nodded. "I'll need to stop by a bank. I found out quite recently that my father actually left me an account." She looked at Charlie, realizing he didn't know that. "I can pay you back some of the money you sent my mother before I knew about the savings."

"Don't be ridiculous," he said. "You don't owe me anything, and you won't pay for anything either. You'll be my wife soon enough."

The thought of never having to pay for anything again—never having to worry about anything again—was a bit foreign to her, and Meg didn't realize Mrs. Ashton was still speaking to her until she was halfway through her statement. "We could have lunch in that little restaurant over there on the corner."

Meg had no idea what she was talking about, but she nodded, even though the idea of going out shopping soon made her stomach tighten. These people were going on about their lives as if *Titanic* had never happened, and while that was all fine and good for them, Meg wasn't ready for that just yet.

"Perhaps Miss Meg would like to get settled into her new place before the shopping spree," Jonathan chimed in, and Meg looked at him with great admiration. "She looks a bit drained to me."

"Oh, yes, dear, I'm sorry. I didn't think... why you must be exhausted as well. It's hard to tell when you're so radiant, but certainly you must be anxious after what's happened. Not just the ship, but leaving your family." Pamela looked at her as if she were a newborn kitten.

"I would love to go shopping and have lunch soon," Meg said. "However, I am rather tired today."

"No explanation necessary," Pamela replied shaking her head and waving one hand in Meg's direction. "Of course you are. Perhaps when Dr. Shaw comes to pay Charlie a visit later this afternoon, he can check in on you as well."

"I don't think that's necessary," Meg said quickly. "I'm not ill —just weary."

"I know that, darling, but the last thing we need is for you to come down with something."

"I think she's fine, Mother," Charlie interjected, squeezing Meg's hand.

Pamela looked at him and seemed to bite her tongue for a second before she forced a smile onto her face and said, "Well then, Carrie can go out this afternoon and pick up a few more things for you. That way you'll have some choices in attire for the next few days before we can go out together."

"That would be quite lovely," Meg said, smiling in return.

"I'll take Meg over to the apartment then." Jonathan was on his feet, a signal that this conversation had ended.

Meg was thankful to have it over with. A little over a week ago, she assumed she'd never even meet these people since she'd been planning to run away from her arranged marriage with Charlie. The last few days, she'd been dreading sitting across from them and giving them a full explanation of what she'd done. Now, thanks to Charlie's insistence on being less than fully forthcoming, she was glad to have the conversation over with and be able to move on with her life.

"Come along, Meg," Jonathan insisted. He was already standing on the other side of the sofa.

She stood, as did everyone else in the room except for Grace and Charlie. She still held his hand, and she knew he wished he could rise to tell her goodbye. "I'll see you soon," she assured him, and he drew her hand to his lips and smiled at her. Thoughts that he might not recognize her the next time she saw him were pushed aside as she turned to face the rest of the room.

"It was lovely to see you again, Grace," Meg said.

"Yes, as always," Grace managed with a fake smile.

Peter hugged her and told her to take care, and Meg thought his hands lingered a bit low and a bit long.

"I will come and check on you soon," Pamela said as she embraced her soon-to-be-daughter-in-law.

Mr. Ashton held her at arm's length for a moment and peered at her face. "It is wonderful to see you again, Meggy." He smiled warmly, and for a moment, Meg thought she knew what it must be like to have a father. Her heart suddenly longed to belong to this man's family. He wrapped his arms around her, as if he were holding a long lost child, and Meg fought to hold back tears as memories of her own Da filled her head.

Once he let her go, she said quietly, "It's wonderful to finally meet you, Mr. Ashton." He chuckled in glee. Meg stepped around the sofa and took Jonathan's waiting arm, one last glance at Charlie over her shoulder as Jonathan led her out of the room. He was smiling at her, and she honestly thought he was returning to his former self. Perhaps this nightmare would all be over soon.

CHAPTER FOUR

Meg was thankful that the carriage house had been completely converted to a guest house since there were absolutely no carriages or horses kept here, and Charlie had an attached garage where he kept his automobiles. (She was shocked when Jonathan said he owned four.) The apartment above the carriage house was nearly as large as her entire house would be if it were placed on one story, and she couldn't imagine why anyone would call this an apartment.

It was immaculate, which didn't surprise Meg at all since she knew Jonathan to be impeccably tidy. The view from one side was of Charlie's house—which she couldn't fathom would soon be her own home—and on the other side she could see the expansive back garden of the house behind them, though there was a large hedge obstructing part of the view. Charlie's own garden, complete with a small pond and fountain, was nestled between the two buildings, and Meg thought it was quite lovely.

Jonathan gave her a quick tour. She was shocked to see the entire house was completely electric. The washroom was unlike anything she'd ever seen, with a large soaking tub and hot water available immediately at the tap. He'd tried to clarify exactly how that was possible, but she didn't understand. The kitchen was also newly renovated and beyond her wildest dreams. There was even an electric icebox. Jonathan explained that this was a product of Peter's factory and that they were actually working on a device that would cool the entire home much like an electric icebox. Meg didn't even know what to say in response; she couldn't even imagine.

"Here's the telephone," Jonathan said, leading her over to where the black box hung from the wall. "I'll write down the number to the main house for you so that you can phone Charlie if you need to."

As he did so, Meg stared at the foreign object on the wall. "How do you..." she stammered, "how do you use it?"

Jonathan looked up at her as if she'd asked how do you eat an apple. "You've never used a telephone before?"

She shook her head, her cheeks reddening. "We had one, but only my uncle was allowed to touch it."

He offered a small smile, as if he realized he'd embarrassed her and was attempting to apologize for it. "It's quite simple." He showed her how to use the receiver and where to speak. He explained that an operator would connect the call. "Do you understand?" he asked when she was done.

"I believe so," she said with a nod, hoping she did. It seemed easy enough.

"Now bear in mind that when it rings, it's rather loud and sudden. If you're not prepared, it could be frightening, particularly since I think you are like me and still a bit... jumpy at loud noises."

Meg nodded, glad to hear him admit he was still struggling with that as well. She hoped it didn't ring at all, even thought it might be nice to talk to Charlie later if he didn't feel like having visitors.

Jonathan finished showing her the rest of the two-bedroom apartment, including the room he wasn't using, which she decided would be hers so that he didn't have to move all of his things out, and then led her back to the main room. "Do you have any questions?"

"I don't think so," Meg replied, thinking about everything he'd shown her. "Will Carrie know how to use all of these appliances and what-not?"

He stifled a laugh. "Yes, she will. Also, there are servant accommodations down the hall."

She nodded again. She hadn't seen precisely what was down the hall or even downstairs as the upstairs apartment had its own entry, but she knew there were no carriage or automobiles below her. "I think I shall be all right then. Thank you very much for your hospitality, Jonathan."

"Of course," he said, dismissively. "I'll take a few of my things now and come back for the rest later. It's a shame my best suitcase is gone," he muttered, looking around the room as if he was checking to see if the rest of his items were still there.

Meg couldn't think about what she'd lost. Only the pink robe really mattered. But then, she'd had nothing left of her own to bring with her. Eventually, she would like to find a way to get Charlie's letters back in her possession.

"You're welcome to eat whatever you'd like. Send Carrie out for groceries." He glanced around the room again before clearing his throat and continuing. "Also, I would expect there will be an inquiry into the sinking soon enough. I'm sure they will want to talk to Charlie, possibly me, though I'm not sure if they will want to talk to Meg West or not."

Meg nodded, not sure what she would say if they did plan to speak to her. "I hope not."

"It will be fine if they do. Just answer their questions as honestly as you can. I worry about them speaking to Charlie, though. He's having a lot of difficulty remembering what happened."

In a way, Meg envied him, though she was certain the memories were there somewhere, locked inside. She took a deep breath and let it go. "He is going to recover, fully, isn't he, Jonathan?"

"Yes, I believe so," he assured her. "Look how much better he is today than he was yesterday."

She nodded again. It was true. He had more color in his cheeks today. His hands felt stronger. He remembered who she was.

"If you need anything at all, give the main house a call. I believe Mrs. Ashton was going to send Carrie out to get your clothing and other items and then she'll send her over."

"What about the few things I left at the hotel this morning? And settling the room?" Meg asked, realizing she'd left the new brush there as well as the old clothes she'd borrowed while on *Carpathia*. She had no reason to want them except for maybe as a remembrance of her own survival.

"We'll take care of all that," he assured her. "Meg, when you are Charles Ashton's wife, you don't need to worry about... anything."

"Right," she said exhaling loudly. "And what about until I am Charles Ashton's wife?"

He laughed. "In Charlie's mind you already are. You may as well believe it too."

She smiled, but it didn't reach her eyes, and in her heart she realized she might still find a way to ruin everything. That was what she seemed to do best, anyway. Part of her wanted to ask Charlie if they could get married right away, while the other half swore she'd never let a penny of her father's money reach her mother's grubby hands. She had just over five months until her birthday. Surely, she could find a way to keep from making enough mistakes to drive Charlie away again in that short amount of time.

"Are you all right?" Jonathan asked, peering intently at her face.

She nodded her head, realizing she'd been lost to the world for a moment. "Yes, I'm fine," she assured him.

He smiled, but she thought he didn't believe her. "I'll come check on you myself after while. Why don't you rest?"

"That's a good idea," she said, looking longingly to the plush chair and sofa nearby.

"Meg," Jonathan said, stepping forward and squeezing her arm gently, "everything is going to be all right. I promise."

She smiled. She wanted to believe him. But she didn't.

CHARLIE WAS ALL ALONE in his own bedroom, sitting on the edge of his own bed, looking out the back window at the carriage house, wondering what Meg was doing. There was no way he could see her from here, partially due to the heavy drapery that covered the windows of the second story across the yard, but he imagined she was resting or possibly reading a book. He wondered if she felt all alone when there was no one with her or if she was suffering from the same sensation he was experiencing.

The voices wouldn't stop. Even when other people were talking to him, even as he formulated responses to their questions, he could hear the constant noises of screaming, crying out, in the back of his mind. While having other people nearby lessened the effects to some degree, it never made them stop. When he was completely alone as he was now, there was nothing to dull the effect, and he could distinctly hear the individual voices, make out what they were saying, and envision their faces. It made him feel as if he were back in the water again, and the longer it went on, the more he could feel panic rising up inside of him. It was maddening to feel both all alone in the world and surrounded by others at the exact same time.

"Charlie? Did you hear me?"

He spun around to look over his shoulder, not even having realized Jonathan had entered the room. "Oh, Jonathan. I'm sorry. I didn't know you were here."

"My apologies. I knocked and announced I was coming in."

"I didn't hear."

There was a heavy silence for a moment, and Charlie imagined his friend was debating whether or not an inquiry as to how that was possible was polite or if he should just let it go. "The doctor is here to see you," Jonathan said, clearly choosing the second option.

Charlie nodded and resituated himself on the fully made bed so that he was leaning back against the headboard, one leg crossed under the one still resting on the floor. "Have you been to check on Meg?"

"Not since I took her over. It's only been a few hours."

"Right," Charlie nodded, his eyes returning to the carriage house.

"Charlie, is it going to bother you having her so nearby?"

He returned his gaze to Jonathan's familiar face. "I honestly don't know how it will affect me. I'll be happy when we are married. I feel like no one else can possibly understand all that we've been through —except for you."

Jonathan nodded and looked at the floor. Charlie knew he was fighting his own battle, but he wasn't the sort who would want to talk about it. Meg, on the other hand, would be more forthcoming with her feelings, even if she didn't quite handle them the same way most people did.

"Dr. Shaw is waiting downstairs. I'll see him up." Jonathan's response was short, and Charlie realized he'd likely never break down the hard exterior to reveal whether or not Jonathan was having any lingering effects from the disaster. He'd have to watch his friend for other indications that all was not well.

Charlie observed him as Jonathan walked out the door. A few moments later, he heard the loud footsteps of Dr. Robert Shaw approaching his room and braced himself for yet another examination. He couldn't have counted all of the inspections he'd undergone these past few days if he'd tried, and he knew he hadn't even been awake for all of them. At least Dr. Shaw was familiar, and Charlie was more comfortable with him than the doctors he'd only just met because of the disaster.

Dr. Shaw was tall and rather large. He had dark black hair and chose to wear a full moustache and beard even though the latter wasn't in fashion presently. He carried his medical bag and greeted Charlie with a jovial smile. "Mr. Ashton, it's a pleasure to see you," he said. Charlie began to rise, but the doctor insisted he stay seated. "Please, don't get up. You know I've come to see if you're well; there's no reason to exert yourself."

Even though Charlie was getting around much better now that he was home and had gotten the opportunity to walk around a bit, he was thankful not to have to stand just for standing's sake. "It's nice to see you, Dr. Shaw," he said, managing a smile.

"Are you feeling better?" he asked as he took various tools out of his medical bag, including a stethoscope. "It's been quite the ordeal, I hear. My cousin had a friend whose wife lost her best friend's brother."

Charlie wasn't sure he followed all of that, but he imagined the doctor was attempting to say everyone knew someone who was affected by the disaster. "I'm feeling much better now, doctor, thank you," Charlie assured him.

"Very good," he replied. He sat down on the edge of the bed, causing the mattress to shift, and Charlie felt a bit off balance again. He took deep breaths to calm himself, reminding himself that the bed was not listing.

The doctor listened to his heart and other organs. He inspected his digits for frostbite and commented that he seemed to be healing nicely. "I have a salve for this," he commented, pointing at the spots on Charlie's finger that looked dead beyond repair. "No cough or congestion?" Dr. Shaw asked as he listened to Charlie's chest and back.

"No, not that I am aware of."

"Very good," Dr. Shaw remarked. "And you're able to get around well?"

"I suppose so," Charlie shrugged. "I needed help to climb the stairs, but I managed."

"Is your balance normal?"

"Most of the time. I haven't walked much without holding onto someone or something just yet."

The doctor nodded. "Well, Mr. Ashton, I think you should be just fine in a few weeks. I'd recommend you stay close to home at least for a while. Nothing strenuous. Your body is still trying to recover from the shock of it all. But you seem quite healthy to me. It probably helped tremendously that you were so fit before the experience."

Charlie nodded, thinking it was rather odd to reduce an ocean liner sinking, killing over two thousand people, to "the experience." But then, he had no idea what he might say if he were trying to carry on a conversation with someone from the other side either. "Dr. Shaw, I've been sleeping a lot recently, thanks to the medication they were giving me. Do you think I should be able to fall asleep on my own now that I'm no longer taking it?"

"It depends on what they were giving you, but I should think so," the doctor nodded. "Do you happen to know what it was?"

"No," Charlie admitted. He thought he might mention that it made him forgetful, but he kept that information to himself. He also thought he might mention the voices, but then, he didn't think there was anything in Dr. Shaw's black bag to help that either.

"I'd say give it a go when you feel tired, and see if you can go to sleep on your own. If not, there are remedies I can provide for you."

That was exactly what Charlie was hoping to avoid. The last thing he wanted was another prescription that would make him feel like he wasn't himself. He only nodded, and the doctor drew the salve he'd mentioned out of his bag and explained how to apply it and how often before setting it on the nightstand next to Charlie's bed.

"Is there anything else?" Dr. Shaw asked, his eyebrows raised. He wore the same friendly expression he always did, and Charlie was tempted to trust him with the secret he was carrying—that even as the doctor stood before him, his mouth closed tightly, there were voices in the room. Charlie shook his head. "Very good then. I shall be back tomorrow to check on your progress. In the meantime, if anything comes up, ring the office."

"Thank you very much, Dr. Shaw," Charlie replied, offering his hand, which the large man enveloped before he let go and gathered up his bag.

"Your mother mentioned a young lady is staying in the carriage house who was also aboard the boat. Would you like for me to check on her while I'm here? Has she any injuries?"

So many phrases in the statement stood out to Charlie, he wasn't even sure where to begin. A young lady? The boat? Any injuries? Charlie opened his mouth, as if he might attempt to explain away all of those misunderstandings, but instead he closed his mouth and continued to shake his head.

"No? All right then. I'll see you tomorrow, Mr. Ashton."

"Have a good afternoon, doctor," Charlie replied, and he watched Dr. Shaw make his way back into the hallway, where he was certain Jonathan would scoop him up and see him out of the house.

Charlie rested his head against the headboard and glanced out the window. Perhaps Meg did need to see a physician, but he knew she wouldn't want to see Dr. Shaw. She'd made that clear earlier. She was fine physically, but Charlie didn't think it would be possible for her to be fully recovered mentally. Even now, in a room that should've been perfectly still, there was no silence. He took a deep breath and resituated on the bed, thinking perhaps a nap might be in order, if he could find a way to make his mind quiet enough to find sleep. He closed his eyes and saw their faces and knew in his heart his mind would never be quiet again.

CHAPTER FIVE

C harlie's dining room table was large and opulent, like most of the other furnishings in his house. However, Meg had come to learn that his mother had chosen most of the décor, and when Charlie said he'd just as soon be surrounded by simpler things, Meg believed him. Nevertheless, seated next to him at the baroque revival dining table made her feel small and insignificant. Luckily, whenever he smiled at her, she felt like the most important person in the world.

"How was your day?" he asked as they sipped bowls of freshly made soup. Meg had learned that there would be at least four courses, sometimes as many as seven depending upon who was present, so she paced herself. "Did you do any shopping?"

"Not today," Meg replied, setting her spoon aside to take a sip of water. She'd declined the wine she'd been offered. Drinking anything stronger than tea made her head ache. She was happy to have Charlie to herself for once. Every other night this past week, at least a few members of his family had been present, if not work associates and friends as well. Charlie had been modest about his valor and quiet about all that he had endured, and Meg had been less than forthcoming about who she was and how she'd come to be living in Charlie's guest house, but most people didn't pry, though everyone wanted to know exactly what it was like to be aboard *Titanic*, and neither of them could ever answer that question to their satisfaction.

The servants brought in the next course, and when Meg recognized lamb and potatoes on her plate, she knew this would be a less elaborate meal than some of the others or else this main course would've been served later.

Charlie looked a bit paler than he had the last few days when he had seemed almost himself again, though not quite. There was always the lingering jumpiness they were both experiencing, the timidity at new or unfamiliar noises or sudden outbursts. Tonight, he seemed a few shades whiter than he had recently, and she knew his interview must have taken its toll. "Do you want to talk about it, or would you rather put it out of your mind?" she asked before she took a small nibble of the well-done meat on her plate.

He exhaled and took a sip of his wine before setting his glass down and offering his hand to her, which she took. She knew Jonathan was nearby, though she couldn't see him, and if there was even the suggestion that something inappropriate might be about to happen, he would suddenly be in the room, but Meg had learned from experience that hand holding was not an alarm to the liegeman.

"It was not pleasant," Charlie admitted, looking off in the distance as if he was trying to remember, or trying to forget. "I'm glad I got to speak with them today because I hear they are moving the interviews to Washington in a few days, and I'd rather not travel again any time soon if it can be avoided."

Meg nodded. "Did they ask you all sorts of questions you didn't want to answer?"

"They asked me all sorts of questions I *couldn't* answer," he confessed with a shrug. "I haven't the foggiest idea how the ship came to hit the iceberg. Nor do I know how the crewmen determined how many people to put aboard each lifeboat. I just know it wasn't nearly enough.'

His voice trailed off at the end, and Meg squeezed his hand reassuringly. "Did they ask you how you came to be on the collapsible?"

"They did. I told them the truth. I honestly don't remember."

She nodded. He hadn't been able to tell her either, though she'd asked while they were still aboard *Carpathia* and then again a few days after they arrived in New York. He said he remembered kissing her goodbye, spending time below the main deck unlocking gates and trying to help some of the Third Class passengers find the lifeboats, but those who spoke little English had no idea what he was saying, and once the boat became so submerged she was noticeably listing, he'd given it up and went back to where the boats had been launching. He remembered seeing the collapsible fall into the water, and then he couldn't remember anything else. He said there was a loud cracking noise, and he remembered being cold. After that, he was aboard *Carpathia*, and everything was sketchy. It came and went. Sometimes, he could remember talking to Meg, asking her to marry him all over again. Other times, she'd had to remind him of that conversation. Thankfully, he hadn't forgotten who she was since that day in hospital when they'd just arrived.

"At least it's over with now," Charlie said with a sigh. "You know, I went to several such hearings after the fire in the Triangle Shirtwaist Factory, and those things are never pleasant. They ask such demanding questions with little or no concern for what the person they're speaking to has been through. I wish all of those people had to go through a similar situation before they could be placed on those boards so that they could be a bit more... understanding."

"Was it mostly people from the government and the shipping industry?" Meg asked as he released her hand so they could return to their dinner.

"I'm not sure. There were reporters, too, I think. I recognized a few other businessmen in the galley and wondered if they were selling tickets." He scoffed and took another drink, almost draining his glass. Even though he'd been drinking quite a bit the last few days, Meg had yet to see him intoxicated, and she hoped tonight would not be the first time. Thoughts of drinking too much immediately led her mind to her uncle, and she pushed him back inside his box.

"I hear they've raised quite a sum for the passengers who need it, particularly the Third Class widows," Meg commented, taking a sip of her water. The lamb was delicious but she hadn't had much of an appetite lately, and she set her fork to the side of her plate hoping whatever the next course was it wouldn't be too heavy.

"Yes, they've collected quite a bit. I should like to contribute as well. I just haven't gotten to it yet."

"It seems odd that you would, in a way. That is, being a victim yourself."

"While I see your point, I feel as if I owe those families. It could just as easily have been one of their husbands or fathers clinging to the collapsible instead of me."

Meg swallowed hard. He'd made other such statements, but this time he had that far off look in his eyes again. "It could've been one of them in my seat as well. Or Jonathan's or Daniel's. There's no way to say how God decided who lived and who did not."

At the mention of God, Charlie's head whipped around and his eyebrows raised. "Do you think He chose?" he asked. His voice was calm, but there was an air of amusement in it. "Do you think He was looking down at the Atlantic that night and put us into categories of who deserved to make it and who did not?"

She put her hands in her lap, absently tugging at the stitches in the hem of her dinner napkin, not sure how to respond. She had little knowledge of Charlie's religious beliefs except for the few he'd mentioned in a letter from time to time. Since they'd arrived in New York, he had given no indication as to whether or not those sentiments had changed. She'd certainly done her fair share of swearing off all things of faith over the years. But she knew that night, as she sat on the unsteady lifeboat in the middle of the ocean, God had heard her prayers. "I believe we all have a reason for making it out of the Atlantic," she said quietly.

"The reason most of the people who made it out alive were able to do so was because they were First Class passengers. It was their wealth that won them their seats." He folded his hands above his plate and looked across the room at a large painting on the wall of an English fox hunt.

"Money wasn't everything, though, Charlie. JJ Astor, Ben Guggenheim, there are others who could've written a check large enough to pay the salaries of every crew member for the rest of their lives who didn't find a seat in the lifeboat and didn't have the capacity to hang on until they were rescued as you did."

"Capacity?" Charlie asked, looking at her with wide eyes. Again, his voice wasn't angry, but that condescending tone was present. "I didn't do anything miraculous or spectacular, Meg. I was just... lucky."

The servants came in again, and Meg set her napkin down. "I won't be having anything else, thank you," she told one of the servants she'd learned was called Victor, and he nodded as he took her plate. Once they were alone again, she said, "Charlie, I have no idea what happened to you while you were in the water. I have no way of knowing. Unfortunately, neither do you."

"I'm not sure that's unfortunate," he remarked quietly as he leaned back in his chair.

"It would be nice to know you have a full memory, I would think," she said. "Anyway, my point is, I spent hours praying that you would be spared, and you were. I don't know if that was divine intervention, luck, or something else. But I won't be ungrateful for it."

He was quiet for a long time before he turned to her and took her hand again, this time a bit more forcefully. "I'm not asking you to be ungrateful, Meg. I'm just questioning... everything now. I don't know how a God could stand by and watch newborn babies freeze to death in the middle of the ocean while boats floated nearby less than half full of women wrapped in enough furs to clothe an entire apartment building full of factory workers. I don't know how a God could pick and choose who lives and who dies and not send the *Californian* over to rescue passengers aboard another ship before she even went down at all. I don't know how a God could've allowed an idiot like Bruce Ismay to order an untested cruiser to pick up speed while plowing through ice fields without giving the lookouts proper tools so that they could see the icebergs. But that's what happened, I suppose. So... if there is a God, and I'm no longer convinced there is, I guess He must've had His reasons."

Meg stared into his green eyes for the longest time, and while her initial reaction was to hurl the same sort of comparisons at him—who was he to sit here in all this finery while somewhere out in the night, a little girl was too afraid to close her eyes for fear a monster would shadow her doorway?—she knew the pain that caused him to make such statements wouldn't respond to her logic. "I don't blame you for questioning God right now, Charlie. And I suppose He probably doesn't either. All I know is that I am thankful that you're here, that we are finally together, that I never have to step foot in Southampton again, and that for once in my life, I finally feel safe, even though I can also remember the terror of that night as clearly today as I could when it was happening."

He leaned in closely and licked his lips, but she could see the pain in his eyes. "Meg, do you hear them?" he asked quietly, his voice just a whisper.

She felt her heart catch in her chest. She'd hoped that it had finally stopped. He hadn't mentioned the voices since he'd been home, but she knew now he'd only been trying to go on about his life like everything was all right. They'd never stopped at all.

Meg slowly shook her head. "I don't, Charlie. But I believe you. And I'm sure you're not the only one. The others who were in the water—they might hear them, too."

His face fell, and he stared at her hand for the longest time. "I can't talk to them. There were only a handful, and they're scattered now. I don't even know any of them. I ...." His voice trailed off. She knew he wouldn't finish that sentence.

"What can I do?" she asked, lifting his face and slowly stroking his cheek as she met his eyes again. "How can I make it better, Charlie?"

"I don't know," he admitted, his other hand resting on hers. "I wish I did, Meg. They never stop. Even now, as I'm talking to you, they don't go away."

She wished with all of her heart she could take it away from him, but there was nothing she could think of to make the voices quiet. "Did you talk to Dr. Shaw?"

"No," Charlie admitted. "I'm afraid they'll drug me once more, and I don't want to forget you again."

"Maybe there's a different medication they can give you."

"Possibly. Or they could lock me up in an asylum somewhere with the other loons."

"You're not crazy, Charlie. You froze to death along with two thousand other people. That isn't insignificant. It's quite traumatic. Everyone else might think we can just be thankful to be alive and go on about our business, but it isn't that simple, now is it? You need to give yourself some time."

"They're driving me up a wall, Meg." His eyes narrowed, and she could see exactly how much he meant it. "It takes me hours to finally fall asleep, and when I do, they wake me several times each night. I give up."

"Then tell Dr. Shaw that you need something for sleep," she suggested, hopeful that it might be a helpful alternative.

He shook his head and she removed her hand, which he clasped in his. "I told you, I don't trust any of those medications now. I don't want to discover I've missed you again."

"Maybe Dr. Shaw will have a different suggestion, then," she said with a shrug.

He let go of her to run a hand through his hair, and she knew that meant he was anxious and disregarding her statement. "Perhaps." He looked like he might want to say more.

"Well, tonight, if you can't sleep, telephone me, and we'll talk," she said with a shrug.

A half grin pulled at one corner of his mouth. "Telephone you? In the middle of the night?"

"Why not?" she asked. "It's not as if I have something I need to do tomorrow. No one cares if Meg West has important information about *Titanic* to share." She had been lucky to escape the inquisition. None of the men running the interviews seemed to realize who she was at this point, and she wanted to leave it that way, though Mr. Ashton had informed her that her mother had sent him a telegraph a few days ago asking if he'd heard from Mary Margaret. He had yet to respond.

"You really wouldn't mind?"

"Not at all," Meg assured him. "In fact, I'd say come over, but something tells me Jonathan would immediately awaken and appear in my apartment the moment your slippers hit my living room floor."

He laughed, and Meg was glad to hear the sound. "I honestly don't think Jonathan would care at all, if it weren't for my mother."

She nodded. "Yes, well, Mr. Lane seems to be of the opinion that you and I cannot be trusted to conduct ourselves as responsible upright youths."

"Mr. Lane might be on to something," Charlie admitted, and Meg realized his mouth was quite near to her own now. She took a deep breath and his lips were on hers. His hand slipped up to cup her chin, and he drew her to him. There was a screech of wooden chair legs on the floor, and Meg found herself on his lap, her arms wrapped around his neck, her fingers in his hair. Charlie's hands had slipped down to her waist, and just as she was hoping they might find their way elsewhere, the door slammed closed behind her, making them both jump.

"Well, I can't say that I'm surprised that leaving the pair of you alone for dinner has had this result, but I am a bit disappointed."

She turned to see Jonathan's words didn't match his amused expression. Meg climbed off of Charlie's lap and straightened the light green dress she was wearing, one Carrie had gotten for her the week before. "Jonathan—you frightened me. Don't you know we still can't handle loud noises?" she asked, breathing hard, though she didn't think the startle had much to do with that.

"I'm aware, Miss Westmoreland, and I apologize. Perhaps more discretion on your part next time won't lead me to have to make such grand entrances."

"Jonathan," Charlie said, shaking his head, "just because you promised my mother you'd serve as chaperone doesn't mean you have to be so overly... present."

"Of course it does," Jonathan disagreed. "I've made her a promise, and I intend to keep it. Otherwise, my reputation might suffer."

"That's all right," Meg shrugged. "In my experience, reputations come and go at the drop of a dime." She winked at him, hoping he'd catch her drift. She was certain all the high society papers in Southampton had her painted as quite the hussy.

He laughed. "I can't just change my identity and go off to another country."

"Of course you can," Meg replied, turning to face Charlie who was now standing behind her. "It's easy enough if you've a mind to." She smiled at her fiancé, realizing that Jonathan was about to sweep her away. "Remember what I said." She held his gaze, and he nodded, letting her know he understood she meant he truly could call her if need be. She hoped that he would.

"Jonathan, avert your eyes," Charlie teased, and then he stepped forward to softly kiss her lips. "Have a good night, Meg. I'll see you tomorrow."

She smiled at him and turned to see Jonathan's eyebrows raised, realizing he hadn't averted his eyes at all. And she didn't care. "Good night."

"Miss Westmoreland?" Jonathan offered his arm.

Meg stepped forward and slipped her arm under his before giving Charlie one more smile.

"Jonathan, we've a few things to discuss when you get back," Charlie called after him.

"Yes, we do," Meg's escort agreed, and she felt her stomach tighten, wondering if they were simply talking about the factory or if there was more.

She waited until they were away from the dining room and they were nearing the back door that led to the path to her apartment before she asked, "Does whatever you have to discuss have anything to do with me?"

Jonathan looked at her out of the corner of his eye. "Why would you ask that?" They stepped outside into the cool spring air, and Meg shuddered, not sure if it was the shift in temperature or Jonathan's lack of a quick declination that made her do so.

"It's been a few days since we discussed meeting with the lawyers, and I'm of the inclination to think that I wouldn't be privy to much of that conversation until I absolutely had to be," she replied as they made their way around the small pond that sat between the two houses. The moon was up and a sky full of stars twinkled above them, but Meg paid little attention to the night sky these days; she'd spent enough time studying it while aboard the lifeboat there was no reason to pay it any mind now.

"It does have to do with the lawyers," Jonathan admitted. "They want to meet with Charlie tomorrow to talk about your options."

"And why do they not want to meet with me if they are my options?" she asked as they neared the stairs that led to her apartment.

"I suppose that is a valid question," Jonathan admitted. "But they said they wanted to meet with him first, get a sense for exactly what has transpired, what your preferences are, and then meet with the pair of you."

"Is the meeting here?" she asked, nodding at Charlie's house.

"Yes."

"When you go back to speak with Charlie, will you inform him that I'd like to come?"

"I will."

"Good."

"What if he says he'd rather you weren't there?" Jonathan asked with an eyebrow raised.

Meg chuckled. "Do you think that's a possibility?"

Jonathan opened the door for her. "I'll see you tomorrow, Meg," he said as she went inside and closed the door behind her. He knew Charlie wouldn't deny her access to such a discussion if she wanted to be a part of it. Meg never imagined she might marry a man who would see her as a partner, but it was quite clear that was the vision Charlie had for their future, and she felt very blessed to have escaped her own reckless behavior. Charlie might be doubting there was a God, but Meg was quite certain there had to be divine intervention at work; it was the only way she could explain how she'd gone from a foolish little girl making damaging and dangerous decisions to the fiancée of one of the most amazing men who'd ever lived over the course of a few weeks.

MEG WAS REPOSING on the sofa, in and out of sleep, letting the worries of the day wash over her, sometimes more than one at a time, when an alarming buzzing noise jarred her fully awake. She jerked upright, thankful that she wasn't on the bottom bunk of the Third Class passenger accommodations any longer or else she would've surely knocked herself unconscious on the bunk above her.

She looked around the living room and realized the irritating noise was coming from the telephone. A glance at the grandfather clock across the room told her it was past two in the morning. She assumed that meant it must be Charlie calling, and she gathered her wits and crossed to pick up the receiver as Jonathan had demonstrated for her, hoping she reached the device in time.

Clearing her voice, she spoke into the piece protruding from the wall. "Yes?" she asked. An operator, she assumed, said something that sounded like, "One moment please," and then she heard Charlie's familiar voice on the other end of the cord. It was quite remarkable.

"Meg, I'm sorry to wake you," he said, his voice hoarse and so quiet it was hard for her to make out his words. "You said to call. Perhaps you didn't mean it, but, I have done so, nevertheless."

She knew her face must be flush. Even the sound of his voice over the wire made her lightheaded. "I'm glad you did. How are you?"

He said nothing for a moment, which made her scrutinize the telephone, thinking perhaps somehow she'd managed to disconnect the call. At last, he said, "I couldn't sleep. I thought... perhaps, you might want to meet me outside. By the pond. There's a little bench there. We'd be out in the open, should anyone question our motivations."

Meg wondered if anyone else was even awake, but she assumed there was little chance of Charlie getting out of the house without Jonathan knowing about it. Not that she cared. Her discretion was more for his mother's benefit than anything else. "Yes, of course," she replied without hesitation. "I know that bench well. I pass by there at least twice a day." He knew that, obviously. She was chattering on for no reason.

"Very good. I'll meet you there in five, ten minutes then?"

"Five minutes?" she repeated. "I'm not sure I can dress in that amount of time."

"That's all right. Just put on your coat. I promise to be respectable."

She giggled. "All right then." She replied before she even allowed herself to process what she was agreeing to. Meeting her fiancé in the back garden in the middle of the night wearing only her dressing gown and a coat? How scandalous! Unfortunately, it wasn't the most outrageous behavior she'd participated in lately, but she pushed those thoughts aside.

"I'll see you shortly, Meg," he said, and she said goodbye before she attempted to hang the earpiece back on the wall. Her first try was not successful, as it clattered loudly off the hook, banging into the wall. She fumbled with it again, and this time, managed to make it stick.

"Miss Meg, is everything quite all right?" Carrie was standing in the doorway between the living room and dining room, wearing a robe, her hair in a nightcap, poking out every which way. Clearly, she had been in a deep sleep.

"Everything is just fine, Carrie," Meg assured her, scurrying around to find her warmest slippers. "I'm going out for a bit, but I'll be back shortly."

"Out?" Carrie repeated, obviously awake now. "How's that now, miss? Outside? In your nightdress?"

"Yes, but I'm only going just there," Meg said, pointing to the little pond. "If you feel compelled to do so, you may spy on me from the window."

"No, of course not, miss," Carrie said, though even in the dim light, Meg could see that she was contemplating her options. "It's a bit chilly out."

"I know," Meg nodded. Even though it was almost May, the nights were still cool. She grabbed her new black coat Carrie had picked out for her at the shop and slipped it on, Carrie smoothing the back and pulling out the collar. "I don't think I'll be long."

"Is Mr. Ashton meeting you, then?" Carrie asked.

"I hope so," Meg replied, "or else he'll have quite a bit of explaining to do in the morning." She stepped past her new friend toward the door.

Carrie yawned. "Why aren't you sleeping?" she asked as Meg placed her hand on the doorknob.

She wished she had an answer. "We both find it quite difficult, dear," she replied. "It's not something I can readily describe."

Carrie nodded, indicating there was no need to try. "Well, miss, if I may be so bold, make him work for it."

"What's that?" Meg asked, tugging the door open.

A sly grin slid across Carrie's face. "He isn't your husband yet. I know he will be soon, but don't give him too much for free, or he'll think he doesn't have to pay for it later."

Meg's eyebrows arched. She wasn't quite sure what Carrie was saying, but she thought she understood enough. "We will just be talking, I assure you."

"Umm hmm." Carrie winked at her, and Meg shook her head and stepped out onto the stairs that led to the ground wondering if Carrie was speaking from experience and deciding she probably was. No one was what they seemed.

She had made it about halfway around the pond when she saw Charlie step out from the shadows near the back door. As soon as he was close enough for her to actually see him clearly, she noticed he was dressed and she immediately wanted to smack him. Why hadn't he given her a chance to put on a gown?

As soon as she saw his smile, all was forgiven. "You look lovely, as usual, Meg," he said, his hands shoved deep into the pockets of his long dark coat.

"Thank you," she said. "I'd likely be lovelier in clothing, however."

"I'll assume you're not implying I think you are loveliest with no clothing on?" He was teasing, and she was glad it was dark since she was certain her face was bright red. "Have a seat won't you?"

She was glad he hadn't given her the opportunity to respond. Thoughts of being undressed in front of a man flitted across her stream of consciousness, but they were soon captured and returned to the box. She sat down next to him, being sure to leave ample space between them since she was certain Carrie was watching if Jonathan wasn't. Though he likely was, too.

"Did you sleep any at all?" she asked. Her coat was buttoned and she felt warm enough, but she took a cue from him and kept her hands in her pockets for safety's sake.

"Not much," he admitted. There was a slight breeze that stirred up his soft brown hair, and she wanted to run her hand through it.

She dug her nails into her legs through the layers. "Perhaps for an hour or so."

She cleared her throat, not sure what to say, but then she realized she was safe to say whatever she liked with him, so she asked, "Was it the screams again?"

"Yes," he said readily, holding out the sound of the "s" a bit longer than necessary.

"Can you hear them now?"

He nodded, once.

"Are there times when they are louder than others?" She thought perhaps talking about it might help, but if he indicated he'd like to change the subject, she was willing to comply.

"When I am alone. When it's quiet."

Even though she knew it wasn't wise, she drew her hand out of her pocket and pressed it against his arm. "I'm so sorry, Charlie."

"Don't be," he replied quickly, turning to face her. "I don't want you to be sorry for me. I just... didn't want to be alone."

"I know. I wish you didn't have to be."

They were quiet for a long time, and she started to withdraw her hand, but before she could take it away, he reached across and caught it in his, pulling her closer so that her hand was resting on his thigh, encircled in his. "Did I wake you?" He wasn't looking at her now; his eyes were fixed on something by the house, perhaps nothing by the house.

"I'm honestly not certain," she admitted. "I was in and out of sleep."

"Thoughts of *Titanic*?" He turned to face her now, and he was sitting more closely than she thought prudent.

"Sometimes," she shrugged. "Most of my ghosts reside elsewhere."

He closed his eyes and turned his head away. "I'm sorry, Meg."

"I don't need your sympathy either," she reminded him, though her tone was just as innocent as his had been.

"I suppose not," he admitted, turning back to face her. "But you have it just the same."

She wasn't sure how to respond to that. Had he been the one who had lived through such a tumultuous past, she assumed she'd feel similar. She'd want to take it all away and make it better, though obviously that wasn't possible.

"Can I ask you something? Something personal?" he asked, his green eyes seeming to peer right through her.

"You can ask me anything." Her voice was a whisper fluttering on the wind.

His lips didn't move for a long while, as if he still wasn't sure whether or not he should ask. Eventually, he said, "When I kiss you, when I touch you... is it... difficult?"

Her answer came quickly. "Not at all," she replied, and she could see surprise in his eyes at first but then acceptance that she was being honest. She broke the trance and looked away. "I thought at first it would be. That is... for all of those years, I thought I would never be able to be intimate with anyone. But then, as you know, there was Ezra. And that was not at all what I was expecting either. But it wasn't the same as... before." The box was attempting to open, and she needed to find a way to slam it shut and still assure him that she was not uneasy about his caresses. She turned to look at him. "Charlie, when you hold my hand, when you kiss me, it comes from a place of love. That's something I've never experienced before. I don't know what it might be like later—when we are married. But for now, I can tell you not to be concerned about that."

"Good," he said, and she realized he was much closer than he had been, much closer than she expected. "If it ever becomes a problem, you'll let me know, won't you?"

"Yes, of course." It was barely audible, but his lips were on hers, and she felt a longing in his kiss that echoed through her every fiber. He ran his hand through her hair as her lips parted, and breathing escaped her. She needed to feel his strong arms around her, feel his hands on her body reminding her that they were still alive, that they were still together.

Charlie pulled back, not just from her kiss, but his entire body shifted, and he suddenly slid nearly a foot away from her on the bench, leaving her staring after him, one hand still in the air, her eyes half closed. "My apologies," he said. "I shouldn't have.... That's not why I asked you here."

Meg put her hand down and adjusted her coat. Of course, she knew that, and Carrie's words rang in her mind. "I know it's not," she agreed.

"It's only... I discovered this evening at dinner—when I'm kissing you, I don't notice the noise so much."

She turned to look at him, certain her eyes were double their normal size. "Is that so?"

"I suppose it's because I'm so lost in you, I don't hear them as prominently."

Spinning around so that her knees were nearly pointed at him, Meg said, "Well, then I guess Jonathan and your mother, and whoever else has an opinion, will simply have to put their thoughts aside."

Charlie tilted his head so that he was almost looking up at her, despite the fact that he was over a foot taller than her. "What's that now?"

"If kissing me makes the voices stop, then you will have to kiss me much more frequently."

A grin spread across his handsome face. "While I'm all for it, I don't think I can kiss you all day and all night."

"No, I suppose you won't get much work done that way, but I'm willing to sacrifice as much of my day as necessary to help you with the situation." She let out a loud, fake sigh. "If I must."

Shaking his head in disbelief, Charlie said, "Meg, you are something else."

"I love you, Charlie," she reminded him. "It took me way too long to realize that, but now that I do, it's not an idea I'll be letting go of anytime soon."

He scooted back over so that he was next to her and fished her hands out of her pockets. "I love you, too, Meg. With all of my heart."

"Good. Then, it's settled. We shall make kissing sessions part of your health regimen."

"Very well. But I will need to explain this to Jonathan tomorrow. Otherwise, he's liable to fall out of the second story window trying to prevent me from taking part in a therapy session."

Meg looked up to where his eyes now fell and saw a shadow looming in the window. "Does he sleep in that hat?" she asked.

Charlie broke into a resounding laugh that echoed through the garden. "I don't know, but quite possibly."

"All right. I'll give you until tomorrow to explain, but it doesn't matter what Mr. Lane says. If it helps, it must be done."

He was still laughing as he turned to face her. "I concur."

She was tempted to lean in and kiss him again, partially just to see if Jonathan would open the window and shout at them, but she could see Charlie was fighting it and decided to honor his wishes.

"Would you like to go pay Kelly a visit tomorrow?" he asked, changing the subject before she could try to persuade him further to ignore the liegeman.

"I'd love to," Meg said, smiling. She hadn't seen Kelly at all since *Carpathia*. While it hadn't been all that long, it seemed like an eternity.

"Good. I'll arrange to take you over in the morning."

"What about the lawyers?" Meg asked, remembering the conversation from earlier.

"They don't come until the afternoon."

"You'll go with me?"

"Yes, of course. I need to see the girls."

Thoughts of Ruth and Baby Lizzy warmed her heart. "They will be so excited to see you."

She thought from his expression he might be remembering how

darling Ruth had been when they were looking for dolphins and octopuses on the ship. "I'll have to stop by and get them a gift before we go."

"Perhaps a doll with real eyes?" Meg suggested, referring to the old doll she'd given Ruth when she was a toddler that now had marbles for eyes

"Not a bad idea. Dolly New Eyes almost cost us dearly."

"You don't have to remind me." It had been leaving that doll behind that caused Ruth to go back into the depths of *Titanic* and almost lost all three of them their lives.

"I suppose we should go in now before Jonathan comes out to check on us." He gave Jonathan a little wave, but there was no gesture in return, an indication that the chaperone wasn't happy at their sneakiness.

"It might be entertaining to see him traipse all the way down here," Meg noted, but she was already standing, knowing she should go back inside and try to sleep again if she was going to be visiting friends the next day.

Charlie rose as well, and turning to face her, he made a big show of extending his hand. "Lovely to see you again, Miss Westmoreland."

Laughing, she shook his hand with as much animation as she could muster so that Jonathan could clearly see their antics. "Likewise, Mr. Ashton."

"I shall call upon you on the morrow." He continued to pump her arm.

"Very good then."

"Sweet dreams.'

"And to you."

He finally released her, and she turned to go, giggling. A few steps away, she spun to see if he was still watching her. He was, but he was also backing slowly toward the door. Glancing up at the window, she saw Jonathan still standing there sentient, and burying her hands deep in her coat pockets, she rushed toward the apartment, wondering why she suddenly felt the tables were turned and the servant was such an influence over their decisions.

As she approached the stairs, she took a chance and looked up at the heavens. She knew Charlie was doubting God's existence, but when she looked up at the sky, there was no doubt in her mind He was there. Despite all that she'd gone through, she finally felt she had found favor in His eyes. None of this had happened by chance.

CHAPTER SIX

Meg had hoped Charlie might feel up to driving, but he had declined stating he still didn't feel as coordinated as he would like in order to captain a motor coach. It ended up working in her favor anyway, however, since she was able to sit in the back with him, holding his hand, as the driver he introduced as Bix steered them along the streets of New York.

She had gone out once a few days earlier with Mrs. Ashton to a dress shop and lunch, though Grace had declined, so some of these buildings looked familiar. However, she truly had no idea if this was the same way they had come or not. She'd been so concerned with leaving a good impression on her soon-to-be mother-in-law, she'd not been paying as much attention as she'd have liked. Now, the top was down on the automobile, and she was able to peer up at buildings that seemed to touch the sky, wondering in awe, and thankful for a multitude of hatpins.

"The toy store is just up this way," Charlie explained, leaning in to her ear so that she could hear him above the wind. "Shall we go in or send Bix?"

"I think we should go in," Meg replied, shouting back. "Ruth will want to know you chose her present yourself."

He nodded, but the coloring in his face gave away his concern. She knew he wasn't feeling well today, and whether it was still recovery from the ordeal or a lack of sleep, clearly he was concerned at being seen in public less than himself. "I don't think it will take long," Meg assured him, tightening her grip on his hand. "I know our girl well enough to find a doll she'll like quickly."

Again, he only nodded, and she supposed he simply didn't want to yell over the wind. She was thinking perhaps Bix should put the top up while they were in the shop.

There were crowds of people walking by on either side of the street, men and women of all ages. Meg had never seen anything like it, particularly in the middle of a week day. She wondered where they were all going. Newspaper boys stood on the corner, and when they slowed at an intersection, she glimpsed the headlines, still focused on *Titanic*. She looked away.

Eventually, they passed the little café where she and Mrs. Ashton had eaten. She recognized the sign in the window, which was written in French. They'd laughed about the translation. Mrs. Ashton had been quite pleasant, and Meg was relieved to know she'd finally have a proper mother figure in her life, as long as she didn't find a way to alienate her between now and the wedding. Mrs. Ashton hinted time and again that, while she trusted Meg to stay in the apartment, proper ladies knew how to conduct themselves.

Meg's eyes shifted to Charlie. To her surprise, his eyes were fixed on her face. She assumed he'd be gawking out the window like she was, but then this scene must be ordinary to him. She smiled, wondering why he was staring at her, but she didn't attempt to ask over the wind. Thoughts of their discussion the night before made her cheeks rosy. He'd assured her he meant to try her theory this morning when he'd come to her door and kissed her in front of Jonathan and Carrie.

They came to a stop just in front of a shop with bright red, yellow, and blue signage, carved toys protruding from the large over-hang. "Dudley's Toy Chest," Meg read aloud. "This looks like just the sort of place Ruth could literally get lost in."

Charlie chuckled. "Ruth could get lost anywhere. We will bring her here one day, when things calm down."

She knew he meant when he felt up to driving and chasing around a little girl with too much energy. She nodded and patted his leg as she heard Bix opening her door.

He was a short man of about fifty or so, she thought, with specta-cles and kind eyes. He smiled as he held the door for her, giving a little bow. "Thank you, Bix," Meg said as she stepped from the motor coach.

Charlie followed, and she waited to see if he preferred to take her arm, which he did. She'd noticed he seemed to have trouble with transitions from one type of surface to another, one height to the next, and he'd need to step out and onto the curb. To others, it would appear that she was simply waiting to take his arm so that he could lead her inside, but the smile of appreciation he flashed at her was not missed. "Bix, while we are inside, would you mind putting the top up?"

"Yes, sir," he replied, closing the door as the couple stepped onto the sidewalk.

"I'd thought you'd like the view of the city, but it's so damn loud I can't even hear you," he explained into Meg's ear.

The feel of his breath on her neck sent tingles down her spine, and she only managed to smile a response, fighting the urge to embar-rass both of them by lunging at him right there on the sidewalk.

Charlie held the door open for her, and Meg gasped as she entered. There were dolls and toys of every variety imaginable lining shelf after shelf, some even hanging from the high ceiling, like zeppelins and other aircraft. She'd known from the outside that this place would be heaven to her little niece, but she had no idea the wonders that lay inside.

"It's a bit overwhelming, isn't it?" Charlie asked, leading her toward the doll section. "I came here once to get a present for the daughter of one of our foremen. It took me hours to decide what to get her, there's so much to choose from."

Meg nodded. "Luckily, I already see exactly what you should get for Ruth." She began to walk toward a doll with blonde ringlets and a lavender dress that nearly matched the shade Meg happened to be wearing. The doll had bright blue eyes and plenty of frilly lace and bows on her gown. "This doll looks very much like Dolly did before she lost her sight."

"Really?" Charlie asked, taking the doll from the shelf. "And you think she'd want one just like the one she has—only with eyes."

"And a full head of hair. And a beautiful dress. Yes, I suppose she will."

"Should we get this new doll some gowns to change into?" Charlie asked, looking at the array of dresses hanging nearby.

"That is a splendid idea," Meg agreed. She picked out a few gowns and accessories for the new doll, thinking Ruth would still want to play with her old doll as well. Both of them could wear the new clothes.

"What about Lizzie?" Charlie asked, looking around at some of the other toys available.

A stuffed bear caught Meg's attention. "She would likely chew on it, but the eyes seem tight. What do you think?"

"I think I wish you'd been with me the last time I was in here," Charlie replied. "Perhaps they wouldn't have found me curled up in the corner crying."

Meg laughed aloud at the thought, assuming he was just joking, especially when he raised his eyebrows at her playfully. They began to walk over to the cash register to pay for their gifts, and Meg remembered her other doll, Lilac, and thought of her father. "After Da passed away, I don't think I ever received another toy of any sort."

He looked at her with arched eyebrows. "Really? You were only six."

"I know. My mother thought toys and playing were a waste of time."

Charlie greeted the shopkeeper before he turned back to Meg. "I'm sorry, Meg. If it's any consolation, I was thinking of you, even then."

Meg couldn't help but smile at the thought of a little Charlie all the way across the ocean wondering what she was like. If he'd known the truth, he might not have been so excited to meet her. Nevertheless, it was evidence of his kind heart. "Thank you," she said quietly, placing her hand on his back as he paid for their purchases and the shopkeeper wrapped them up in bright colored paper so that Ruth could be surprised. They didn't bother to have the bear wrapped since Lizzie wouldn't be able to tear the paper anyway, and Meg scooped it up and held it in her arms as they waited. She would've loved to have had a bear like this one. Someday, she'd have her own baby and spoil him or her with all the bears and dolls or balls in the world.

Once they had their packages, they headed for the door, and Bix immediately took everything but the bear and slid it into the trunk, as Charlie and Meg returned to their seats in the back, the bear sitting on Meg's knees.

"You're quite fond of that fellow, aren't you?" Charlie asked regarding the bear as Bix started the automobile.

"He's adorable," Meg replied with a shrug. "Look at his cute little nose."

Charlie studied him for a moment. "He doesn't look much like a Teddy to me, but then I was never good with names."

"Teddy?" Meg asked, looking at him with wide eyes. "What do you mean?"

"All stuffed bears in America are named Teddy, don't you know?"

"What's that now?"

"Yes, they're named after President Roosevelt."

Meg could scarcely believe her ears. "You name stuffed bears after presidents here?"

"Yes. We're an odd bunch of ducks, aren't we?" he asked, that same playful expression in his eyes.

"Indeed," Meg replied, giggling. "And what if Lizzie wishes to call him something else? Does the president's personal detail come and take her away?"

"No, don't be ridiculous," Charlie replied waving her off. "It's a local jurisdiction issue. The New York City police will arrest her, and throw her in baby jail."

The way he made such a ridiculous statement with absolute sincerity had her laughing so hard she was afraid she might split the seams in her dress. "It's nice to see you're coming back to your old self, Charlie," Meg finally managed to say once she'd caught her breath.

"Do you think so?" he asked, and any hint of joking was brushed aside.

She stopped laughing and held his gaze. "I do," she assured him. "You'll get there, Charlie. I know you will."

"If I do, it's because of you," he replied, and even though Meg didn't know how that could be true, she didn't have long to think on it before his lips were on hers. She was thankful it was Bix driving the car and not Jonathan, because not a sound was made from the front seat as Charlie continued to kiss her until the motor coach pulled to a stop in front of its next destination. She was so lost in the embrace Meg wouldn't have even noticed the auto wasn't still moving if Charlie hadn't whispered in her ear, "We're here."

It took her a moment to realize what he was saying, but when she did, she pulled away enough to look over her shoulder and see a large apartment building. Once again, she was surprised as the façade was not at all what she was expecting. This was a building that housed many of the workers from the factory, which was just a few blocks away. Meg expected it to be old and dingy, though she knew Charlie wouldn't allow his workers to live in filth. Still, the outside was a pristine limestone, and even the windows were clean. Flowers grew on either side of the front steps, and an older woman sat on the stoop, dressed nicely with a shawl around her shoulders. She waved at the few people passing by on the sidewalk.

Bix had the door open, but it took Meg a moment to straighten her hair and hat after Charlie's sweet kisses had mussed them a bit, and while she was righting her outfit, he got out on the other side and came around so that he was the one now waiting for her, his hand outstretched and a jovial grin on his handsome face.

"Am I a mess, thanks to you?" she whispered as she drew close to his ear.

"No, you look lovely, as always," he assured her. "I'm only amused that there was a possibility that you might be a mess."

She wasn't certain she believed him, but she knew Kelly would let her know if she looked at all disheveled. It had been one of her jobs for many years to keep Meg looking her best.

Meg held the bear in her free hand and took Charlie's arm, Bix behind them with the rest of the gifts. The woman on the front stoop spoke to them, and Charlie called her by name, which Meg found impressive. They took the lift to the eleventh floor, which was nearly the top of the building, and Meg steadied herself as the floor beneath her began to move. She may have been on such a contraption at one point in her life, but she couldn't remember it, and she was glad to have Charlie's arm to keep her grounded even if she was no longer on the ground.

Once the elevator came to a stop, and the operator opened the door, Meg was happy to be back on a non-moving surface. The hallway had lovely carpeting, and she was again in awe at how well the Ashton's cared for their workers.

"It's just over here," Charlie said as he led her around the corner and knocked on the door of number 1107.

It took a moment for her to answer, but even before she opened the door, Meg recognized Kelly's voice as she spoke to someone, perhaps Ruth. She was both nervous and excited to see her friend, not sure what memories might come to the surface once they were face to face again.

Kelly pulled the door open, and a warm smile spread across her familiar face. "Meg!" she shouted. "Charlie! How wonderful to see you!" The redhead opened her arms wide, and Meg stepped into her embrace, entering the apartment as she did so.

Releasing Meg, Kelly hugged Charlie as well and then led them into a small entryway that opened up into a living area. Meg couldn't believe how spacious the apartment was. There was a small dining area and a kitchen, and it looked as if there were at least two bedrooms as well. The windows were wide with thin drapes that let the sunlight pour in, and Meg was instantly grateful that her friend was able to make such a nice place her home.

"How are you?" Kelly asked, ushering them in.

Before Meg had a chance to answer, Ruth, who had been playing on the floor nearby, crashed into her knees, nearly knocking her backward. "Aunt Meg!" the little girl shouted, her red curls bobbing about. "You've come to visit at last!"

"Hello, Ruthie," Meg said, scooping the child into her arms. "It's so nice to see you." She squeezed her as tightly as she dared. "How have you been?"

"Good," Ruth answered, but soon she was wiggling away, her arms outstretched, shouting, "Uncle Charlie!" and Charlie took her out of Meg's arms, laughing at her excitement.

"If it isn't my little friend, Ruth. Have you seen any dolphins out your apartment window?" he asked, teasing her.

"No, silly," Ruth said, wrapping her chubby arms around his neck. "There's no water out there."

"Oh, that's right." Meg noticed Charlie's face brightened almost immediately upon seeing his favorite little girl, and she absently wondered what had taken them so long to stop by. He set the little girl down, but she stayed right there, eyeing the stack of presents in Bix's arms.

"Lizzie's sleeping," Kelly said, gesturing for them to come into the living room, "but she should be up soon."

"This bear is for her," Meg said, handing over the stuffed animal which looked a bit less fluffy now that Ruth had been in Meg's arms as she tried to hold onto him.

"Isn't that cute," Kelly said as she took the bear from her. "She'll love it. Thank you. Please do have a seat."

"What's for me? What's for me?" Ruth bounced up and down, and Meg couldn't help but chuckle at her antics.

"What makes you think we brought you anything?" Charlie asked.

"Because I'm your favorite girl," Ruth reminded him, making them all laugh.

Charlie had no argument for that, so he took the gifts from Bix, who promptly excused himself back to the waiting motor coach, and as Meg sat down on what appeared to be a brand new sofa, Charlie set the stack of presents down on the floor in front of Ruth. "All right, Ruthie. Here you are."

She opened the large one first and marveled at the doll. "Now Dolly New Eyes shall have a sister!" she proclaimed. Each of the outfits also made her giddy with excitement until Meg thought the little girl might burst. She ran over to Charlie and flung herself at him, hugging him tightly and thanking him over and over again, proclaiming him the, "Best uncle in the whole world."

"All right, Ruthie. Take your toys and go to your room so that grownups can talk," Kelly instructed. "And be careful not to wake your sister."

"Does she have her own room?" Meg asked as Charlie sat down next to her on the sofa.

Kelly collected the last scraps of wrapping paper and walked toward the kitchen. "She does for now. Lizzie's crib is in our room, but we'll move them together when she's a little older."

"Your home is so lovely," Meg said, glancing around.

"Thank you," Kelly replied, sitting in a chair near the sofa. "Thanks to Charlie."

He waved her away. "Nonsense. Daniel is doing remarkably well. All of the workers at the factory say he's just splendid, the best foreman they've ever had."

"He's working very hard," Kelly nodded. "He wants to do good work for you. After all you've done for us...." Her voice trailed off as if she might get emotional if she wasn't careful.

"My father is a firm believer that, if you treat workers well, they're more loyal and will do their best work. I agree." He said it as if it was obvious to everyone, and yet Meg knew her uncle didn't have the same philosophy, nor did many other factory owners. Perhaps that's why Westmoreland Textiles continued to lose business every year.

"We absolutely love it here," Kelly continued. "I thought we'd be living with my cousin in a little flat across town for a year or so. This is not at all what I had in mind, but it is so much better."

"Perhaps your cousin needs to find a new place of employment," Charlie pointed out, hinting that he might be willing to offer her cousin a job.

"I'm sure he'd appreciate an opportunity. He's a hard worker, too."

"He'd have to be if he's your cousin, I suppose," Charlie said, making Kelly blush.

"The Irish don't get enough credit for the work we do."

Meg agreed. She knew there was still a lot of racial tension and hatred against Kelly's people here, something she didn't quite understand. She cleared her voice, hoping to change the subject but not wanting to ruin the chipper mood, either. "Have you heard from your mother?"

"Yes," Kelly nodded, folding her arms across her lap. "I let her know we were all safe, my family that is, and that she shouldn't worry about you."

"But she knows we are together, doesn't she?" Meg asked.

"I never told her for certain before we left what our plan was, but I'm sure she does."

"And she sent a telegraph back?" Charlie clarified.

"She did. It was short. She only said she was so thankful to hear we were safe. I don't think she knew for certain what ship we were on, but I'm sure she assumed the worst when she heard about *Titanic*."

Meg nodded. It would be just like Patsy to think the worst, though in this case she was right to worry.

Kelly continued. "I've sent her some money, but I don't know that it's gotten there yet. I'd like for her to be able to stay home now that she's getting up in years."

"Of course," Charlie said quickly. "I'm happy to send her whatever she needs."

"Oh, no!" Kelly objected. "I didn't mean... Daniel's salary is more than enough for us to afford to send some money back home."

"Nevertheless, if your mother needs anything..."

"You're too kind, Mr. Ashton," Kelly said, her face reddening.

"Mr. Ashton?" he repeated, looking at her like she'd lost her marbles. "Kelly, you're practically family now. Please. If your mother needs anything, I'm happy to help. If she wants to come here, I'm glad to do that as well. Of course, I can't recommend White Star Line."

They all chuckled at the joke, but it still stung a bit as well, and Meg remembered her father used to say, "Sometimes you have to laugh so you don't cry."

"Have you seen the papers?" Kelly asked, her face quite serious again, and Meg felt her stomach tighten as her friend stared into her eyes.

"What papers?" Meg asked. "The ones about *Titanic*?"

"No, the ones about you," she replied, her eyes flittering to Charlie.

"She hasn't seen them," he muttered, and Meg realized he must have read the newspapers himself.

"What do they say?" Meg asked, feeling a bit of panic rising in her throat, wondering if someone had discovered where she was or had decided she'd committed some sort of violent crime or other atrocity.

Kelly cleared her throat. "I have one. It's weeks old, since it had to come across the Atlantic, and we all know how hazardous that can be."

"May I see it?"

Kelly glanced at Charlie, who nodded at her, and then she crossed to her kitchen and returned in a moment with a well-worn newspaper. Meg pulled her hand away from Charlie's and took it. The headline read, "Westmoreland Believed to be Dead." She swallowed hard at a photograph of her uncle's automobile slammed into the trunk of a tree.

"You can read it if you'd like," Kelly said as she regained her chair. "Essentially, two days after *Titanic* sailed, Ezra showed up at your mother's house, saying you'd stolen Bertram's auto and forced him and Charlotte to go with you. He said he was finally able to get away from you, but Charlotte stayed, and he didn't know where you were going. A few days later, they found the auto crashed into a tree near Exeter, and there was blood all over the front seat."

Meg glimpsed the article briefly but didn't read it word for word. "And no one knows where Charlotte is?"

"Not the last I heard," Kelly said, shaking her head.

Meg looked to Charlie, and she could tell by the expression in his eyes he knew more. "What are they saying now?'

He cleared his throat and looked at the floor for a moment. "They think the blood is yours. Possibly Charlotte's too. But right now, they're saying she might have killed you and is now running from the law."

Meg shook her head violently. "That can't be. I mean—I know, obviously, you're aware that she didn't kill me. But Ezra and Charlotte left well before I did, and they took the motor coach."

"They found your bag, and no one seemed to know the timeline exactly," Kelly clarified.

That made sense. It was possible no one noticed Ezra and Charlotte left the night before Meg did. For that matter, her mother may have thought she managed to sneak out earlier than when Meg left with Kelly. "What about you?" Meg asked, scanning the article for mention of Kelly and her family.

"My mother told yours we had left for New York once she was certain we were gone. She didn't tell her we were together. But it was enough that the police aren't questioning our whereabouts."

"Doesn't it seem odd to anyone that this many people have gone missing from the same household in such a short amount of time?"

"Your uncle is under investigation for other reasons now as well," Charlie explained. "Several women, including some socialites, have accused him of scandalous behavior. The banks are making cases against him for money laundering. So, yes, the police do find it odd that so many people left so quickly."

Meg was discovering it was difficult to breath. "Do you think... do you think Charlotte is all right?" She was looking at Kelly, but she would've taken an answer from anywhere.

"No," Kelly said, her eyes flickering between Charlie and Meg.

Gulping for breath, Meg said, "Do you think it was an accident?'

"I honestly don't know," Kelly said, shrugging, though her eyes revealed she thought otherwise. "You knew Ezra better than anyone. Do you think he was capable of... hurting her?"

She hadn't allowed herself to think about Ezra since she'd stepped foot on *Titanic*. The way he'd treated her had been unfathomable. She would've never thought he could use her the way that he did. And yet he had. Was he capable of harming Charlotte? She prayed not, but she didn't know. "I hope not." It was the only answer she could muster. "But as long as they assume the blood is mine, they won't be looking for her properly."

"That's a possibility," Charlie admitted.

"Then... that means I need to reveal my identity," Meg said with a loud sigh.

"It's probably for the best." Charlie's voice wasn't as strong and reassuring as she would've liked, but she knew he was right. "Meg, you don't need to worry, though. Nothing can happen to you now. You're here. You don't have to go back to Southampton to let everyone know you're alive, and you're with me."

She turned to look at him, fighting back tears. "I do have to go back, Charlie," she said, her voice shaking. "If others are coming forward and accusing Bertram, I should be there, too. I have more to accuse him of than anyone."

"Meg," Kelly interjected, "you can't be serious. They would put you on a witness stand and make you relive all of those terrible experiences. In front of a crowd of strangers."

She looked to Charlie, a question in her eyes.

"It's quite possible," he agreed. "I know you're strong enough to do that, Meg, but are you sure it's worth it? I mean, he's likely to go to prison for a very long time based on the crimes he's committed against the banks alone. He's not a young man. He'll likely die there."

The idea of sitting in a room full of strangers and reliving the atrocities her uncle had committed against her made Meg feel like her stomach was caught in a vice. And yet, she couldn't imagine having other women—ones she knew, ones she'd grown up with—testify to similar events and not stand up with them and speak the truth. "I need to go back." Her voice was a whisper.

Charlie's arm was around her shoulders, and he kissed her temple. "Let's speak to the lawyers about it this afternoon, Meg. You don't have to make a decision now."

"Perhaps you can sign some sort of documentation and submit your testimony that way," Kelly offered, though they all knew that likely wouldn't be sufficient.

"I need to help Charlotte," Meg reminded them.

"That you can do from here. We'll decide how best to announce your presence, and then you can give everyone the true timeline so that Ezra can be questioned. Clearly, he's made up a story, and the police will want to talk to him again after they know what he's saying isn't true."

"I wonder how much time they've to devote to this now. You know we lost over five hundred men when *Titanic* sank?" Kelly asked, eyeing Meg.

Meg's eyebrows shot up. "Five hundred? From Southampton?"

"Yes," Kelly nodded. "Mostly crewmen."

Meg hadn't realized that, though it made sense. Her hometown was the last port of call for *Titanic* before the voyage, though they'd stopped briefly in Cherbourg. The vice grip had let go of her insides, but now she felt as if she might be ill all over Kelly's pristine carpet.

"Are you all right, Meg? You look a bit... green."

It was only slightly amusing to her that Charlie was so concerned about her coloring considering how many times recently she'd been worried that he had no color at all. "I'm fine, darling," she said, quietly.

"I'm sorry what was supposed to be a happy reunion has become so morbid and disconcerting," Kelly offered. "Let me get you some water."

Before Meg could even respond whether or not she wanted any, a glass was thrust into her hand. She took a slow sip, and she vaguely heard Kelly going on about how lovely it was to have both cold and hot water from a tap in her very own kitchen, though she supposed it wasn't really *her* kitchen since they were only living there on Charlie's good graces, but it was still nice, as was the radiant heat and the bathroom facilities. They'd also met some lovely neighbors with a daughter Ruth's age....

Meg knew she was simply trying to draw her attention away from the weighty topics they'd been discussing, but it really wasn't working. Thoughts of returning to Southampton made her stomach lurch again, especially if the city was broken after such a loss of life. Not to mention she'd have to go by passenger liner, and Charlie had already said he'd never step foot on another ship again, though she thought he might be exaggerating since he did so much business in London.

"Meg?" His voice was soft against her ear. "Would you like to go back to your apartment and lie down for a bit?"

She turned to face him, his lips brushing her cheek as she did so. "I'd like to stay and see Lizzie if we could," she reminded him.

"I think it might be best if you came back another time. You don't look well. We can't both be stumbling about like drunken fools."

She knew he was teasing, but there was truth behind the statement. Meg was about to protest again when a soft whimper from the back bedroom caught her attention. She looked at Kelly.

"It sounds like the princess might be awake. Let me go see."

As soon as Kelly was out of the room, Charlie's lips found hers, and Meg was relieved to have the opportunity to think of nothing but him for a few moments. His hand softly caressed her cheek, and she leaned into him, hoping he understood just how much these stolen kisses meant to her; it wasn't just the voices in his head that needed taming.

She heard Kelly in the hallway as she spoke in a sing-song voice to her youngest daughter. Ruth's voice tinkled through the air as well, and Meg managed to pull herself away from Charlie, who straightened her collar and then his own tie, giving her a wink, which made her giggle despite the situation.

"Look who's here, Lizzie," Kelly said, stepping around the end of the couch.

The baby's face lit up, as if she recognized Meg, and as Meg opened her arms, she swung into her embrace. "Hello, sweet girl," Meg said, and Lizzie cooed at her. "She's growing so much."

"I know," Kelly agreed, standing nearby. "She'll be scurrying about, running after this one before we know it."

Ruth made herself comfortable on Charlie's lap, her new doll clutched to her chest. "Are you leaving soon, Uncle Charlie?"

"I'm afraid so," he replied, wrapping his arms around her little waist. "Would you like to come and visit at my house one day?"

Ruth's face lit up as she turned to face him. "Could we?"

"Yes, of course. Any time."

"She'd get lost in five minutes at your house, I suppose," Kelly laughed.

"We'll assign Mr. Jonathan as your personal assistant then," he said into Ruth's ear but loudly enough for everyone to hear.

"Mr. Jonaffin is my friend!" Ruth reminded him. "I miss him."

"I know you do, darling," Charlie replied. "And he wanted to come, but he's been quite busy at the factory this week."

"Daniel mentioned he'd seen him. I'm surprised he's back to work already."

"We can't all lay about all day long without doing anything productive." Charlie was poking fun at himself, but Meg felt the need to jab him in the side, a reminder that he wasn't just lying about for the sake of being lazy.

"You do seem much better than the last time I saw you, though your color is still a bit pale," Kelly observed.

"I feel much better," Charlie said. "I think I shall go back soon enough."

"I feel better, too," Ruth chimed in. "But I have bad dreams sometimes."

"You do?" Charlie asked, leaning forward so she could see his face when she turned her head.

"Yes. About the boat."

"Me, too," Charlie admitted.

"I think we all do, love," Kelly said. Lizzie made a fussing sound, and Meg handed her back. "Except this one. I don't think she has any idea." She kissed her daughter on the forehead.

"Lucky duck," Charlie said, as he tickled the babe-in-question's big sister until she laughed aloud.

Meg didn't mention that she was also nightmare free when it came to the ship; her nightmares still contained spindly fingers and monsters that shadowed bedroom doors.

"I'm afraid we need to be off," Charlie said, still looking at Meg with great concern.

She gave him a reassuring smile. "I am a bit tired."

"It was lovely to see you," Kelly said, bouncing Lizzie.

Charlie slid Ruth off of his lap onto the couch and stood, offering his hand to Meg, which she used to pull herself up off of the plush sofa.

"Can we really come to your house?" Ruth asked grabbing his other hand.

"You can." He turned his attention to Kelly. "Ring the house and let them know when you'd like to come over, perhaps sometime next week. You have the number?"

"Yes, it's over there by the telephone." Kelly nodded in the direction of the contraption on the wall in the dining room. Meg wondered how she hadn't noticed it before, as if it was commonplace now.

"It was lovely to see you," Charlie said, giving Kelly a hug and a peck on the cheek before telling Lizzie goodbye in a sweet voice that made Meg melt just a bit on the inside. He scooped Ruth up and held her for a moment before kissing her cheek and making her promise to be a good girl.

"You don't have my number, do you?" Meg asked as she hugged Kelly.

"I don't," she admitted.

"Just ask the operator for number four-forty-five Fifth Avenue," Charlie explained.

"That's a bit of a tongue twister, but I think I have it," Kelly smiled.

"Goodbye, Aunty Meg," Ruth said as she extended her hands from Charlie and Meg took her in her arms.

"Goodbye, darling. Be a good girl. I will see you soon."

"Aunty Meg, don't be afraid of the next boat. It'll be safe," the little girl assured her, and Meg looked at the other two adults in the room, wondering if there was any way Ruth may have overheard their conversation. Their wide eyes told them they didn't think so. Ruth leaned in so that she was whispering directly into Meg's ear, her breath tickling her so that she jumped. "Also, don't worry about the monsters. Uncle Charlie will protect you."

When she was done, Meg pulled back to look at her. "Thank you, Ruthie. I will remember." She knew she'd never used that word aloud —monster—even though she'd thought it several times since she'd entered the room. She set the little girl on the floor and spied her suspiciously for a moment. Ruth had known *Titanic* would sink long before it did; if she felt assured that Meg was safe, she would try to take the message to heart.

"We'll see you soon," Kelly said, taking Ruth's hand.

They said their goodbyes, and Meg stepped out into the hall, taking Charlie's arm. They were silent all the way to the lift, and only then did Charlie greet the operator and ask him to take them to the ground level. It wasn't until they were outside in the fresh air that Charlie asked, "What did she whisper in your ear?"

Meg swallowed hard. "Nothing important." She wasn't willing to tell him anymore about the monster just then. He kissed her hand and helped her into the car before going around to get in on the other side. Meg suddenly realized she was much more exhausted than she had noticed. She was hopeful that she could manage a nap, though there were voices in her own head now, ones she hadn't heard for a long time—ones she'd hoped she'd never hear again. Charlie was talking, and it helped to lessen the sounds of a little girl crying and an old man's raspy whispers, but it wasn't enough, and she suddenly knew exactly what Charlie had been living with these past few weeks. It could only be described as pure hell.

CHAPTER SEVEN

Charlie's bed was large and plush, the sort of mattress you could sink into and never be found again if you tried hard enough. The furniture was opulent—much like the dining room table—and Meg wondered at how such a humble person could sleep surrounded by such finery. Surely, he hadn't picked this décor out himself either.

They were both fully dressed, the only parts currently touching were her hand and his forearm, though she would admit there had been some other contact earlier before he fell asleep. Carrie was seated on a settee just outside of the door, which was open, and she stood every once in a while and poked her head in, though Meg was well aware by her crooked grin they'd picked a chaperone more partial to their side than Mrs. Ashton's. Nevertheless, when Jonathan arrived home from work, if he knew what they were up to, they'd both be scolded unmercifully if they had no chaperone whatsoever.

Charlie had been asleep for at least an hour now. It was difficult for her to see the clock at this angle, and she wouldn't risk adjusting to look for fear she might wake him. As much as she would've liked to join him in a deep slumber, the idea that this would soon be her bedroom, that they would share it as man and wife, had her head in a tizzy, and she wasn't able to rein in her thoughts to anything that might lead to sleep. She could see her own apartment out the back window, and it was comforting to know that Charlie could look out his window and see her, in a way, as he lay here in his bed.

The lawyers would be there soon. She was tempted to tell them to go away, that Charlie's rest was more important than anything they needed to discuss, but she doubted he'd sleep much longer anyway. Every once in a while, he stirred quite violently, and she questioned whether or not to wake him. Each time, she'd squeezed his arm, and he'd readjusted and gone back to sleep. She was hopeful that his dreams were not nightmares, but it was difficult to be optimistic when he began to thrash around like that.

She'd watched him sleep frequently aboard *Carpathia*, but that seemed quite different. He'd been drugged at the time, and while it had been necessary to calm him, it wasn't natural. Now, she had the pleasure of gazing at his handsome face in a natural sleep, and doing so brought a smile to her face. She really was quite lucky her father had chosen such an attractive man to be her husband.

It was all a bit surreal, if she was honest. She knew in her heart none of it had really been due to chance. Not only was he unwilling to step aside after she'd been noncommittal for years, he'd come all the way to Southampton to see her, and even came to her house after she'd purposely stood him up at Alise's ball. Then, they just happened to both purchase last minute tickets aboard *Titanic* and spot each other on board. If Ruth hadn't picked Charlie out of the crowd and run to him when she got lost, Meg would've done everything she could to avoid him, since she knew exactly who he was, but he had no clue of her true identity. She attempted to evade him time and again, but he pursued her anyway. Even after he discovered the truth of who she was, and she was certain he'd never speak to her again, he'd given her another chance. Now that they were finally together, she would never do anything to lose him again. She'd acted like a fool for the last time.

She must have been staring at him more intently than she

intended because she soon realized he was looking at her, a small smile forming on his lips. "This is the most beautiful sight I've ever opened my eyes to," he said, his voice raspy.

Meg blushed. "I'm sorry. Did I wake you?" she asked, turning onto her side so he could hear her better with her voice still lowered.

Charlie scooted back onto his pillows a bit so that he was sitting up slightly. "I don't think so. I was just dreaming of you, and then I awake to find you really are here."

She could still feel the heat in her cheeks. "Dare I ask what you might have been dreaming?"

His face began to match the color in hers. "Since you are a lady, I'm afraid I can't say."

Meg smiled at him, contemplating leaning over and kissing him, but she knew that doing so would be very dangerous, and just as she was formulating a response, Carrie stood and stuck her head in the doorway. "I believe I hear Mr. Lane's footsteps on the stairs," she said in a hurried whisper.

"It seems I've awoken just in time," Charlie managed, sitting fully upright.

Meg scooted off the edge of the bed on the side nearest the window, straightening her gown as she did so. She hadn't even removed her boots, though her hat was hanging on a hook by the door. She decided she didn't have time to pin it back to her head, but she could still sit it in place. "I don't suppose you have a sitting room on this floor we can hurry to?" Meg asked as Carrie helped her with the hat.

"We do, but I'm not overly concerned about it." He was also fully dressed and only needed to slip on his jacket and straighten the comforter on the bed, which he did.

Carrie had just finished with the hat and stepped back when Jonathan rounded the corner, coming to a full stop in front of the door. "What's this now?" he asked. "Up to no good?"

"Don't be ridiculous," Meg replied, turning to face him. "Carrie has been with us the entire time."

Jonathan eyed her suspiciously, and Carrie managed a small smile. "I'm not quite certain that means anything," the liegeman stated.

While Carrie thrust out her bottom lip, as if she were greatly pained to hear that Jonathan thought her an unworthy chaperone, Charlie stepped forward and looped his arm through Meg's. "Unfortunately, Carrie is a better chaperone than one may think." Then, changing the subject, he asked, "Are the lawyers here then?"

"They are. Four attorneys, stuffed in suits, in the parlor, ready to do your bidding, and offer their best advice regarding what to do about Miss Westmoreland."

"Well, let's get on with it then," Charlie suggested. "No reason to prolong the inevitable."

Carrie stepped out of the way so that Charlie and Meg could follow Jonathan down the hallway toward the stairwell, and then the lady-in-waiting trailed until they reached the bottom of the stairs.

"Are you certain you're ready for this?" Charlie asked, pausing in the foyer to turn and face her.

Meg nodded. "I assume it's not the most difficult task I'll be called upon to complete in the near future." Thoughts of what it would be like if she had to testify against her uncle in court made her stomach lurch again.

"True," Charlie replied with a shrug. "You are planning on marrying me."

That was enough to make her giggle, and she playfully nudged him in the arm. "That wasn't quite what I was referring to."

"Nevertheless...."

"I'll just wait for you here, miss," Carrie said as she stepped out of the way.

"You can have a seat," Charlie informed her, gesturing toward a sitting area at the end of the hall.

"Any questions before we enter?" Jonathan asked, looking at Meg.

She noticed his eyes were a bit bloodshot, and she wondered if he'd also been having trouble sleeping. It would make perfect sense that he would be struggling as well. She shook her head, and the three of them made their way to the parlor.

Meg hadn't been in this room yet, although it resembled the library with its dark mahogany furniture and red velvet cushions on all of the seating options. There was a large table, and four men sat around it, encircled in a cloud of cigar smoke. It took them a moment to halt their conversation and notice the door was open. By then, Jonathan was most of the way across the room, Meg and Charlie just behind him.

"Gentlemen, may I introduce Mary Margaret Westmoreland," he said, gesturing in her direction.

"How do you do?" Meg asked, giving a nod in their general direction.

Jonathan continued with the introductions. "This is Tom Halsey, Charlie's primary attorney, and these are his assistants." Tom Halsey was a rather large man with gray hair and a protruding belly. Meg nodded directly at him. "This is David Whicksmith, Clyde Overton, and Stanley Brubaker." Each of the men made quiet niceties as Meg looked from one to the next. Mr. Whicksmith was rather short with red hair and a kind smile, which made her instantly like him most of all, while Mr. Overton and Mr. Brubaker were taller with dark hair. Mr. Brubaker was the only one who wore spectacles, and they were quite large on his thin face.

Charlie greeted each of the gentlemen before pulling out a chair for Meg and sitting down himself between her and Mr. Brubaker. Jonathan found a seat on the other side of the table next to Mr. Overton.

From the head of the table, Mr. Halsey said, "Miss Westmoreland, it is our understanding that you would like to know the specificities of the contract your father put together with Mr. Ashton before his death. Is that correct?'

"Yes," she replied with a nod. "I'd like to know what my options are. And I'd also like to know how one best goes about letting the world know she is still alive."

Mr. Halsey had a stack of paperwork in front of him, and Meg wondered if one of the documents was the original contract, the one that would have her father's very own handwriting on it. "I'm not exactly sure what you know, so I will go over the terms of the contract with you, miss. Firstly, the contract calls for you to marry Mr. Charles Ashton by your twenty-first birthday. If you do so, the sum of fifty thousand pounds will be released to your mother, Mildred West-moreland, and to your uncle, Bertram Westmoreland. At that time, full title to your father's company, Westmoreland Textiles, will transfer to Charlie."

Meg nodded. She knew that part very well.

"Your father was quite clear that this is what he wished to have happen. Not only is it noted in the contract, but he expressed that desire to Mr. John Ashton both upon requesting the agreement and when the contract was signed.

Meg swallowed the lump in her throat. Would her father have still wanted it to go that way if he knew what her uncle had done? How her mother had treated her?

"Secondly, there are provisions for what must happen should you fail to marry Charlie before or during your twenty-first year."

"And those are?" Meg asked, though she had a bit of an idea.

"If you do not marry Mr. Charles Ashton at all, the company becomes yours upon your thirtieth birthday, but the money will go to charity."

"That's not really a concern," Meg reminded him, and Charlie's reassuring smile let her know he wasn't interested in dwelling on that condition either.

"Very well," Mr. Halsey nodded. "If you marry Charlie after your twenty-first birthday, the money will be yours, but Charlie will still own the factory."

Meg looked from Charlie to Jonathan, who didn't appear to be as interested in the discussion as she thought he would be—perhaps because he already knew all there was to know about the situation. "And what should happen if either my mother or uncle passes away or is incarcerated before we wed?"

Mr. Halsey's brow furrowed. He glanced down at the paperwork and back at Meg. "Well, there is a contingency within the document that says if one of them were to pass, the totality of the funding would transfer to the other. There's no recommendation for what happens if one of them is incarcerated."

Charlie was looking at her curiously, too, but Meg wasn't quite sure why. He must know the reason she'd asked the question. "Legally speaking, what might happen?"

The confused expression still sat upon the lawyer's face. Mr. Whicksmith spoke next, looking at Meg as he asked, "Do you fear that is a possibility, Miss Westmoreland?"

She appreciated the fact that the attorney spoke straight to her without looking to Charlie for permission first. "I believe my uncle may be in some trouble."

"What sort of trouble?" Mr. Halsey asked Charlie.

Rather than answer, he deferred to Meg, glancing in her direction to let her know he assumed she could respond for herself. "The papers are reporting he is being investigated for money laundering amongst other things."

The lawyers looked at one another for a few moments before Mr. Halsey cleared his throat and said, "Generally speaking, under such circumstances, a convicted criminal appoints someone to handle his finances. I would assume your uncle would choose your mother, in which case she would essentially receive all of the contracted amount."

Meg thought that would likely be the case, and she wasn't sure how she felt about it. She knew she could simply wait a bit longer before marrying Charlie so that neither of them got any of the money, but that was becoming less and less of an option with every moment she spent with Charlie.

"What other questions did you have?" Mr. Whicksmith asked in his caring voice that made Meg feel more at ease than the tone in which the other lawyers addressed her.

"Obviously, I am alive, while my mother and the Southampton police continue to look for me. Will I be in any sort of trouble for running away?"

"You're twenty, yes?" It was Mr. Brubaker this time, this being the first time he had addressed her at all. Meg nodded. "Then, by British law, you're an adult. You can come and go as you please."

"The fact that your mother has sent the police off to investigate your whereabouts under false pretenses is not your doing," Mr. Overton added.

"There is another girl missing, though," Meg reminded them, and all of the gentlemen nodded along, as if they were aware of Charlotte's disappearance, which she found odd since none of them seemed to know of her uncle's legal problems. "I feel that announcing that I am safely residing in America will give the police more information so that they can continue to search for her. Do you think I could be linked in any way to whatever has become of her?"

"I wouldn't worry on that," Mr. Halsey said with a chuckle that made Meg feel as if her question was silly. "They should know you weren't involved. They found the auto well after *Titanic* had set sail."

"That doesn't mean that they won't suspect I had something to do with it," Meg reminded them.

"Did you?"

The question came from Mr. Overton, and Meg's eyebrows raised in offense. "Of course not," she replied quite quickly.

"Then I should think you wouldn't have anything to worry about." He wiped his brow with a handkerchief from his breast pocket.

"I plan to travel back to England soon, and I want to be sure that I won't be in any sort of trouble with the law when I arrive there," Meg further explained.

"I can vouch for her whereabouts from the moment *Titanic*

sailed. That should be enough, don't you think?" Charlie was looking at Mr. Halsey, but all four of the lawyers nodded.

"Miss Westmoreland, you may rest assured that you have the best legal counsel in all of New York at your service, and we work quite closely with Mr. Ashton's attorneys in London as well. You will be fully protected." Mr. Whicksmith smiled confidently as he looked into her eyes.

Meg was happy to have the soft spoken man as part of the conversation, and she absently wondered how he even became a lawyer in the first place. "Thank you," she said with a nod.

"Is there anything else?" Mr. Halsey seemed to be in a rush.

"As far as letting the world know that Meg was aboard *Titanic* and was among the survivors, how do we proceed?" Charlie asked, looking around the room.

"I believe it would be best to make a simple statement to the newspapers. I know a reporter at *The Times*. He can help us put out a press release. I think mentioning it further back in the paper is the best way to go, not to aim for a headline," Mr. Overton suggested, wiping at his brow again. Meg wondered if it was really that warm in the room or if he always had this sort of perspiration problem.

"We certainly don't want a headline," Charlie agreed. "But how do we prevent that from happening? Isn't any reporter going to jump at the opportunity to announce Miss Westmoreland was aboard *Titanic*?"

"And that she's with Charlie?" Jonathan asked, suddenly becoming part of the conversation.

"Must I make any sort of announcement? Can't I simply telegraph my mother and the police station in Southampton?" Meg wondered.

"You will have to make some sort of a statement," Mr. Halsey said, looking at her as if she'd gone half mad.

Meg scooted her chair back a smidge so she could turn to look at him better. "Why is that exactly?"

"It's to be expected," the larger attorney replied with a shrug.

"Anyone could send a telegraph to the authorities. We'll need photographic evidence."

"So a statement and a photograph?" Jonathan asked, looking from the lawyer to Charlie.

Meg shook her head. "No, I don't want to make a fuss. I just want the police to know that I'm not with Charlotte and that the blood they found in my uncle's motor coach isn't mine."

"I'm afraid the only way they will know that for sure is if you go there and tell them. In the meantime, a photograph will be enough to show them that you are here." Halsey had a way about him that made Meg want to wipe the self-righteous smirk off of his face.

"Meg, we can ask one of the photographers to come here. It doesn't have to be a production," Charlie said quietly, his hand sliding up her arm to rest just below her elbow. "It will be all right."

"I've spent my entire life trying to stay out of the papers," she said between clenched teeth.

"Perhaps you shouldn't be marrying an Ashton then," Mr. Halsey laughed.

"Perhaps you should reexamine that document in your hand," Meg shot back, bringing his laughter to an abrupt halt. Her eyes met Charlie's to make sure she hadn't offended him; obviously, she wanted to marry Charlie—now.

He looked amused, perhaps proud of her ability to put the pompous lawyer in his place. "It will be more difficult for you to stay out of the papers now that you're here, Meg, but we will make sure that whomever we invite to take the photograph is trustworthy."

"I have a fellow in mind," Mr. Overton said.

Meg met his eyes and then returned her gaze to Charlie, who was clearly waiting on a response from her. "Fine," she managed.

"Very well, then," Charlie said. "We'll arrange it. In the meantime, Jonathan will send a telegraph to your mother and to the police in Southampton to alert them that you are here. If you have anything specific you'd like the messages to say, let him know."

Meg shook her head. "I trust your ability to be concise and tactful more than myself."

Jonathan offered a weak smile.

"We have other business to attend to," Charlie said, surveying a sea of nodding heads before he turned back to Meg. "I'd like for Jonathan to escort you home."

"That's not necessary," Meg began. "Carrie is here."

"I'd like Jonathan to go with you."

Jonathan was already up, and Meg wondered why it was so important to Charlie that he send his man with her. "If you insist," she said, knowing there must be some reason. Turning to the attorneys, she said, "Thank you all for your assistance. It was lovely to meet all of you." She nodded at each of them in turn but held Mr. Whicksmith's gaze a bit longer, hoping he realized she was more thankful to him than the others.

"I will see you soon, Meg," Charlie said, squeezing her hand once more as she stood. She rested her hand on his shoulder for only a moment before turning to take Jonathan's arm. He led her out of the room without a word.

Once they'd reached the hallway, Jonathan signaled for Carrie to follow them, which she did at a distance. Turning to Meg, he asked, "Are you well?"

"I'm fine," she admitted. "I must admit I've never sat in a room full of lawyers before."

"You handled yourself quite respectfully," Jonathan assured her.

When he turned to speak to her, Meg noticed more than the scent of mint she usually associated with him. There was another familiar smell as well, and she realized why he wasn't quite himself. "Are *you* feeling well, Jonathan?" she asked.

"Yes, of course. Why do you ask?" He held open the back door for her and she was happy for the cool breeze that brushed away the smell of whiskey, a scent she could've done without.

"I don't know," she replied, taking his arm again. "You just don't seem quite like yourself today. You didn't say much in the meeting."

"There wasn't much to say," he replied. "I'm not an attorney."

"No, but you are an expert on most things, including high society. I'd assumed you'd have had more to say about what Charlie and I should do to announce my presence."

"There's a reason I didn't say anything," he explained as they made their way around the pond. "Whatever you decide will be overridden by Mrs. Ashton anyway."

Meg stopped in her tracks. "Whatever do you mean?" Perhaps this was the reason Charlie insisted he walk her home, so that he could break the news.

He turned to face her. "I mean... as soon as Pamela Ashton learns you are willing to let the world know of your engagement to Charlie, there will be a ball in your honor. And there's nothing you can say or do to get out of it."

Meg felt as if a ton of bricks had just come crashing down on her insides. "A ball?" she asked, her voice weak.

"Yes, and I'm sure that Charlie realizes that as well, but there was no reason to mention it in a crowded room, especially since he knew you'd stop breathing, the way that you have just now."

Taking a deep breath, Meg realized he was right, and she wished they were closer to the bench so that she could sit. "I'm not sure I can do that, Jonathan."

"Do what? Go to a ball? I think you can, though I know there are times when you decide not to at the last moment."

She knew he was teasing, but she didn't find it humorous at the moment. "Jonathan, I can't even imagine standing up there in front of everyone, having to answer their prying questions, listen to their sarcastic comments...."

"Meg, you won't have to worry about all that." He was patting her gently on the shoulder. "Charlie has a way of handling those sorts of situations. It will be fine."

"But what if he can't?" she asked, leaning in a bit and using a sharp whispering voice as if she thought Charlie might somehow overhear. "What if he isn't well enough to handle it himself?"

"All the more reason to get it over with now so that you don't have to worry about it once we don't have any excuses."

His words made sense, but they didn't make her feel any better. Suddenly, a stiff drink sounded like a good idea, and she wasn't one inclined to drinking after she'd witnessed what it did to her uncle.

"Come along, Meg," Jonathan said, taking her arm and leading her in the direction of her apartment. "We need not worry about it just now. Let's wait for the hammer to drop before we become too uncomfortable. After all, there are lots of other things to spend our time dwelling on."

Unfortunately, what he said was true. "Do you know what you'll say when you send word to my mother?"

"I was thinking, 'I'm alive, you miserable excuse for a mother. Now stop looking for me and leave me the hell alone.'"

Meg burst out laughing and had to take a moment to catch her breath, pausing just before the door that led to the stairwell. "That actually isn't half bad."

He was laughing too, but mostly at her, she assumed. "I was just going to say something to the extent of, 'I'm alive and in America. You will hear more from me soon.' To the police, I would say, 'I wanted to inform you that I set sail on *Titanic* on April 10 and have arrived safely in New York on *Carpathia*. I was not with Ezra Bitterly or Charlotte Ross when they left my mother's home and have no knowledge of the whereabouts of Miss Ross. I am happy to answer any inquiries you may have.' Does that sound about right to you?"

She nodded, but she wondered how he happened to know the last names of the pair in question. She had known Charlotte for quite some time yet had no idea what her surname was. "Yes, that sounds perfect." She wasn't surprised that he would know precisely how to word it.

"All right then, Miss Meg. I shall leave you to your quarters," he said, holding the door and gesturing for her to climb the stairs on her own.

"What? You're not going to escort me up?"

"I'm afraid I have quite the boring business meeting to get back to," Jonathan replied with a sigh.

"I see. I don't envy you there."

"I am sure Charlie will want to call on you soon, or else have you over for supper."

"He'd better," Meg replied with a sharp nod. "Thank you, Jonathan." She placed her hand on his shoulder, and looking into his bloodshot eyes, she added, "You know, if you ever want to chat about what we've been through, I'm happy to listen. You're not in this all alone."

He managed a weak smile. "I shall keep that in mind, my lady."

She giggled at his forced formality and looked back to see Carrie was following her. She wondered why Jonathan felt he had to be immune to any sort of feelings. Hoping she'd find a way to reach him eventually, she entered her living area and collapsed onto the sofa, pondering how she could be so tired just from thinking.

MEG DID FIND a way to doze off, and it was nearly supper time when Carrie finally roused her, insisting she get up now and get dressed or else she would be late for the evening meal. "Mr. Lane stopped by and said that it is important that you are well dressed this evening," the brunette informed her mistress as she dragged her from the living room into the bedroom.

Though her mind was still a bit foggy from her nap, Meg yawned and asked, "Why do you insist on calling him Mr. Lane? He is also in the employment of the Ashtons, the same as you."

Carrie was digging through the armoire and only turned to look at Meg briefly before shrugging and saying, "Everyone calls him Mr. Lane. He's... more important than most of the other servants. Just as everyone calls Mr. Ashton's second Mr. Pointer and Mrs. Ashton's lady Ms. Dumont."

Sitting down on the edge of her bed and contemplating rolling over onto her side and going back to sleep, Meg said, "I suppose overly well-to-do people have servants for their servants."

"Miss! You can't go back to sleep!" Carrie tugged on her arms and began dressing her in a lovely sapphire blue gown Mrs. Ashton had picked out for her. For a moment, Meg was reminded of Charlotte dressing her just before she went downstairs to face her mother for the final time.

"I'll do it! I'll do it!" Meg shouted, standing up and pushing Carrie aside. That last thing she needed was memories of that morning or thoughts of that particular young lady. She pulled the lilac gown off, and despite her insistence that she could do it herself, Carrie helped her work the blue one on over her undergarments.

"Your hair is quite messy. We'll have to redo it." Carrie gestured at the vanity Mrs. Ashton had purchased which occupied the corner nearest the window facing Charlie's house.

"Can't we just pin it up?"

"Miss, Mr. Lane was quite clear when he said you must look nice."

Carrie's voice was as insistent as she had ever heard it before, and Meg's stomach began to twist into knots. "What is Mr. Lane on about, Carrie? Has he something up his sleeve?"

"I honestly don't know, miss, but I'm not about to be blamed for your refusal to attend supper as polished as possible. Now, please, have a seat so I may work on the bird's nest on your head."

Meg pursed her lips together but had a seat anyway. "It isn't half as bad as it was when I disembarked, is it?"

"No, miss," Carrie replied, taking the pins out so that she could start over. "It isn't so bad, but it simply won't do when Mr. Lane insists...."

"I understand, Carrie," Meg cut her off. They were quiet for a moment, and as her mind continued to linger on Jonathan, a question began to formulate in her mind. She wasn't one to gossip, but she was a bit concerned. "Carrie, do you happen to know, does Jonathan have a reputation as... a drinker?"

"A drinker?" Carrie repeated as she combed Meg's hair out. "No, not that I know of. However, he did used to work in a tavern, I believe."

"Really?" Meg asked. Carrie was tugging at her hair so hard, her head nearly snapped back.

"Yes, I believe that's where he and Mr. Ashton met."

"Charlie frequenting a tavern? That seems odd to me." She couldn't imagine him wandering into a common saloon.

"I don't think it was the sort of establishment Mr. Ashton visited regularly. I'm honestly not sure. Why do you ask?"

It was a good question. Meg wasn't sure why she'd brought it up. It did seem like the sort of topic she would discuss with Kelly, but Carrie was not Kelly. "No reason, I suppose," she replied as Carrie began to pin her hair up. "He just smelled a bit like alcohol this afternoon, and I guess I'd never noticed it before."

"Maybe he's upset about the boat."

She assumed she meant the sinking of the passenger liner, and wondered why everyone insisted on calling it a "boat."

"Or the wedding."

Meg forgot that the girl had a handful of her hair and turned her head rather sharply, which stung a bit. "What's that?"

"Oh, nothing," Carrie said quickly, giving a nervous laugh. "Nothing at all."

"Carrie?" Meg was still looking at her, and Carrie attempted to walk around to the other side so that she could continue to work on her hair.

"It really isn't something I should repeat, miss," she said, and she bit her bottom lip in a way that let Meg know she wanted to tell but thought she might end up in trouble over it. Meg continued to turn so that her hair was facing the mirror, a position in which Carrie couldn't possibly reach it. The girl let out a sigh. "All right. I'll tell you what I've heard—but it's only speculation, and it's probably not even true."

Again, Meg said nothing, only stared at Carrie expectantly.

Carrie licked her lips and swallowed hard. She glanced over her shoulder, as if she thought Jonathan might suddenly appear in the room. In a quiet voice, she said, "Some folks say that Jonathan is secretly in love with...." She stopped, waiting to see if Meg could guess where she was going. Meg's face was frozen. Even though she already knew what the last word in the sentence would be, she didn't move, not even an eyelid. "Charlie."

Meg had guessed as much herself while on the cruise liner. She'd even hinted at it to Jonathan, but she had put it out of her mind, thinking that if it were true, surely he would attempt to stop the wedding. But he'd done nothing of the sort. "Why would anyone say that?"

"I honestly don't know," Carrie admitted. "I've just heard some of the other servants joke about it. No one thinks it's requited mind you. In fact, some of them jest that Charlie is so oblivious to it, he doesn't even notice."

"What is there to notice?"

"Would you... can I work on your hair, please?"

Meg reluctantly spun around, and Carrie took another deep breath and began to pin up the rest of Meg's hair. "Some say it's just a look now and again in Mr. Ashton's direction. Mr. Lane has never been seen with a woman, and he's nearly forty, you know? He has been seen with other fellows though, or so I'm told. All of this is simply rumor, mind you, Miss Meg?"

"I understand, Carrie. And you should know the only reason I ask is because Jonathan is quite important to me, and I'd hate to do anything to upset him."

"Yes, miss," Carrie answered. "Would you like face powder?"

Meg hardly ever used the substance, though many of the girls back in Southampton had done so. "No, thank you," she replied. She let out a deep sigh. If her marriage to Charlie really was heartbreaking to Jonathan, she wished she could speak to him about it, but then there was nothing that could be done. Perhaps she could find a way to let him know just how important he had become to her.

Carrie went over to Meg's jewelry box, which still had very little to choose from since she'd brought nothing with her from England, and pulled out a few of her newer pieces. Simple drop earrings and a necklace with blue stones were enough to compliment the outfit and the combs in her hair without overwhelming. After helping her into a pair of slippers that better suited her dress than the boots she'd been wearing all day, Carrie stated, "I believe you're ready, miss."

"Thank you, Carrie," Meg said, standing, and turning to face the girl. "I appreciate your help, and thank you for trusting me with the information you disclosed."

"You won't say anything to anyone, will you?"

"No, of course not," Meg replied, knowing that was true partially because there would be no one to tell. She may say something to Charlie, given the opportunity, but that hardly counted since they were practically married.

"I'll ring the house and let them know you're ready."

"Thank you, Carrie," Meg said again. As the young woman walked away, she added "and I'm sorry I yelled at you when I was tired."

Carrie giggled. "If you think that was yelling, you should see my grandmother when someone's late for Sunday meeting."

Meg couldn't help but smile at the retreating form as Carrie made her way down the hall. She was lucky to have found someone else who could be a potential friend. Filling Kelly's shoes was hard, but she did like Carrie, and she was good at her job. Before long, Meg thought Kelly just might need a lady herself, an idea that surprised her but also made her quite proud of everything her best friend and her family had accomplished. With one last glimpse in the mirror, Meg made her way out into the hall, hoping that whatever it was that made Jonathan insist she get gussied up wouldn't be too overwhelming to her already nervous stomach.

CHAPTER EIGHT

"We can have that lovely orchestra that Josie and Walter used at their daughter's coming out party, what are they called? The Moonlight Waltz, or something or other. Oh, and when you officially propose at the engagement party, we can do it outside so we can use firecrackers, just like they did at that wedding we attended in France. It'll be wonderful."

Meg's fork was poised over her salmon, but her eyes were glued to Charlie's across the table from her, neither of them even blinking.

"Mother, I really don't think all of that is necessary. At all," Charlie began, not losing hold of Meg's eyes.

"Please, Charlie. My only son will only be getting engaged once," Pamela insisted.

Meg cleared her throat but said nothing, and rather than taking a bite she moved some of her carrots around on her plate so that it might appear as if she were eating.

"Honestly, Mother, I appreciate the fact that you want to make it a memorable affair, but really, just close friends and family should be sufficient."

"I wish your sister were here. Perhaps she could talk some sense into you," Pamela replied. "I spoke to her on the telephone earlier, just as soon as you rang me, and most of these are her suggestions. You know her parties are always so popular in Buffalo. There's no reason why we can't make this engagement the talk of New York City."

"Trust me, dear, it already will be," Mr. Ashton finally chimed in from his seat at the head of the table. Charlie was sitting next to him on his right with Meg on his left. Pamela sat at the other end. It would've been quite awkward if all of the leaves had been left in the table, but they were much closer now that the dining table was only a speck in the grand scheme of the formal room.

"I'm only saying...."

"Mother, perhaps we should talk about this later," Charlie said with a small smile. "I'm not sure your vision, and Grace's vision, is in line with what Meg and I want, but we've both had a tiring day, and I'd just as soon not discuss it this very moment."

She let out a sigh. "All right then." She was quiet for a few moments before she muttered under her breath, "There will be an awfully lot of people who will expect to attend."

Charlie looked at her but said nothing, and Meg silently applauded his ability to bite his tongue, something she wished she had been better at with her own mother.

"How did your meeting with the lawyers go?" Mr. Ashton asked, looking at Meg, which caught her off guard.

She put her fork down, banging it a bit too loudly which made her jump. "Pardon me," she said under her breath. "It was... enlightening, I suppose."

Mr. Ashton nodded and gave her a small smile. "Do you know what you intend to do then?"

"Not yet," Meg admitted. "Charlie and I are still discussing it."

"Luckily, Grace and I have been discussing the wedding for several months," Pamela chimed in, and Meg envisioned the release of thousands of doves at the conclusion of the ceremony. "Should you want to get married in the next few months, we will be able to pull it all together."

"Wonderful," Meg said, smiling at her and letting a nervous laugh escape her lips before she caught Charlie's eyes. She felt his shoe gently tap against her slipper and knew he was signaling for her to humor his mother but not to bother to argue, something she wouldn't do anyway.

"Well, hopefully we will have a response to Jonathan's telegraph to your mother soon. I'm sure you're anxious to know her reply." Mr. Ashton offered Meg another reassuring smile, and she felt drawn to him as she would if he were her own father.

Charlie cleared his throat. "It is possible we may need to return to Southampton soon. Mr. Westmoreland has gotten himself into a bit of a financial bind, and Meg may be called upon to testify."

Pamela stopped eating and stared at her son in shock. Meg waited for her to say something, but she didn't. Her eyes shifted to Mr. Ashton, and he looked as if he knew even more than what Charlie had mentioned.

"Of course, neither of us is looking forward to re-crossing the Atlantic, but if it can't be helped...."

"Perhaps I should accompany Meg, and you should stay here," Mr. Ashton offered. Meg could tell by the look in his eyes he was concerned for his son's well-being. She imagined if it had been her child who had nearly died in such an undertaking, she'd never let him out of her sight again.

"Thank you for the offer, Father, but I would like to go with Meg myself. It will be difficult, I won't deny it, but if she can do it, so can I."

"I've heard some fellows already went back to London," Mrs. Ashton stated, shaking her head. "One was said to have gotten on the next boat out. I can't imagine."

"Neither can I," Meg admitted, looking at her plate. The food was delicious, as it always was when Charlie's cook, Lois, prepared it, but Meg found it difficult to eat while having stressful conversations, possibly the reason she'd been described as a "twig" most of her life.

"We will plan the engagement announcement for next weekend, then," Mr. Ashton suggested, "and then, if you should have to go back, you shall have it out of the way."

"I'm not sure that will give us enough time...."

"Actually, I believe it needs to be quicker than that," Charlie explained, interrupting his mother. "The point is to let the world know that Mary Margaret is alive so that the authorities in Southampton will... stop looking for her."

Meg thought he was about to mention Charlotte, and while she was unsure as to why he hadn't shared that information with his parents, she didn't question it. Surely his father knew; he must read the papers.

"Didn't the telegraph accomplish that?" Mrs. Ashton's question was a valid one.

"Yes, but the lawyers suggested a photograph be taken of the pair of us together so that they will know for sure that the telegraph was sent by Meg and not someone simply pretending to be her," Charlie further explained.

"That does make sense," Mr. Ashton nodded.

"So... we'll discuss the details tomorrow, Mother, but I'd like to do it the night after next. Here. With only a small number of guests."

Mrs. Ashton had a smile frozen on her face. "We'll discuss it tomorrow. I'm not even sure if your sister is free and can make it down that quickly."

"She'll manage," Charlie assured his mother. "I apologize for leaving dinner before it's finished, but I'm not feeling well, and I'm afraid I'll need to excuse myself."

Meg had seen the color in his face draining layer by layer as the meal progressed. "Of course," his father was saying. "Shall we call someone to escort you out?" He looked at the servants standing nearby, and one of them, a young man Meg didn't know the name of, stepped forward.

"No, that won't be necessary," Charlie said with a weak smile. "I'll send Jonathan in for you, Meg." She realized he didn't want to abandon her to his parents, though she didn't mind so much, as long as he was all right. She only nodded. He shook his father's hand and wished him good night and stooped to kiss his mother's cheek before he gave Meg one more look and slowly walked out of the room.

Once he was gone, Mr. Ashton said, "I'm quite concerned, Pamela. I don't think he should be getting on another ship anytime soon."

She nodded her head in agreement. "Meg, surely you wouldn't mind if John accompanied you to speak to the police in Southampton, rather than Charlie?"

Meg's mouth suddenly felt dry, and she couldn't formulate a sentence for a moment, Eventually, she pried her tongue off the roof of her mouth. "It's not that I mind so much, Mrs. Ashton. It's only, I'm certain Charlie won't let me face my mother and uncle without him."

"Please call me Pamela," the mother reminded her. "And why is that, exactly?"

She wanted to tell them, or at least give them a logical explanation, but once again the words wouldn't exit her mouth properly.

"It's all right, dear. If you don't wish to talk about it...."

"I do wish to talk about it. But I don't seem capable," Meg admitted.

The Ashton's exchanged looks that Meg recognized as sympathy. "Well, dear, whatever you and Charlie decide is best, we'll try to accept it. I only worry that he will end up making himself more ill."

"I understand. I am also concerned."

"He isn't as strong as he thinks he is sometimes," Mrs. Ashton muttered, moving her own food around on her plate.

Before Meg could say anything else, Jonathan stepped into the dining room, and without crossing to the table, which she thought was odd, he called, "Meg, are you ready to go, or are you still dining?"

"Don't let us keep you," Mr. Ashton insisted as Meg looked at each of them, wondering what she should do.

"I'm certain we will see you soon, darling," Pamela said with a smile.

Meg stood, and Mr. Ashton rose to peck her cheek and wish her goodnight. Meg wished them both well and then met Jonathan at the door. With one last glance at Charlie's parents, she went out into the hallway, her hand on Jonathan's arm, but immediately, she recognized why he'd kept his distance. "Jonathan, you're intoxicated," she whispered sharply near his ear, though she wouldn't dare get too close. The smell was enough to make her gag.

"Yes, I am," he admitted. "And I apologize for that."

"Why?" she asked. He was able to walk in a fairly straight line, but as they approached the back door, she felt that she was doing more of the leading than he was.

"I didn't realize Charlie would ask me to escort you home. I thought I was done for the evening."

His answer made sense; he was able to do whatever he liked on his own time. Still, she was surprised. "Did Charlie realize you were drunk when he asked you to bring me home?"

"I doubt it since he looked as if he were about to pass out himself."

She stopped and looked at him, and he gave a loud guffaw. Meg wasn't sure if he was telling a joke or not. "You know, Mr. Lane, I can see my apartment from here. I suggest you head back to your room, and I'll make it the rest of the way myself."

"Now, don't be silly, Meg. I can walk you to your apartment. It's just over there."

"I know that—but it really isn't necessary."

"Meg..."

"Jonathan... thank you, but this is quite far enough." She pulled her arm away from him, and he looked at her for a moment with a hint of something invidious behind his eyes, causing her to take a step back. Just as quickly as it came, it faded.

"Very well then. Have a good night, Meg." He spun on his heels and headed back toward the main house, covering the ground quickly. Meg would've been certain she'd offended him if she thought he would even remember it in the morning.

A few hours later, Meg awoke to the sound of the ringing telephone. Unlike the night before, she recognized the sound now, and only choked on her own heart for a split second before she sprung from the sofa to answer. Less than ten minutes later, she was sitting next to Charlie on the bench, her coat wrapped tightly around her. She was fairly certain Jonathan would not be checking on them this night.

"I wanted to apologize for my mother," Charlie said with a sigh. "She's never been much of one to throw such social spectacles until my sister's engagement party and subsequent wedding. Since then, she's become enamored with making as much of a show as she can. It's like a ... contest or something."

Meg couldn't help but scoff. "I suppose that makes you lucky then if its only started recently. Most of the women I grew up knowing did anything and everything they could to outdo each other when it came to such get-togethers. My mother never had the money for such things until my coming out party—which you paid for."

Charlie smiled at her. "Too bad I wasn't invited."

"It would've been much more fun if you'd been there." She remembered the night well, even though it'd been several years ago. Not as many people had come as her mother would've liked, thanks to her uncle's reputation as a womanizer.

"Well, I wanted to apologize nonetheless, and to tell you I'm sorry I left you."

"No, it's all right. I understand. You weren't feeling well."

He inhaled deeply through his nose, held it for a moment, and then let it go. "Meg, I've been thinking... it's been a few weeks now, and nothing seems to be improving. Perhaps, when we return from

Southampton, if things aren't any better... perhaps I should... see someone."

She raised an eyebrow. "What do you mean? See whom?"

He pursed his lips together, as if he wasn't sure whether or not he could tell her. "I mean a specific sort of doctor who specializes in this sort of thing."

Her other eyebrow shot up. "You mean... a psychiatrist?"

He nodded. "I know it might sound desperate. It's only... I don't know what else to do. I don't want anyone to think I'm crazy...."

"A psychiatrist would be the one to say that, though, wouldn't he?"

"Possibly," Charlie shrugged. "I think I'm sane enough to stay out of an institution. I hope I am anyway. But I've been reading, and some of the techniques these doctors have come up with might help me. Have you read anything by Freud? Or Jung?"

She had heard of Freud but not that other person. "I don't know much about psychiatry," she admitted.

"They both have several theories, and they're both quite different. But perhaps if I see a psychiatrist, they might be able to help me better understand what is going on in my mind and why I am hearing voices that aren't there."

Meg opened her mouth and closed it again. She didn't know what to say.

"Do you think I'm crazy?"

"No!" She said it quickly, turning to face him. "Not at all."

"Then why are you against me seeking help?"

"I'm not," she reassured him. "I'm not. Charlie, if that's what you need to do, I'll support you. I suppose... I just wish I could be enough to fix it for you, that's all."

"Oh, Meg," he said, brushing her hair back behind her ear. "You are enough. Believe me, you're more than I ever expected. But... this has nothing to do with you. That's the problem. I don't know why I'm doing this to myself. From what I've read, I have to sort out why it's happening in order to be able to stop it."

She wanted to understand what he was saying, but she couldn't. She had her own ghosts, her own voices, and they all fit nicely into the little box in the back of her mind. They were there just now. Why couldn't he simply do that—build a fortress to keep them inside so they couldn't surface? She didn't ask. "Charlie, I love you, and if you want to see a specialist, I will do whatever I can to support you."

"Thank you," he smiled at her and then leaned forward and kissed her on the forehead before pulling her head to rest on his shoulder. He held her in silence for a long time before he finally said, "You know, Meg, you've been through an awful lot as well. Perhaps, if this method works for me, you could consider seeing a psychiatrist, too.."

Meg's head shot up off of his shoulder. "Do you think I'm mad?"

"No, I don't. I didn't mean that. Not at all, Meg. I only meant, surely with all you've been through, you must have difficulty sleeping. I know you don't eat as well as you should. I just thought... perhaps it could help you feel better about what's happened. That's all."

She pursed her lips together. "I don't need a psychiatrist, Charlie. I need answers." She squinted her eyes for a moment, contemplating whether or not she should say what was on her mind. He looked at her expectantly. "Perhaps a gun."

"A gun?" he repeated. "Is that why you asked what would happen if one of them was deceased?"

"Possibly," she admitted with a shrug.

"Meg, you can't be serious. You couldn't kill your uncle."

"No, of course not," she said. The words came out easily. The thought did not fade as quickly. It hadn't been the first time killing him had crossed her mind.

"Meg, darling, don't be silly. You know he'll never hurt you again, don't you?"

"Yes, I know." She rested her head back on his shoulder. She didn't want to kill Bertram so that he would never hurt her again. She wanted to kill him for what he'd already done.

"We'll go over there and tell the police all that we know, and they will lock him up for a very long time. He'll get what he deserves."

"You're right," she said quietly. But she knew there was no possible way Bertram could ever get what he deserved until he was burning in hell. She hoped one way or another he'd be there soon enough.

Meg's eyes fell on the window upstairs where they'd seen Jonathan watching them the night before. He wasn't there tonight. She assumed he was likely passed out on the bed. Her stomach tightened at the thought. He was certainly having trouble dealing with the memories as well.

"I'm rather surprised not to see Jonathan there," Charlie said quietly, as if he had been reading her mind.

Without raising her head, Meg said, "I'm not."

"Why is that?"

She took a deep breath and let it go slowly. "He was a bit... tipsy when he walked me home earlier."

"Tipsy?" Charlie asked, clearly surprised. "Jonathan?"

"I'm afraid so. I think he may be trying to drown his sorrows in a different sort of ocean, one that consists mostly of Johnny Walker Red."

Charlie pulled back so that she was forced to remove her head from his shoulder and look at him. "Meg, what are you talking about? I've never known Jonathan to drink excessively. In fact, there's been more than a few times when he's had to pull a bottle of brandy out of my hand."

While that information was less than appealing, she wasn't about to get into a discussion of why she hoped her fiancé wouldn't drink anymore. "I'm sorry, Charlie. I only mention it because I'm worried. I'm sure you haven't noticed anything, but Jonathan has smelled of liquor frequently of late. I realize he assumed he was off-duty this evening when you asked him to bring me home, but clearly he wasn't himself. I'm afraid he's not dealing with all this as well as he's letting on."

Charlie slowly shook his head. "I can't imagine. Are you certain?"

"I'm sad to say I certainly know how to tell when someone is intoxicated—and the smell of whisky cloaked with mint will be ingrained in my brain until the day they bury me."

"I suppose I've been so preoccupied with my own problems that I hadn't even noticed."

"I know, and no one can blame you for that."

"Possibly. But what sort of a friend am I if I didn't even notice that he was suffering?" He ran his hand through his hair, and Meg wished she hadn't said anything at all.

And yet, she found herself pressing on into dangerous territory. "Charlie, I think there might be other aspects of Jonathan's life you're not quite seeing."

He tilted his head to the side and looked deeply into her eyes as if he were trying to read what she was getting at. "No, I think that's a popular myth perpetrated by servants with too much time on their hands and not enough to talk about."

Her eyebrows arched. "What do you mean?" she asked slowly, cautiously.

"I mean... I'm not a fool, Meg. I know."

Somehow, her eyebrows raised even higher so that she thought they might touch the combs on the back of her head. "You do?"

"Of course I do."

"Then... why haven't you ever said anything?"

He scoffed, the corner of his mouth crinkling up into a smirk. "Exactly what would you like me to say? 'I'm flattered—but I love you like a brother, not like a wife?' I mean, really, Meg, what is there to say? If you were in his position, would you want me to say anything?"

She dropped her eyes to the ground. "No, I suppose not."

"That's just not who I am, you know? Even if it was—which i isn't—but if it was, I'm engaged to you. He knows that. It's never bee an option."

Meg only nodded, understanding but not sure what to say.

"I do try to be supportive, however," Charlie continued.

Meg looked back at him, hoping the surprise didn't show too much on her face. "You do?"

"Yes, of course. There've been lots of women I've suggested he ask on dates over the years, even talked him into it a few times."

Meg couldn't catch the guffaw that escaped her lips quite in time, and Charlie looked at her as if she had insulted his mother. "I'm sorry. It's just—you only just said that isn't you—that you could never have those sorts of feelings for him. What makes you think he can change who he is?"

Charlie began to stammer. "I only... I mean, it's just... well, people don't...."

"I'm aware of what most people think, Charlie, darling, but we are not most people. We are his friends. We should love and support him no matter what. It must be an awful position to be in—to know that society thinks there's something wrong with who you are on in the inside to the point where you feel you must hide it at all costs, don't you think?"

"Yes, I suppose so," Charlie nodded. "I don't think I've ever stopped to think of it that way."

"I believe a lot of people haven't stopped to think of it that v. Perhaps instead of encouraging him to date women he's not ested in, you should let him know that you will always accept ppreciate him no matter whom he chooses to spend his h."

began to shake his head slowly from side to side, and she e might rebuke her, but instead, he quietly said, "You're rkable, Meg. You see people so clearly. You understand thers in a way I've never seen before."

taken aback and literally leaned away from him. "I do?"

had never heard that about herself before.

se you do."

so. I mean... I had no idea that Ezra would do what

ne the benefit of the doubt. You see the good in

everyone. I think that's why it surprises you to see the evil in anyone," he continued.

"I certainly don't see the good in my mother or uncle," she argued.

"Unfortunately, I think that is because there's none to be seen."

She opened her mouth and closed it. She couldn't think of a single word to say in response to that truth.

"I wish there'd been some way for you to let me know," Charlie lamented.

"What's done is done," Meg replied, scooting back over and slipping her hand into his. "Now, all we can do is hope to get some sort of justice."

He kissed the crown of blonde hair on her head. "We will. But not by shooting him, as tempting as that may be."

Meg rested her head on his shoulder. She said nothing in response. She knew she wouldn't really shoot her uncle, but she wasn't willing to let go of the fantasy just yet.

"We should get back," Charlie finally said. "We will need to plan the engagement announcement tomorrow, and that could be exhausting.'

"I'd like to ask Kelly over, if you don't mind," Meg said, tilting her head up to face him. "I think she could help. At the very least, she could keep me calm."

"Whatever you'd like," he said, kissing her forehead. "You know," he continued, his voice changing just a bit, becoming softer, huskier, "Jonathan isn't watching us. I don't suppose Carrie or anyone else is either."

"Are you asking for another therapy session, Mr. Ashton?" she asked, smiling coyly.

"It does seem to help." He kissed her softly on the tip of her nose.

"I'd hate to see you suffer if I can prevent it," she said with a sigh, and Charlie found her mouth with his. Meg lost herself in the feel of his soft lips, his hands caressing her cheek and gently brushing her hair away from her face. He was calm and reserved, though he kissed her much longer than he ever had before, and Meg realized soon enough that the true testament to her healing would come. She prayed she'd be ready, though the idea made her nervous. Nevertheless, kissing Charlie was unlike anything she'd ever experienced before, and she knew it wasn't just his mind that was healing; her heart was as well.

CHAPTER NINE

Not only was Grace able to make it back in time for the proposed date Charlie had in mind for the engagement party, she made it back by mid-morning the next day to meet with Meg, Mrs. Ashton, and Kelly, along with a team of designers and other professionals Meg wasn't quite sure she understood the purpose of. There were two older women who were to be responsible for decorations, a middle-aged man who'd be working on Meg's gown (though he had no idea how he would manage such an extravagance on such a short timeline) and a group of chefs and bakers who would be responsible for the menu. Meg said very little, mostly listened to Grace prattle on about exactly what she envisioned. It was only when she began to talk about the number of guests that Meg found her voice.

"We can easily expect three hundred guests, possibly more," Grace was saying, as her mother nodded along.

"Three hundred?" Meg said, her eyes as large as the dinner plates they'd already decided would be simple white china with a pink accent to match the gown and flowers. "I apologize—but I'm quite sure that's not what Charlie and I had in mind."

Grace looked at her as if she'd just announced the party should be held in the cellar. She cleared her throat. "We have several families who would be greatly offended not to be invited." Her words were short and clipped, as if she assumed Meg otherwise wouldn't understand their meaning.

"I apologize," she said again, "but they'll simply have to wait for the wedding. Charlie and I were thinking more like forty or fifty people, including family."

"Forty or fifty?" Grace said. She looked at her mother and then burst into laughter. Though Pamela was trying to be more polite, she also had a small grin on her face.

"Now, Grace, let's remember, this is Meg's engagement celebration."

"Yes, mother, I know. But there are certain expectations she can't possibly understand," Grace replied. "Charlie is an Ashton, after all." She was looking at Meg now; of course their mother knew Charlie was an Ashton.

"We could cut the list down a bit, I suppose," Pamela said, and Meg was thankful she was playing to the middle a bit. "Possibly—two hundred?"

Meg opened her mouth but no sound came out. It wasn't much of a compromise.

"If I may...." It was Kelly, and Meg could tell by her friend's expression that she had been biting her tongue almost as long as she could handle, and a wild Irish explosion might happen at any time. "I thought the main purpose of this event was to let the papers know Meg is alive. Would it not be possible to have a small gathering for that purpose, let Charlie propose if he so chooses, and then do a larger party later—when Charlie and Meg are feeling better?"

Meg thought Grace's looks of disdain were only reserved for her until she saw the expression the elegant brunette gave her friend. "Perhaps it would be better if the help weren't involved in the planning."

With one hand on Kelly's leg to keep her from leaping off of the couch in Charlie's sitting room and launching her petite frame across the expanse at his sister, Meg said, "Kelly isn't the help. She's my friend—more like my sister. She's here because I value her opinion."

"With all due respect," Grace continued, "I'm not quite sure you should be here yourself. Clearly, you're not feeling well. You should just let us handle it. Let Maurice take your measurements and then retire to your apartment." Her voice was flat and even, each word measured, like she was weighing Meg's value and coming up short.

"Grace," Pamela said, an air of light in her voice, "let's consider the suggestion."

"What's that mother?"

"Perhaps Mrs. O'Connell has a point. Your brother isn't quite himself. Scaling back our plans now will also give us the opportunity to make a more splendid affair later on."

"For the wedding," Meg spoke up. "While I do agree with Kelly that this should be a simple get together, Charlie and I don't want another engagement party on top of this. A simple engagement announcement, a bit of dancing and music, a lovely meal, and a few friends to enjoy the evening with—that's what we want. For the wedding, I shall keep my opinions to myself and let you follow through with everything you've been planning, so long as we can simplify this event tomorrow evening." Meg kept her tone calm. She knew she had more power in the situation than the Ashtons were willing to admit; at the end of the day, she was certain Charlie would take her side should it come to that. She hoped it wouldn't. Hearing Kelly's opinion made Meg bold enough to insist they see things her way this time.

"Very well then," Pamela said with a smile of admiration. "If you'd like to limit the number of guests this time, we can rein things in a bit."

Grace looked disgusted. "Mother?"

"Grace, honestly, you haven't had the opportunity to visit with your brother much these past few days. If you had, you'd understand. We really need to be... considerate of his condition."

"Mother, you're speaking of him like he's an invalid."

145

Pamela cut her daughter off and dismissed all of the merchants and bakers from the room. "If you will wait just outside in the antechamber, I shall call you back in when we have reached an agreement." She smiled, but it was clearly forced, and Meg watched in awe, wondering what her purpose was.

When the last of them had left, and all of the servants were out of the room as well, Mrs. Ashton looked at her daughter sternly and said, "Grace, Charlie is not quite himself."

Grace's nose wrinkled, and for a moment, Meg thought she might see a bit of concern. It was soon replaced with disbelief. "Mother, I'm sure he's fine."

"He's not fine," Meg interjected. "He's not well at all."

"And there's a distinct possibility he may be going back to Southampton soon."

Grace looked from her mother to Meg, her mouth agape. "Whyever would he do that?"

"My family is having some problems," Meg explained, quietly. "I will have to go, and Charlie insists on accompanying me."

"If he's so ill, he can't possibly," Grace said, her eyes like daggers. "Can't you go by yourself?"

"Your father offered to go, but Charlie wouldn't hear of it," Pamela explained.

"I don't understand then. If he's well enough to go to Southampton, he should be well enough to attend a ball in his honor," the older sister insisted.

"We simply cannot overwhelm him," Pamela said, clutching her daughter's hand. "Grace, you know I'd like more than anything to throw Charlie a lovely, grand affair. But Meg's right. We do need to be more sensitive to his condition. You wouldn't want to appear in public when you were less than yourself either, I'm sure."

"All right, whatever you'd like," Grace said, pulling her hand away and crossing her arms, her nose in the air. Before Meg could even manage to thank her for her understanding, she turned to look at Meg and said, "I suppose we are all to consider ourselves lucky that you've suddenly taken an interest in Charlie when all you wanted from him for the last fifteen years was our money."

"Grace!" Pamela shouted, her hands covering her mouth.

"I can't blame you for saying that," Meg said after she got over the initial shock. "But I have to tell you, that's not true at all."

"Certainly it is..." Grace continued.

"No, it isn't," Meg interrupted, her hand on Kelly again to keep her from jumping up. "I assure you, Mrs. Buckner, I wasn't interested in Charlie at all until the tenth of April. It wasn't until we were aboard *Titanic* and I saw what a kind and wonderful person your brother is that I began to realize how extremely lucky I am that my father chose so perfect a match for me, and how incredibly foolish I'd been for not seeing it before. You have every right to be angry at the way that I treated Charlie before I came to know him in person, but if he's found a way to forgive me, I should hope that you can, too. I apologize most sincerely to you, to your entire family. But I will say, it wasn't me who was constantly asking for money—that was my mother and uncle. And I am not like them; not at all."

Grace's face flickered between surprise and a fire that indicated she was ready to argue if she was able to get a word in edgewise or find fault in Meg's declaration. Once Meg had finished, Grace only managed to say, "I suppose we shall see," and Meg didn't know if she was implying they would see if she meant her apology or if she wasn't like her mother and uncle.

Kelly was fuming next to her, and Meg realized it was time to go. Unfortunately, this had not been the courteous planning session she had hoped for, but then, rarely did anything come easily in Meg's experience. "I should like to leave the preparation to the pair of you, then, if you understand our wishes to have the number of guests limited." She looked at Mrs. Ashton as she spoke, no longer wishing to address Grace.

"Yes, of course. You look worn. Perhaps you should retire to your room, and when Maurice is ready, we will have him escorted over to take your measurements."

Meg nodded and thanked them before saying her goodbyes and heading for the door, Kelly on her heels. They had to slip between the waiting designers to reach the library on the other side of the house where Charlie was entertaining the girls—with Carrie's assistance. Kelly mumbled under her breath the entire length of the hallway, most of it words Meg wouldn't repeat in church or polite company.

As soon as she entered the library, all of the frustration melted away, and Meg stood in the doorway, gaping at the sight in front of her. Charlie sat before the unlit fireplace, Ruth poised on his knee, a picture book in front of him, and he was reading to her. The little girl giggled and pointed at the pictures, and Charlie made little animal noises to represent whatever was portrayed in each picture. Meg was reminded of a similar book Da used to read to her when she was Ruth's age. She'd loved those moments on his lap, surrounded by his books, the smell of leather and book binding emanating from the volumes around them. Meg felt Kelly's hand on her shoulder and knew she appreciated the scene as well.

Charlie looked up from the book first, followed by Ruth, whose face broke into a wide grin. "Mama!" she exclaimed. "Aunty Meg! You're back so soon!"

"We are back early," Meg admitted as the women crossed the room. Carrie sat in a rocking chair near the window, Lizzie on her lap. The infant cooed and waved for her mother who went to pick her up.

As Meg lifted Ruth from Charlie's lap and hugged her, he asked, "Did everything go well?"

Meg shook her head slowly, but forced a smile, mostly because of the little girl she was holding. She could let him know what had transpired later, after little ears were gone.

"We went for a walk," Ruth said, "and I saw all the big rooms in Uncle Charlie's house. This will be your house soon, won't it Aunty Meg?"

"It will," Meg agreed, and she saw Charlie's face light up as she said it.

"There's a picture of horses and dogs in the dining room, a big one."

"I know."

"And in the hallway, there's lots of pictures of old people."

Meg laughed. "I know that, too."

"But they are 'portant." Her face was quite sincere, and Meg couldn't help but giggle.

"This one is gettin' bleary-eyed," Kelly noted crossing the room as Lizzie yawned as if to prove her mother's point. "I suppose we should be headed back home."

"I'll have Bix bring the motor coach around," Charlie said.

"I'll get him, sir." Carrie was out of her seat before Charlie even had the chance to stand, and Meg was thankful to have such an attentive lady in her service.

"I'm sorry I wasn't much help in there," Kelly said, a sympathetic look in her eyes.

"On the contrary, you were invaluable," Meg assured her. "I never would've had the courage to say what I did if it weren't for you speaking your mind first."

"I'm afraid I just riled things up," Kelly muttered.

"Not at all."

"Do I even want to know?" Charlie asked, looking from one lady to the other.

"No," they both said at the same time. Then, Meg added, "I shall let you know shortly."

"Are we having a party tomorrow?" Ruth asked.

"Grownups are having a party tomorrow," Kelly corrected. "Little girls are having a sleep over at Mrs. Wagner's house down the hall from our place."

"Awww!" Ruth moaned, her shoulders falling.

"When you're a bit bigger, you can come," Meg reminded her,

kissing her on the top of her head and setting her down on the ground.

Carrie was back. "Mr. Bix is ready when you are, Mrs. O'Connell."

Kelly looked around. "Is my mother-in-law in the room?" she sniggered. "I'm not used to bein' Mrs. O'Connell."

"I'll walk you out," Meg said, but as she turned to go, Carrie chimed in.

"Actually, miss, Mrs. Buckner says they are ready to measure you, if you'd like to return to the parlor."

"Oh," Meg said with a sigh.

"I'll happily walk your guests out," Carrie added, and Meg noticed she was careful not to use Kelly's surname again, as if she was embarrassed by Kelly's comments.

"Very well then," Meg said. Turning to Kelly, she said, "I will see you tomorrow." Her voice was as threatening as she could muster; she couldn't attend this lavish event without her best friend by her side.

"I'll be here. In my best dress." She glanced down. "This is it!"

Meg couldn't help but laugh. "I will make sure you have an appropriate gown." She hugged Kelly and kissed her cheek, careful not to squish Lizzie, who also got a kiss. "Goodbye, Ruthie, darling," she said, stooping to kiss her favorite little girl.

"Goodbye, Aunty Meg. I want to see you and Uncle Charlie again soon, too."

"You shall," Charlie assured her, pulling her into his arms before he hauled himself slowly to his feet and kissed Kelly and Lizzie good-bye. He walked with them as far as the library door, and then Carrie escorted them out.

Once they were gone, Meg let go a breath she hadn't realized she was holding. "It really didn't go well, then, did it?" Charlie asked.

"Let's just say, if your sister hated me before, she hates me even more now--if that's even possible."

He managed a crooked smile. "She doesn't *hate* you."

"Loathe. Despise. Detest."

Charlie laughed. "Possibly."

Meg sighed, and he wrapped his arms around her. "I don't suppose I can blame her."

"Oh, no, you can," he said into her hair. "She has no reason to do so."

"Doesn't she, though? Wouldn't you if you were in her position? She honestly doesn't have enough information to forgive me the way that you have."

Charlie shrugged. "I don't know. But the fact that I love you should be enough to make her stop this nonsense."

"I don't even want to go back in there," Meg admitted.

"Come along. I'll go with you," Charlie replied, taking her by the arm.

"Oh, no, I can't ask you to do that," Meg said, but he was already headed in the appropriate direction, and Meg went along, having little choice.

"My sister decided she didn't like you way back when you didn't even know I was writing to you," he explained. "She had a few friends she thought would make perfect sisters-in-law. And when I didn't see things the same way, she decided to hold it against you."

"I can hardly blame her for being overly protective of her younger brother. If I had a little brother, I'm sure I'd feel the same way." The parlor door loomed ahead, and Meg's stomach became a clenched fist.

"This has much more to do with her getting her way than it has to do with her feelings for me, I assure you," he replied. "In fact, I would wager she'll try to send me out of the room so that she can better control something as simple as a dressmaker taking your measurements."

Meg swallowed hard, not particularly excited about the idea that some strange man she did not know would be measuring her or Grace's potential attempt to throw Charlie out of his own parlor.

"It'll be fine, I promise," Charlie said, standing in front of the parlor door. "Meg, as long as we are together, we can get through anything. Surely, you know that by now."

She gave him a small smile. There were not too many things in this world she was sure of, but the fact that his words were the gospel truth was one of them. With a deep breath, she went back into the frying pan, hoping things would go more smoothly now that Charlie was with her. Perhaps, compared to this, the actual party would be a piece of cake.

"Cake, my lady?"

Meg turned to find a servant she did not recognize offering her a dainty pastry barely the size of a postage stamp, and she wondered how it could possibly be described as cake. She shook her head and mumbled a polite, "No, thank you," watching him scuttle off to the next crowd of people.

The rules had certainly changed over the years. Meg remembered when she first started attending social events how she had to wait for a gentleman to offer to escort her to the refreshment table, and then she'd been scoffed at for actually eating. Though this wasn't a ball exactly, as that had been, times had certainly changed, and she marveled at the young ladies who crossed the room without an escort, wondering how it had ever been a travesty before.

"You look lovely."

She spun around to see Charlie had somehow managed to sneak up on her. She'd seen him only briefly when the party had first begun, and after that, he'd been swept away by one guest or another. While it was customary for couples not to spend too much time with each other at a ball, she kept reminding herself this was something else altogether, and she was happy to see him.

"You said that already. Earlier." She couldn't help but smile at him. He was wearing a full tuxedo with tails, much like he wore the night she'd attended dinner in the First Class dining hall with him, and she bit her bottom lip in an attempt to fight back the urge to kiss him right there in front of the hundred or so guests Grace had eventually whittled the list down to.

"It isn't so bad, is it?" he asked, stepping close to her so that his breath was in her ear.

"Not so far," she admitted. Kelly had been by her side for much of the event, though now she was across the room with Daniel speaking to a couple Meg had met but couldn't remember. She'd been introduced to so many people that night, it wouldn't be possible for her to keep them all straight.

"Maurice certainly did lovely work completing that gown so quickly."

Meg glanced down at the rose colored dress she wore. Grace had insisted the gown be the same color as the flowers and the rest of the décor, though she had no idea why she'd insisted on pink, which seemed more like a color for an announcement of a new baby than an engagement. "I think so. It is a bit tighter than I'd like."

"That's what happens when your soon-to-be sister-in-law insists you don't breathe while you're being measured," he reminded her.

She could only shake her head. If Charlie hadn't been there, the dress would likely be even tighter. "Have you any idea why we are all to gather in the garden after dinner?"

"I haven't the foggiest why they picked the garden, but I believe that is where I am to formally ask you to be my wife," he explained. "I am glad that the photographs will be taken inside at least."

"Well, assuming it's quite dark outside, I suppose they'd have to be. It's not as if they have a way of sufficiently lighting a photograph at night. Flash bulbs can only do so much."

"Wouldn't it be extraordinary if they could?"

She knew she'd lost him for a moment as he pondered an impossibility, and she couldn't help but laugh. "Is there anything you don't want to invent?"

"No," he said quickly. "Anything you can think of, I shall make it happen."

"Hmmm," she accepted the challenge, "what about a telephone that allowed you to actually see the person you were talking to? You could just peer into it and see into their home? Wouldn't that be something?"

"Can you even imagine?" Charlie asked, shaking his head. "Or books that moved like nickelodeons that you could hold in your hand?"

"What's this now? Are you imagining the future in your head again, old boy?"

Meg looked up to see a tall, handsome man with blond hair she was fairly certain she'd not yet met. A woman with short, curly, brown hair stood behind him, a slightly annoyed, half amused look on her face.

"Quincy Cartwright!" Charlie exclaimed, embracing the man and clapping him on the back several times. "How are you? I haven't seen you since the wedding." With those words, he glanced back at the woman standing behind Mr. Cartwright, and Meg noticed a shift in Charlie's expression. She didn't know what it was, but she didn't like it. It was gone almost as quickly as it came. "Stella. How are you?"

Charlie hadn't stepped in her direction, but the woman threw one arm around his neck; the other held a drink, which she thrust out in an attempt not to spill and almost hit Meg in the face with it. "Charlie, darling! It's lovely to see you." She had an audacious look about her, and Meg instantly knew she did not like this person.

"It's nice to see you, too, Stella," he remarked. He placed his hand on her back, but Meg noticed it seemed as if he were touching something fragile, like spun sugar, and he didn't seem to want to apply any pressure lest she break. Either that or he simply didn't want to touch her at all.

Once the woman, who was wearing an elegant black gown and a ring on her finger with a stone larger than the ones in Meg's earrings, stepped back, Charlie said, "Quincy, Stella, this is Meg."

"It's lovely to finally meet you," Quincy said, taking the hand Meg offered and pressing it to his lips.

"Thank you," Meg said with a polite nod.

"Yes, it is lovely to *finally* meet you," Stella agreed, taking a sip from her glass. "I have to admit, I wasn't sure this day would ever come."

Meg laughed nervously, not sure what to say since she had no idea who these people were or what she may be implying.

"It's been a tumultuous journey, but I assure you, Meg and I are together for the long haul now," Charlie spoke up.

"This fellow used to smile for weeks after getting a letter from you," Quincy offered, punching Charlie lightly in the arm.

"Is that so?" Meg asked, smiling at the playfulness.

"*When* he got a letter from you." Stella's mumble was just barely audible, but Meg caught it.

"We went to Cambridge together," Charlie explained. "And Stella's brother, Ralph, and I went to high school together. Where is Ralph? Is he here?" Charlie looked around the room as if he might have overlooked him.

"No, he's out of town on business," Stella explained. "I believe it's London this week."

"Oh, that's too bad," Charlie said.

"So you've known each other since high school?" Meg asked, still trying to figure out what she was missing.

"Charlie and I know each other very well," Stella said, looking Meg directly in the eye.

Meg glanced at Charlie and could see he looked quite uncomfortable. Quincy leaned in toward Stella's ear and whispered, "Darling, please, take it easy on the gin and tonics, won't you?" He looked back at Meg and laughed nervously, and she could sense the tension between the couple.

"How long have you been married?" Meg asked, trying to make conversation.

"It will be two years next week," Quincy said through gritted teeth.

"Is that so?" Charlie asked. "I don't suppose I realized it had been that long."

"One year, eleven months, three weeks, and five days, to be precise," Stella said, and Meg could see for certain in the way she turned to face Charlie that she had already drank too much.

"Stella always was good with numbers," Charlie laughed, clearly trying to clear the tension between them. "She studied chemistry at Cambridge."

"You don't say?" Meg asked, turning back to Stella for one more try at cordiality. "That's quite impressive."

"Yes, I was one of the first women to graduate with a degree from Cambridge," she nodded. "And now I live in a fancy house on Twelfth Street, spending my days making sure my husband's home is in order and spending my nights fulfilling his every need."

"You'll have to excuse my wife," Quincy said, putting his arm around Stella and pulling her back away from Meg a bit. "I'm afraid she's had a bit too much to drink this evening."

"You don't need to apologize for me, Quincy. I'm not drunk," Stella said, her jaw set tightly.

"I believe you might be," Quincy said, a fake smile still plastered on his handsome face. Meg took a step toward Charlie, who put his arm around her in reassurance.

"No, I'm not," Stella insisted. "You know, Mary Margaret," she continued, stepping around her husband, "if I had been a wagering woman, Charlie would be even richer today. I would've bet anything you'd never have shown up. In fact, I'm still not completely convinced you'll actually get married."

"Stella...."

"No, let me finish, Quincy. Do you have any idea what you did to this man for so many years? It really is a shame." Her voice was low, despite her accusations, but a few people standing nearby turned to look.

"Stella, I think it might be best if you go outside with Quincy and get some fresh air," Charlie recommended.

"Wait," Stella insisted, pulling away from her husband, who was tugging on her arm.

"It's all right," Meg said quietly. "Let her finish. She's certainly got a valid point."

Stella's eyes widened. "You think so?" she asked, as if she was surprised to hear Meg's admonition.

"Yes, of course," Meg agreed. "I absolutely treated Charlie terribly before I met him in person. I will certainly acknowledge that."

"Meg, really, that's not necessary." Charlie looked more uncomfortable now than he had the entire time they'd been home.

"Good." Stella nodded her head and finished her drink. "Good. I'm glad you admit that. And... you'd better be sure it doesn't happen again. He has friends you know, lots of them, and we'll take up for him."

"I see that," Meg nodded. "I'm glad to have the opportunity to meet the people Charlie holds so dear."

Stella laughed, loudly, which drew more eyes. "You haven't any idea." She was shaking her head, her brown curls dancing about. "You haven't any idea."

"Stella!" Quincy had her by the arm again and this time he was pulling hard enough that she had no choice but to retreat.

Before she disappeared into the crowd, she shouted, "I'll see you soon, Charlie," and winked at him in a way Meg couldn't quite decipher.

"What in the world?" Meg asked, looking to Charlie for some answers.

He opened his mouth as if he might explain, but just then there was the loud clank of metal on glass, and they both jumped. The Master of Ceremonies, a gentleman Meg had met earlier by the name of Mr. Hill, was calling for everyone's attention. "Ladies and gentlemen, if I can have Mr. Ashton's immediate family and Miss Westmoreland to the library, please, the photographers have assembled there. The rest of you, please make your way outside to the garden, and we shall join you shortly."

While in theory it seemed a good idea to have the guests begin to make their way outside as the family prepared to be photographed, doing so caused Meg and Charlie to have to cross through a throng of people who were crowding through the exit. Most people were willing to let them pass if they were paying attention, but it seemed Stella wasn't the only one who may have had too much to drink, and Charlie kept Meg close behind him as he threaded his way through, an attempt to keep her from colliding with anyone or having a drink spilled upon her new dress. Eventually, they arrived in the library.

There were several photographers assembled here, their cameras set up pointing at the fireplace. Meg immediately felt her stomach tighten. She'd been under the impression it would be one photographer from one newspaper. Once Grace entered the room, she explained, "I could hardly show favoritism to one paper over the others."

Meg disagreed, but she said nothing. Mr. Hill situated the family just how he wanted them, with Charlie and Meg in the middle, his parents on his left side, his sister and Peter on Meg's right. She refused to note the fact that she had absolutely no family in the world she'd want to be in the photograph even if they'd been on the same continent, and she forced herself to smile her best fake smile for the camera, thinking of Charlie and nothing else in order to muster as much happiness as she could.

A barrage of flashing lights began to go off, and the photographers shouted at them to stay still, and then to move closer together, or further apart, and Meg did her best not to lose herself in the flashing lights, her head growing dizzy with each explosion from the flashes, the smoke burning her nose. After what seemed like forever, Mr. Hill shouted, "All right then. Last one!" Most of the photographers complied, and as they took their last shots, the older gentleman ushered them from the room, and Meg hoped, from the building. A few shouted questions at them as they went, but neither she nor Charlie answered.

"Well, that was certainly an experience," Mr. Ashton joked, rubbing his eyes.

"I do think it would've been better if we'd had it in the daytime," Grace mused, "so that they didn't need to use those terrible flashbulbs."

"I concur," Pamela agreed. She was wearing a lovely gown only a shade or two darker than Meg's and Meg couldn't help but hope she would look just as pretty when she was Pamela's age.

"Shall we head out back then and get on with it?" Charlie asked, absently checking the pocket inside of his jacket.

"Yes, let's do," Grace agreed, and since she still seemed to be the one in charge of this affair, they began to follow her out, Mr. Hill leading the way.

Meg had Charlie's arm, and she slowed so that everyone else went around them. Leaning in so that only he could hear, she teased, "If that rock in your pocket is even half as large as the one on Stella's finger, I'd think you needn't check to see if it's still there. You'd feel it thumping against your chest with each step."

He chuckled. "I know that it's still there; I just can't help but make sure from time to time. You know, I've been thinking about this moment for more years than I can count, and never in my wildest dreams did I think there'd be a hundred and fifty people staring at me when I gave you this ring."

She glanced up at him out of the corner of her eye. "I knew it," she said, making him raise his eyebrows. "I knew there were more than a hundred people here."

He began to laugh so hard she had to stop, though she was surprised no one in front of them seemed to notice. "This is precisely why I love you so much, Meg. I never know what you're going to say, but I always know it will be perfect."

Realizing no one else was paying them any attention at all, Meg turned to face him. "Charlie, you've already asked me to marry you, and I've already said yes. This is just a formality."

"Yes, I know, but this is my grandmother's ring. She gave it to me specifically to give to you before she passed away."

Meg felt her heart flutter. "She did? For me?"

"Yes, of course. She knew I'd marry you one day. She wanted you to have it."

"No wonder your sister hates me," she muttered.

"Don't be ridiculous," he replied, giving her a crooked grin. "There are lots of reasons why my sister hates you."

She punched him in the arm, harder than she would've dared a week ago for fear he'd fall over.

"Listen, all of this will be fake, a production for my family's friends and business associates, but I want to give you this ring in private afterwards. I want to ask you to marry me properly without everyone staring."

Looking into his eyes, Meg could see how sincerely he meant those words. "Then do it now," she said, glancing before them to see his family had reached the hall that led to the back. There was no one around.

Charlie raised his eyebrows for only a second, as if he wasn't sure. But then, dropping to one knee, more carefully than Meg would've originally envisioned, he pulled a box out of his pocket. "Meg, I didn't believe in fate or chance before I met you in person. But with every-thing we've been through, with all the coincidences and chances we've encountered, I've never been more certain of anything in my life than the fact that you and I are meant to be together. Mary Margaret—Meg--will you do me the honor of being my wife?"

Tears were rolling down her cheeks as Meg nodded and said, "Yes." He slipped the ring on her finger, and with Meg's help, stood to catch her lips with his.

A few moments later, they heard a distinct throat clearing at the end of the hallway and realized Jonathan was waiting for them. Pulling themselves apart, Meg brushed the tear streaks from her face, and Charlie looped his arm through hers and led her down the hall, as if they were walking to the firing squad instead of a group of alleged friends.

Once they reached the end of the hallway where Jonathan stood, the liegeman whispered sharply, "Your sister is about to have a conniption thinking you've snuck off somewhere."

"We are just slow walkers," Charlie assured him, amused.

"I'll let you explain yourself to her. She assumed you were right behind her."

"We were. Right behind her—far, far behind her." Charlie looked at Meg, a twinkle in his eyes.

"I believe you will need the ring back if you're to give her the ring in front of everyone," Jonathan reminded them.

Meg shrugged and let go of Charlie's arm so she could work the ring off and hand it back. The diamond wasn't nearly as large as the ostentatious one on Stella's finger, but it was lovely with a princess cut diamond in the center surrounded by dozens of smaller stones, and Meg was reluctant to take it off.

Jonathan nodded his approval and began to slowly back toward the exit. While she noticed he smelled a bit like alcohol, she was glad it wasn't nearly as overwhelming as it was the other night, and she assumed it was because he was technically working.

Once Charlie had the ring back safely in his pocket, they went on their way to the back garden where Meg thought she'd be forced to pretend she was somewhere else for a while in order to keep from hyperventilating with every wealthy eye in New York City on her. Unfortunately, she had plenty of practice with the art of being somewhere else.

"There you are!" Grace proclaimed, a fake smile plastered to her face. Her satin and lace blush gown caught the flicker from the gas lights and seemed to dance around her as she approached them.

Mr. Hill was standing in an open area in front of most of the guests, and Grace led the couple over. Looking around, Meg was relieved when she saw Kelly's reassuring smile in the crowd, Daniel

161

beside her, his casted arm yet another reminder of what they'd been through.

As they approached the Master of Ceremonies, he made a loud announcement. "Ladies and gentlemen, what we've all been gathered together this night to witness...." He held up his arms, and Meg was reminded of the one visit to the circus she'd made as a little girl with her father and her mother, the latter having been almost as unhappy then as Meg felt now. Charlie looked almost as lost as Meg was, but once his sister guided him into precisely the place she wanted him to stand, and Meg followed, he looked at her, and the rest of the people became much less important.

Grace and the rest of the family stood off to the side with Mr. Hill, as Charlie cleared his throat and momentarily glanced out at the sea of anxious faces. He looked back at Meg, and she was tempted to make a silly face at him to make him feel less nervous, but she didn't do so, only gave him a knowing smile.

Charlie glanced down at the ground and Meg prayed he wouldn't bother to get down on one knee again, since they were standing on brick pavers and she knew it would be difficult for him to get up and down again. Nevertheless, he did so, and she offered her hand to steady him, since she realized he'd need it anyway. There was a loud "oooh" from the crowd as they cooed over the romantic gesture.

"Mary Margaret Westmoreland, we've been planning our wedding for years, but now it is time to make it official." He reached into his pocket and pulled the ring out, leaving the box inside. "Will you marry me?"

"Yes," she said quickly, pulling him up to his feet even before he had the ring completely on her finger. She was thankful that he'd kept it short and to the point. No one need know the other sweet words of affection he'd shared with her earlier in the hallway, or the professions of love he'd made when he'd originally asked her to be his wife aboard *Carpathia*.

The crowd seemed surprised at the hastiness of the moment they'd been waiting all evening to witness, but once they realized it was over, they broke into applause, and Charlie leaned down and kissed Meg's cheek. Over his shoulder, she saw Grace give some sort of signal to someone on the other end of the yard, behind the bushes that surrounded the pond, and a split second too late, she realized what was about to happen.

The first explosion was so loud and nearby, if Meg hadn't had that moment to prepare, she was certain she would've screamed. Instantly, she was back on the water in the lifeboat and a flare split the night sky in half with a loud crack. Fighting the panic, Meg reminded herself it was only a firecracker and tried to keep from running. However, Charlie didn't have the benefit of seeing his sister's secret gesture, and his first reaction was to leap and spin around in the air so quickly, he nearly flung Meg into the pond. She kept her grasp on him as the explosions continued to fill the air above them, but his eyes were wild, and she knew she must have help if she was going to get him to safety before he managed to hurt himself or someone nearby.

Jonathan reacted much the same way Meg did. She could see the panic in his eyes as well, but he moved toward Charlie quickly and precisely, grabbing his friend by the shoulders firmly, and even though Charlie's first instinct was to throw him off, Jonathan held resolutely. Between the two of them, they were able to calm him enough to make him realize the noises were simply fireworks and nothing to be alarmed about.

Most of the crowd was so absorbed in staring at the bright, colorful lights overhead, they likely didn't even notice their host and his bride-to-be had been transported to another time. It wasn't until Meg and Jonathan began to guide Charlie back toward the house that some of them seemed to see something was the matter as the trio had to pass through many of the guests in order to get inside. As she approached the door, her arm around Charlie's midsection as Jonathan held him from behind, Meg realized she'd collected Kelly and Daniel who looked just as frightened as Meg felt.

Once inside, Meg kept right on walking, headed toward the

parlor where she thought guests might leave them be and the fire-crackers might not be so loud, though the popping sound followed them through the house, and each time another burst, all of them jumped to some degree or another.

Meg led Charlie over to the sofa and forced him to sit as he began to stammer out some sort of an apology that made little sense. "I'll get him some water," Jonathan said as he let go and headed for the door. Another explosion caused him to noticeably jump before he reached the exit.

"I don't understand," Kelly was saying as she paced back and forth behind the sofa where Meg was trying to reassure Charlie he was safe. "We know that they are only firecrackers, yet every time one explodes, I feel like my insides are about to come out my ears."

"I don't understand it either," Meg admitted. "But I knew it would happen. It isn't even because of the flare, I don't believe. Any loud noise at all has this effect on me."

"Me, too," Daniel admitted. Meg glanced over at the foreman and saw his face even paler than usual, his strawberry blond hair looking as if he'd pulled half of it out on his way to the parlor.

Jonathan returned and handed Meg a glass of water, which she lifted to Charlie's mouth. "Here, take a drink. It will help."

He complied, taking the glass out of her hand, though his own hand was shaking so violently little droplets spilled on the front of his suit. A few moments later, there was a barrage of popping noises and then a loud applause, and they collectively let out a sigh of relief that the display seemed to be over.

"I specifically asked them not to do this," Meg said through clenched teeth.

"As did I," Charlie finally managed. "I apologize," he said, looking at Meg. "I'm not sure... as you said, any loud noise...."

"You have no reason to apologize," Meg replied, not even allowing him to elaborate. "We all knew you'd react that way. We all wanted to run. Perhaps it's just the sudden, unexpected blare."

He was nodding his head slowly. "The ship... made all sorts of cracking and popping noises before...."

"We could hear it," Jonathan assured him. "Luckily for us, we didn't happen to be standing on it while it was happening."

Charlie had been. Meg felt rage welling up inside of her. She wanted to go scream at Grace for her insensitivity. She wondered if Mrs. Ashton had had any idea that the fireworks show was about to happen.

When Charlie's mother burst into the parlor only a moment after Meg thought to go chase her down, it was clear she hadn't known. "Charlie? Are you all right?" Pamela asked as she hurried to his side. "I'm so sorry... I had no idea."

"Mother," Charlie said, looking at her through glassy eyes, "I'm fine. Whose idea was that precisely?"

"I'm not certain," she said with a shift in her eyes that made Meg think she at least suspected Grace. "I will find out though. Your sister feels just terrible. She didn't realize...."

"She should have." Kelly spoke as if she'd told her herself, which Meg knew she hadn't.

"I don't know that anyone ever mentioned it to her. I thought I knew everything that was to happen this evening, and I would've told her not to do it if I had known she planned to, but she wanted it to be a surprise for me as well."

"It was certainly a surprise," Jonathan muttered from his position across the room.

"I know she feels just awful. She's fled to the library in a fit of tears. Once she calms herself, I'm sure she'd like to see you."

"Yes, of course," Charlie replied. "I'll be fine in a moment. I just need to catch my breath and rest a bit."

Mr. Ashton entered the room then. "Is everything all right?" He had a lost look about him, as if he had no idea what was going on, and Meg couldn't help but find it a bit amusing, though she fought back a giggle. Poor Mr. Ashton. Everyone spending his money and he didn't even know what he was purchasing.

"We shall be in a moment," Charlie assured his father.

"Shall I go back out and let the guests know... something?" Mr. Ashton stammered.

"I'll go," Pamela replied, patting her son on the knee. "You're sure you're all right, Charlie?"

He nodded and took another sip the water he was still clutching so tightly Meg worried for the glass.

"I'll go with you," Jonathan said, giving Meg a knowing glance as if to say he'd handle everything with the guests and she needn't worry about Charlie's reputation. At the moment, it was the last thing on Meg's mind. Yet, she knew it wouldn't do for everyone to assume something was permanently wrong with Charlie. She didn't know what sort of story Jonathan might make up, but she was certain it would get the job done.

Kelly finally stopped pacing and dropped into a chair near the sofa, a sigh of exhaustion escaping her lips. "I'll leave the pair of you in peace in a moment," she began, glancing at Daniel, "but I need a moment myself."

"Take your time," Meg assured her. She had her hand against Charlie's chest, and she could feel his heartbeat starting to slow back to normal.

"I believe I shall return to our guests then," Mr. Ashton said. "Charlie, if you need anything, let me know."

"Yes, Father," Charlie said, giving his father a look of gratefulness before returning his stare to the glass of water.

Daniel must have realized his wife wasn't leaving anytime soon, so he found a seat, as well, in a chair across from hers. He absently rubbed at the cast on his left arm. Meg thought it must be a constant reminder of *Titanic*, and she was thankful she didn't have that sort of badge to wear around every moment of the day.

"It's been a lot more difficult than I've been willing to admit," Kelly said, and Meg glanced over at her friend to see she, too, was staring off into the distance, like she couldn't see the room around her. She was quiet then, and Meg looked from her face to her husband's. Daniel's expression showed that he agreed, though he would never voice his own struggles. Eventually, Kelly took a deep breath and looked at Meg. "It will get easier, won't it?"

Before Meg could formulate a response, Charlie said, "It must. It simply has to." His voice sounded more haunted than Meg could remember ever having heard it, and she scooted even closer to him, wrapping her arms around him. He didn't move, didn't even shift the glass of water in his hand, as if she wasn't even there.

"We should give you a moment." Daniel rose from his chair, approaching his wife, who looked a bit more collected. Kelly glanced in Meg's direction but she didn't say anything, only took her husband's good arm and went out of the room.

Meg wasn't sure what to do or say, she simply held Charlie, hoping she could find a way to bring him back to her. She knew he must be hearing the voices now louder than ever, and his countenance reminded her of all the times he'd forgotten who she was, though she was certain he recognized her, even if he wasn't sure where he was.

"I'm sorry, Meg," he finally said, with a loud sigh. As if a spell had been broken, he set the glass down on the end table and relaxed in her arms.

"Don't be," she insisted as his arm came around her waist and he pulled her into his chest. "I wish I'd known what she was planning. I should've said something."

"It isn't your fault. Hell, it isn't even Grace's fault. It just... is."

"Well, we will have to make certain it doesn't happen again."

"How can we do that, exactly?" he asked, his face in her hair. "How can we ensure there are no loud, sudden noises for the rest of our lives? The factory is full of them. Daniel and Jonathan have been back to work for days now, and they aren't complaining."

"Both of them were just as frightened as you were."

He laughed. "No one was as frightened as I was. Thank goodness the ring was already on your finger or it might have ended up in the pond."

She couldn't help but laugh with him. "I thought for a moment you might accidentally throw me in," she admitted.

"Accidentally?" he teased, nestling her ear with his nose.

She tipped her face to look at him. "On purpose then?"

His face went a bit more serious. "No, I wouldn't toss you in the cold water. It's not at all inviting."

She kissed his temple. "I know you wouldn't."

"Sometimes... I feel like I'm still sinking in cold water, Meg."

She brushed his hair back off of his forehead. "I know. But you're not. You're safe."

"And if I am?"

"Then I'll jump right over with you, Charlie. We are in this together now, through thick or thin, for better or worse." She glanced at the ring on her finger and wiggled her fingers in his face so that he could be reminded as well.

"I'm afraid you'll give up on me, Meg. That I'll become too much work."

"That won't happen, Charlie. I'm not exactly the easiest person to live with either, you know. I may have a few issues of my own."

"You're an angel."

"Are you on some sort of medication again?"

He laughed. "No. I might need to be, though, especially once I get back on another ship."

"So long as you don't forget me this time," Meg replied. The sounds of partygoers echoed down the hallway, and Meg thought the proper thing to do would be to go back out and check on their guests. She leaned her head against Charlie's shoulder instead.

"I'll have to go back out there," he reminded her. "Just like we have to go back across the sea. I have to face my fears and walk into that crowd and pretend like I didn't just react like a small child and run away from a loud noise."

"No one was watching us by then," Meg assured him. "I'm sure they realize we are missing now, but they likely think we are up to no good."

"Well, if that's the case, then let's not disappoint them." He raised her face so that she was looking at him and slowly kissed her. "I love you, Meg. I'm so glad you've agreed to be my wife."

"I love you, too. I'm so glad you asked. Again."

He kissed her once more, and the party, the family, the fireworks, even *Titanic* faded to the background; they could stay there forever as far as Meg was concerned.

CHAPTER TEN

Mauretania seemed eerily similar to *Titanic*, but Meg wouldn't allow herself to think about that. She'd boarded the ship much differently this time, as a First Class passenger, under her own name, and the captain himself had come by to make sure she was comfortable and to assure her there was nothing to fear. While Meg was fairly certain she would manage the week-long voyage well enough, she was worried about Charlie. He had given in to his mother's insistence that the family physician, Dr. Shaw, be brought along, and it was comforting to know someone so familiar with Charlie's medical history was nearby, particularly since this one had not given him any medication that might make him forget his fiancée.

They had opted for interior rooms on the lowest floor possible of First Class accommodations in hopes that there would be less movement and fewer reminders that they were out on the water again, but Meg ended up feeling more trapped than soothed by the lack of a balcony or window. Even the Third Class room she'd had on *Titanic* came with a porthole.

Neither of them planned to attend any meals outside of their rooms, and for the most part they kept to Charlie's quarters, Jonathan and Carrie almost always in their company, the doctor checking in several times a day. The time went by slowly, passed by playing chess, which Meg was a champion at, or checkers, or reading. Jonathan frequently became stir-crazy and would disappear for hours, and occasionally Carrie would go out and about, having never been on a passenger liner before, but they never left the couple together alone. At all.

Meg could see in Charlie's eyes that he was struggling by the fourth day. Jonathan was already out, and she sat across from him pretending to read while she really secretly watched him over the top of her book. Carrie was dozing on the settee nearby. "Perhaps we should go out for a walk," Meg said quietly, closing her book and setting it aside.

His eyes grew wide. "Surely, you jest."

"Why not? Jonathan says it doesn't remind him much of *Titanic*."

He was shaking his head before words even came out. "No, thank you. I shall stay here and pretend that I am in my library at home."

"Maybe you should try opening a book then," she teased. Inwardly, she had been quite concerned at the amount of time he seemed capable of simply sitting and staring at nothing.

"Maybe I should follow Carrie's example and go to sleep. Permanently. Until we arrive."

"I'm awake," the servant girl said, but her eyes didn't open.

"We'll be there in a few days," Meg reminded him. "We're over halfway there, and the captain assures me the difficult part is past."

"What's the difficult part? Are we over shallow water now? Could we get out and walk if necessary?" He was certainly toying with her, but Meg could see the fear in his eyes.

"I believe he meant no more icebergs. It's practically summer now."

"It's not even June."

"The water should be much warmer."

"I'll take your word for it. No need to test it for myself."

She giggled, trying to lighten the mood. "No need for anyone to test it."

"Why don't you and Carrie—who is awake—go for a stroll, and I shall stay here and keep that painting on the wall company?" Charlie suggested, nodding in the direction of a portrait of an older woman sitting in what appeared to be a country home.

"She is quite lovely." Meg couldn't help but make eyes at him when she said it.

"Isn't she though?"

"No, not at all." They laughed, and Meg felt better, seeing some of the color come back into his face. He'd been himself off and on, which is more than she'd hoped for when they embarked upon this trip, but she still longed for him to be Charlie again all the time.

"Please, go. I'll be fine. I don't need a sitter, and you and Carrie may as well get some exercise."

Carrie was sitting up now, rubbing her eyes. "Would you like to go, miss?"

Meg was a bit hesitant herself. She'd only brought it up because she thought fresh air would do Charlie good. Now, faced with the possibility of looking down off the side of a ship again, she wasn't quite sure she was ready. "Go, Meg. Come back smelling like the sea and the wind."

"All right," she said, and even though she was a bit frightened to do so, she set her mind on getting back out there into the world. She stopped to kiss him before she left, and Carrie only giggled, not attempting to intervene at all.

"You really are a horrible chaperone," Charlie called after her as the women made their way to the door.

"You're welcome," Carrie replied, raising her eyebrows and lowering them at him, making Charlie laugh. Meg was glad to hear it and hoped he'd still be in good humor when she returned. Unless he was asleep. That might be even better.

Up on the promenade, it was quite windy, and Meg wished she'd thought to bring a shawl. Her hair was pinned tightly so most of it stayed out of her face, but Carrie was fighting hers. They walked for a bit, and Meg took Carrie's arm, staying away from the railing as best they could. After a few moments, she felt more at ease. It really didn't remind her of *Titanic* as much as she thought it would.

Ahead of them, she spied Jonathan standing alone, peering into the water. He still managed to keep his hat upon his head, despite the wind, and Meg thought he looked haunted. She wondered if it had anything to do with the ship or if it was something else.

"Carrie, would you mind going back to the room to get my shawl? I see Jonathan up there. I'm sure he will keep me company while you go."

"Yes, miss," Carrie replied, pulling a lock of brown hair out of her face as she did so. Meg assumed she'd be happy to have the opportunity to put something warmer on and pull back her hair better.

He saw her coming, which didn't surprise her since he always had a way of knowing what was happening long before anyone else. He may have even been expecting her. "Is everything all right?" she asked as she came to a stop beside him.

"As well as can be expected, I suppose," he replied, smiling at her.

Meg was happy to smell no alcohol whatsoever, though she thought this might be the time when he'd feel the need to drink the most. "It really is a different sort of passenger liner, isn't it?'

"Yes," he replied. "Although now that we are standing here together, I'm reminded of that night when I hunted you down after dinner."

She knew exactly what he was speaking of. "I am also reminded of countless discussions aboard *Carpathia*, wondering if Charlie would be all right."

"I suppose we will continue to have those conversations for months, if not years, to come," he admitted. "I can't believe it hasn't even been two months yet. It seems like an eternity."

She agreed. It was as if *Titanic* had always been a part of her, like even before she boarded the ship, it was ingrained in her soul. "The fresh air seems to be doing you well," she said, nonchalantly.

He looked at her skeptically. "I've not been drinking quite so much, if that's what you're getting at."

"No, I was just saying..."

"Meg, I understand what you were saying that night back home. I knew I was letting it get the better of me. It's all been quite difficult, you know."

"I do," she admitted.

He sighed and looked around, uneasy. He turned to face her. "Meg, did you happen to speak to Charlie about me? About your suspicions concerning my private affairs?"

His tone didn't seem hostile, and yet she felt tension in her abdomen. She hadn't meant to do anything to offend him. "I... yes," she admitted. "I did have a discussion with him. But only for your benefit, I assure you."

He nodded and shifted so that he was faced back out to the sea. "I know you meant well."

"Did something ill come of it?" she asked, resting her hand lightly on his forearm.

"No, not at all," Jonathan replied, still not facing her. "He mentioned something the other evening, after supper, and I thought it must be due to your intervention."

Meg took a step backward, surprised. "Whatever did he say?"

"Only that he wanted me to know that my friendship meant more to him than anything, and, so long as I was comfortable with myself, he would support any decisions I should make in the future."

She couldn't help but smile. "That seems... vague."

"I agree. I asked him what in the bloody hell he was talking about, to steal a line from you Brits, and he said he was sorry for trying to introduce me to young ladies when he realized that wasn't my forte."

The thought of Charlie saying such a thing made her giggle. She was certain it must have been an awkward conversation, but she was proud of him for speaking up, nonetheless. "And how did you take such a proclamation?'

"At first, I was dumbfounded. I had no idea he was aware of... anything."

"He was. I'll admit I was about to mention it to him, but he already knew."

"So... I just thanked him, and then we went on about the card game we had been playing, as if he hadn't said anything at all."

"That sounds about right," Meg nodded. She glanced behind her to see if Carrie was nearby, but she wasn't. "And is this the reason for your newfound sobriety?"

He laughed. "No, I don't think so. Not in its entirety anyway. I feel I need to be on high alert while Charlie is in such a precarious state. But it did make me feel better." He looked far out to sea, as if he was looking for home. "I've thought about bringing it up to him before, particularly when he's suggested I date some young woman or another, but I was never brave enough to do so. I thought he might... treat me differently."

"I can assure you, nothing will change the way Charlie feels about you, Jonathan. You're his best friend as well as the hardest worker he's ever employed. You're family."

He offered her a meager smile. "I can't tell you how much I appreciate you bringing it up to him, Meg. I don't know that I ever would've dared to on my own."

"You're welcome," Meg said with a shrug. "And I'm sorry if I put my nose where it didn't belong. I just want you to be happy, Jonathan. That's all that matters to me."

He turned and opened his arms, and Meg wrapped hers around him, resting her head on his chest. "I wish everyone were as open-minded as you, Meg."

She couldn't think of a single word to say in response, so she only clutched him tighter.

"Miss, here's your shawl," Carrie said, her footsteps stopping right behind Meg. With one more squeeze, Meg let him go.

"I'll go check on Charlie," Jonathan said with a small smile, and Meg took her shawl and watched him walk away, hoping this would be a new beginning for him. Everyone deserved a happily ever after, especially someone who did so much for so many others.

MEG SAT next to Charlie on the settee in his room, listening to Carrie snore on his bed. It was nearly midnight, and she knew she should go back to her room, but she didn't want to. *Mauretania* was due to arrive in Southampton in the morning, and thoughts of what that would mean kept creeping into her mind, along with a host of ghouls from the box. The battle of pushing them back in was exhausting.

"Do you think my sister and mother are enjoying planning the wedding?" Charlie asked, clearly trying to lighten the mood.

She looked up at him with one eyebrow raised. "I'm sure they are, though if it goes anything like the engagement announcement, we shall have to purchase stock in heart medication."

Charlie chuckled. "At least Grace apologized. That's something, I suppose."

They hadn't really talked about the events of the engagement party since that night, the fireworks having marred the entire event, but there were questions lingering in Meg's mind, and she thought now was just as good a time as any to broach them. "Will the same attendees be invited to the wedding—and several hundred more then?"

"I assume so," Charlie shrugged. His arm was draped around her shoulders, her hand on his knee. Their chaperone slumbered on peacefully. "I do hope Ralph is able to make it, though. And my friend Walter. You'll love him. Silly old chap."

Meg had heard mention of Walter before, though she'd yet to meet him. Ralph was the opening she was looking for. "Ralph is... Stella's brother?"

"Yes," Charlie said, though his demeanor changed a bit. She wasn't sure if it was the mention of her name or the realization that he'd given her the opportunity she had wanted since she'd started the conversation.

"She seemed a bit hostile," Meg said, making her voice as nonchalant as possible.

Charlie only nodded. "Ralph was a sort-of troublemaker in high school, but he certainly turned things around. He's working in exports now, I believe."

The change in topic didn't stick. "Charlie, why was Stella so antagonistic?"

"Stella?" Charlie asked, as if he couldn't quite place her. "I'm not sure. She was inebriated I believe. Perhaps that's why."

She let a sly grin spread across her face. "Charles?"

"All right, Mary Margaret. If you must know, Stella and I spent quite a bit of time together for a semester or two, back when you took one of your hiatuses from writing to me."

She raised both eyebrows. "I see. So it's my fault that she fell in love with you and never recovered?"

"Partially," he said, returning her surprised expression. "Although, for most women it can't be helped."

She laughed loudly and threw her hands over her mouth in an attempt to keep from waking Carrie. "That might be the most boastful statement I've ever heard you make."

"And you knew immediately I was joking," he reminded her, kissing her on the forehead.

"I did, only because I know you wouldn't ever say such a thing— that doesn't mean it isn't true."

He shrugged again. "It isn't true for most women, I dare say. But for Stella... we'll just say there was a hope there that you and I would not work out."

Meg nodded. "And did you feel the same way about her?"

He answered quickly. "No. I mean... I cared a lot for Stella. She is unlike any woman I'd ever met before. I met her during a football match where she ran onto the field to take the ball away from me."

"Really?" Meg asked, her mouth agape. "I can't imagine."

"Yes, she's quite unique and interesting. And I believe you know I did go through a short period of time when the idea of controlling my own destiny seemed appealing. But it was short-lived, and my relationship with Stella was ended quite quickly after I realized how much I cared for you."

"Before you even met me?"

"Yes."

"When I was across the ocean pretending you didn't exist?"

"Indeed."

Meg shook her head slowly. "It's no wonder she hates me. And it's no wonder she thought you were mad to believe we'd ever end up together."

"Well, if that's what makes me mad, then I'll accept the label." He kissed the top of her head again, and Meg slid her hand up so that it was around his waist, leaning her head against his shoulder. "Stella and Quincy might not be happy, but that doesn't give her the right to make a spectacle of herself at our wedding."

"No, it's fine if she comes," Meg assured him. "If she'd like to. I don't mind."

"All right then," Charlie said, wrapping his arms around her.

Meg glanced up at him. "You're certain there's no regret, though? You don't wish things had happened differently?"

His only answer was to kiss her in such a way that Carrie might have even had to put a stop to it if she'd been awake. Meg was grateful she could still hear her lady's snores as Charlie's sweet kisses carried her away.

SEEING Southampton from a distance was surreal, and Meg almost wished she'd stayed inside of her room until the ship docked, but she'd been drawn to the upper deck where she could see her hometown unfurl before her. When she'd left, not nearly as long ago as it seemed, she'd done so assuming her future would hold freedom and a new beginning in New York. While that had been the case, it was nothing like what she'd imagined. If she'd had her way, she'd be working her fingers to the bone in a factory somewhere, living in a dirty hole in the wall, who knows where, with dozens of other tenants, barely eating, wearing rags. She'd have been free, but she wouldn't be with Charlie. Kelly and Daniel would be in the same situation—living a meager existence just scraping by to feed their children. While Meg was certain she'd be happier in such a situation than she had been under her uncle's roof, she was thankful fate had other things in store for her.

Charlie was with her. It was the first time he'd come out of his cabin the entire trip, and with the sunshine and fresh air, his coloring did look better, but she could tell he was nervous, and his hand shook where it grasped the railing in front of them. This would be the hardest part for him, she was certain. Going back, he would be more assured of himself. Perhaps he'd even join her on the promenade or frequent the First Class dining hall.

"How do you feel about going home?" he asked, not even turning to look at her since his eyes were fixated on the buildings in the distance.

"Nervous," she admitted. "I'm glad you're here with me."

"I know it will be difficult to face your mother and uncle again, but you can do it."

She agreed. It would likely be the hardest thing she'd ever done, but she had no choice. On top of that, she'd have to speak to Ezra again as well. She needed to know what really happened and if Charlotte was all right. The thought of what she was about to discover made her stomach tangle into knots.

Once they reached the pier and the ship stopped moving, Charlie managed to loosen his grip on the rail and slip his arm around her. "Don't worry, Meg. You don't have to face those monsters on your own ever again."

She leaned her head into his shoulder and steeled herself for what may lie ahead, praying for the strength to bring this nightmare to an end once and for all.

CHAPTER ELEVEN

The motor coach Jonathan had somehow procured pulled to a stop just short of her front door, and Meg was glad to have a bit of a walk to gather her nerves. She could see the front stoop from here, the window to her bedroom that looked down on the front garden where she'd spied on Charlie the day he'd visited and decided she didn't deserve him. Jonathan got out of the driver's seat to come around to her side, but his hand fell short of the handle, and she was certain he would give her all the time she needed.

Another auto parked behind them, and Meg used the mirror at the front of the vehicle to see two police officers climb from inside. One was a plainclothes detective, the sort that might investigate murders and other horrible acts; the other was in a uniform. Again, she wasn't sure how Jonathan had managed to have the authorities meet them there, but she was glad for it.

Meg licked her lips and took a deep breath. She looked at Charlie beside her, and he tightened his grip on her hand. He smiled at her reassuringly but said nothing, which was enough to tell her that she needn't rush.

Jonathan was speaking to the police officers, and Meg could only hear bits and pieces of their conversation. One of the men said they'd been here so frequently over the past month, the kindly servant woman had been keeping his favorite cakes on hand. She knew he must be referring to Tessa, and Meg realized she was the only person in the estate that she even remotely wanted to see.

"I believe... I'm ready," Meg said quietly.

"Are you certain?" Charlie asked. "You can stay here as long as you like."

"Eventually, you'd think my mother might come out to see why there are autos parked in front of her house."

"And if she does, and you're not ready to speak to her, I'll chase her away."

The idea of Charlie scurrying after her mother up the front steps made her giggle, and she was thankful that he always found a way to make her feel better. "I believe it's time."

"All right then," he said, and he pushed his door open. Hearing the noise, Jonathan immediately cut off his conversation and returned his attention to Meg, opening the door for her.

Jonathan offered his hand so that she could more easily step onto the sidewalk. "Are you ready then?" he asked.

"As ready as I shall ever be," Meg said, breathing in deeply through her nose.

He nodded at her. "Miss Westmoreland, this is Officer Gordon Brown and Detective Harry Weber. They will accompany us."

Meg greeted the officers, who both offered pleasantries, and then she asked, "Will you arrest my uncle based on the information I'm about to provide to you?"

Det. Weber nodded. "We actually have several warrants to serve today, Miss Westmoreland. It is our understanding that you prefer to discuss the situation with your family before we take your uncle in, but rest assured, regardless of what you do or do not say today, we will be taking him with us when we leave."

Meg felt relief at their words, but knowing her uncle as well as she did, she muttered, "You may need more officers."

"There are others on the way," Officer Brown said in response. "We are here to speak to Ezra Bitterly as well."

"Now that we know for certain his story isn't true, we need to find out what really happened to Charlotte Ross." Det. Weber scratched the side of his ample nose.

"Indeed," Meg replied. "Well then, let's have at it shall we?" A fleeting thought that she should have stayed back at the hotel with Carrie and Dr. Shaw was pushed aside as she forced herself to turn toward the only home she'd ever known.

Charlie was standing behind her now, and with one more slow inhale, Meg took his arm. Her legs were unsteady, but she made her way to the front of the house. She paused to gaze up, thinking of the happy times she'd had here with Da, trying to block out the other times, the ones that had led them all here. Pursing her lips, she climbed the front steps, and gave two sharp raps on the door.

She expected Tessa to open the door, but instead, the familiar face of her mother, Mildred Westmoreland, stared back at her once the heavy door was pulled open. "Mary Margaret?" she said, grasping her chest. "Oh, thank goodness. We were so worried."

Meg chose not to fall for her charades. She had witnessed them enough over the years. "Mother," she said, her upper lip stiff. "Might we come in?"

"Yes, of course," Mildred said, stepping out of the way and making a sweeping gesture with her arm. "I wasn't expecting you to have such an entourage."

"You've met Charlie. This is his man, Jonathan. And these two officers would like to speak to you and Uncle Bertram once we are done with our conversation. Is he home?"

"He is," Mildred replied, her head tipped up so that her nose was in the air. "Officers, it's nice to see you again. Jonathan, lovely to meet you. All of you are most welcome." Her teeth were clenched, and Meg knew she didn't mean a word of it. As Meg followed her into the parlor, along with Charlie, Mildred added, "Your uncle isn't feeling well. I believe he's in his chambers."

The room was exactly as she recollected. It hadn't been that long on the calendar, but it felt like years. She remembered sitting on her father's knee before the fireplace. She remembered her mother teaching her the tango. She remembered her uncle picking her up off of the floor and carrying her up the stairs....

"I said please have a seat, Mary Margaret," Mildred repeated, and Charlie gently pushed her back toward one of the chairs. He took another, and her mother sat in her usual position across from them. "Are you well, child?"

She wasn't sure if her mother was asking because Meg hadn't been paying attention or if it was because she hadn't seen her since the incident, but either way, she knew the woman didn't really care. "I'm as well as one could be, I suppose."

"We were so relieved to hear that you weren't harmed, particularly when we learned of the disaster at sea. Such a tragedy. Thank God you were all safe."

Meg cleared her throat. "Would it be possible for Bertram to join us? I want to say what I have come to tell you only once."

"Well, as I said, he's resting...."

"Wake him," Charlie said, and his tone was enough to make Mildred recoil slightly, something Meg didn't think she'd ever seen before.

"Very well," Mildred said. "Just a moment."

Charlie stood as her mother rose from her chair to go find her uncle, and Meg felt ill. He reclaimed his seat as soon as it was polite to do so and rested his hand on her arm. "It will be all right, darling. You've nothing to be afraid of."

"I don't want to see him. I don't want to smell him. I don't want to hear the sound of his voice."

"I know. It will all be over shortly."

There was movement in the adjoining dining room, and Meg saw the familiar skirt and apron of the lone servant who still occupied the residence. "Tessa?" she called. "Is that you?"

"Meg!" Tessa proclaimed bounding into the room. "How are you, love?"

"I'm well," Meg replied, standing and wrapping her arms around the older woman. "And you?"

"About as well as can be expected, I suppose. Your mother asked that I stay in the back."

"I understand," Meg said. "I was hoping to see you, though."

"It's wonderful to see you, child. You look just lovely."

"Thank you." She turned to Charlie and said, "This is Tessa. She's been here for several years."

"We've actually met," Charlie reminded her, standing to take Tessa's offered hand. "Nice to see you, Tessa."

"You as well, sir." Returning her attention to Meg, she said, "I'm not sure what I'll do if... well, if Mr. Westmoreland can't keep up with the place, but God willin' I'll find something."

"Don't you worry about that, Tessa. We'll take care of you."

Tessa's face melted. "Oh, God bless you, child." She hugged Meg again. A noise above them made her start, and Meg knew that Bertram's room was just over the dining room, which meant they were likely on their way down. "Take care, sweet girl."

"You as well," Meg replied, squeezing Tessa's hand one more time as she scurried off to the kitchen.

Meg reclaimed the chair she'd been sitting in, though she knew it was her uncle's preferred place. He'd just have to find another spot. "Why aren't the others in here?" she whispered to Charlie.

"I believe they wanted you to have a chance to say what you needed to in private."

"What if he sees them and takes off?"

"I believe Jonathan can outrun your elderly uncle."

"He's a lot spryer than you might think," Meg reminded him. She would've never thought him capable of some of his most recent feats.

Charlie took her hand, and when Meg saw her uncle enter the room, every fiber of her being cinched up tightly, as if someone were pulling at her corset strings.

His eyes were more bloodshot than she'd ever remembered seeing them. His clothing was wrinkled, and she thought he truly must have been sleeping in it, while the gray hair atop his head looked as if it had been wetted and pressed down, likely by her mother. In all the years they had lived under the same roof, he had never said more than a few words to her outside of her own bedroom, so she steeled herself for what he might say now.

Mildred walked in and sat across from Meg, leaving the seat across from Charlie for Bertram. He looked them over and tipped his head slightly. Meg felt Charlie's grip tighten, and she knew he was wishing they'd brought a gun with them just as much as she was.

"Mary Margaret," Bertram said quietly, the sound of his voice grating through her brain like the accidental catch of a fingernail on a slate tablet.

"Bertram," she said, forcing the word out as if it were a curse. "This is Charles Ashton."

Bertram nodded at Charlie, who did not even blink in response.

Meg cleared her throat. "I've come to discuss the contract with the pair of you and the legal circumstances you find yourselves in."

Mildred looked around, as if she wasn't sure why Meg might imply she was in any legal trouble.

"Accessories often go to prison, too, you know, Mother."

"Accessories? To what?" Mildred asked.

Meg shook her head. "Everything. You are more than aware of every single thing that happens at Westmoreland Textiles and in this house."

"Mary Margaret, I assure you, there's nothing to the accusations the banks are making. We've been nothing but compliant with the laws...."

"Funny you are willing to use the word 'we' when you talk about compliance but it seems if the police find otherwise, you suddenly know nothing."

Mildred didn't say a word. Meg supposed it was because there was nothing to say.

"This is the situation. As you know, if I marry Charlie before my birthday, you will each receive twenty-five thousand dollars. If I wait until after my birthday, you won't."

"We know," Mildred said, quietly. "Surely, you will want to honor your father's wishes and proceed with the contract before your birthday. That's what he meant for you."

"Since when do either of you care what my father wanted for me?" Her tone was still calm, but Meg could feel the rage growing under the surface. She was thankful for Charlie's hand or else she may have lost control of herself already.

Mildred looked at Bertram, who was staring at the floor. Meg wondered if he'd drunk himself into oblivion so many times over the years there was nothing left in his head. "Mary Margaret," Mildred said quietly, "I know you are upset about certain events, but I assure you, there's no need to dwell on those things now. What's past is past."

"What's past is past?" Meg asked, struggling to keep her voice down. "No, what's past is present, Mother. It continues to follow me around everywhere I go. Every time I close my eyes. Every time I lay my head down to sleep. You can't honestly think that, can you? That I should simply forget what's happened to me here?"

As Meg's eyes bore holes through her uncle, without looking up, he quietly said, "I didn't mean to hurt you."

She couldn't quite believe her ears. She looked at Charlie and saw his jaw set in such a way she knew he was doing his best not to fly out of his seat and knock her uncle into the next room. "Don't you dare!" Meg said, her tone menacing. "Don't you dare sit there and make it seem like an accident. Like you didn't mean to come into my room night after night to torture me, to make me feel helpless, to invade my personal space, my own body, for your own pleasure. Don't you dare try to make it seem like you didn't know what you were doing, like it wasn't calculated and planned. You are the most disgusting, vile, evil creature who has ever slithered on the face of the earth, and I know I am not the only one who thinks so. I know about the other little girls you tortured under this same roof. They may not be able to gain vengeance, but I most certainly will. So help me God, you will pay for your actions if it is the last thing I ever do."

By the end, he was looking at her, and Meg could see the fear in his eyes. For a moment, he looked like a small child, perhaps one waiting in the dark for something sinister to sneak through the door and torment him. Meg glared at his leathery face, every ounce of rage she had stored up protruding through her searing blue eyes.

For the first time Meg could ever remember, she heard the sound of her mother weeping. She glanced in Mildred's direction and saw real tears rolling down her cheeks. There had been times when she'd put on a show, but this was genuine. The fact that she was crying for this horrible man, not her own little girl, made Meg even more furious. She was just about to turn her lashing to her mother when her uncle spoke, causing her to turn back in his direction.

"Is that all?" he asked, his tone bordering between bored and unimpressed.

Meg opened her mouth in disgust, unable to think of any words she could say to such a statement, but she didn't have the chance. Charlie said, "I believe the officers out front will want to speak to you shortly—before they arrest you, and take you to prison, where I'm sure the other inmates will like to know that you're a pedophile and a rapist."

The fear was back in Bertram's eyes, but only for a moment. He looked just as disinterested in Charlie's remarks as he had Meg's. "When they are ready, I'll be in my room." He stood on unsteady legs and began to exit the room.

"Bertram?" Mildred called, scooting to the edge of her chair. "Bertram?"

"Perhaps you should follow him, let him know how horrible I am for speaking the truth," Meg offered. "Not that you choose to recognize it as such."

"What do you want me to do, Mary Margaret?" Mildred asked, turning to face her daughter. "By the time I knew what was happening, it was too late. We were both reliant on your uncle, on his running of the factory, for our very lives."

"That's not true, Mother," Meg shot back. "You had every opportunity to do something—anything—to save me, to save the other girls. You chose him over me. You never treated me like a daughter, not even when Da was still alive."

"Mary Margaret, of course I did," Mildred argued. "I've always loved you."

"Then you have no idea what love is, Mother!" Meg shouted back, no longer able to keep her voice down. "You were never affectionate, never had any time for me at all. Your idea of showing you cared was to warn me not to eat too many biscuits or else I'd grow plump. The one pleasant memory I have of you was when you were teaching me to dance, and even that is tarnished by the fact that it ended with my confession about what was happening to me and you sending me sprawling across this very floor." By the time she finished, tears were flowing down her own cheeks, which made Meg even angrier. In all these years, she'd never let her mother see her cry, and she hated the fact that she was doing it now.

Mildred folded her arms and said nothing for a very long time as Meg swiped at her tears and Charlie offered her a handkerchief, which she took away from him a bit more violently than she intended and then had to mumble an apology, which he dismissed. They heard footsteps overhead followed by the sound of a door closing, announcing Bertram was back to his nap, and Meg was at least grateful that it would be his last under her father's roof.

"You're right, Meg. I was a louse of a mother," Mildred admitted, quietly. "I was terrible to you. I don't suppose I set out intending for that to be the case, but it was, nevertheless. By the time you were born, I'd given up on being a mother. I'd buried so many of your siblings, I didn't think I'd ever have a child. Then, when you lived past the lengths of your sisters' and brothers' short lives, I spent every day waiting. Waiting to wake up and see that you were ill or that you'd died. Obviously, you didn't pass away, but by then, I'd put so much

ID JOHNSON

distance between us, it wasn't something I could readily remedy. And I was jealous of the affection you had for your father. It all came so easy to him. So... I simply decided not to love you the way a mother should for fear you would break my heart the way the others had."

Meg's tears had dried up by the time her mother finished speaking, and even though the reasoning seemed sound, Meg didn't think it was much of an excuse. Her entire life she had been of the opinion her mother was also evil, just like her uncle, and she wasn't able to budge her stance one bit based on these remarks. "Mother, we've decided we will marry before my birthday on one condition, and one condition only."

Mildred's face perked up just a bit as she turned to face her daughter. "What's that?"

"You will testify to what you witnessed the day Bertram took advantage of me, just before I left to board *Titanic*." The woman was already shaking her head back and forth. "If you want to show me that you truly do care about me, then you will do this. Otherwise, we will wait, and you will get nothing. And you can rest assured there will be no more wire transfers of funds from the Ashtons."

"Mary Margaret, what you're asking me to do... to testify against your uncle... you can't be serious," Mildred stammered.

"I'm quite serious," Meg replied, standing. There was a loud noise overhead, like the sound of a large book or something else heavy falling on the floor, which caused Meg to momentarily look up, but she didn't pay it much mind. "This is your one and only opportunity. You tell those officers everything you know, right now, and agree to testify in court, or else I walk out that door and the next time you see me, you will likely be sitting next to your very own attorney."

Mildred inhaled deeply, her nose in the air, and Meg could see she was considering her options.

"Is Ezra in the carriage house?" Meg asked. "I need to speak with him."

"I'm sure he's out there somewhere," Mildred replied.

190

"Very well. You have until I return to decide."

"No need," Mildred said, exhaling loudly. "I will tell them."

Meg offered a small smile and nodded her head, relieved that her mother was at least motivated by money if not by love for her daughter.

"I'll get Det. Weber and then meet you outside," Charlie said, standing and looking at Meg to make sure she agreed.

She nodded and gave her mother one last glance before she headed off in the direction of the back garden.

Tessa was tidying a counter that didn't need it and looked up and grinned as Meg passed her by with a humble smile in return. As soon as Meg opened the back door, her uncle's dogs began to beg for attention, and she would've loved to approach the fence and scratch the heads of the two foxhounds had she not seen a familiar outline in the carriage house. Glancing behind her to see if Charlie was coming, and seeing that he wasn't there just yet, Meg took a deep breath and stepped down off of the porch steps.

"Meggy? Is that you?" Ezra called as he began to head her direction. "Oh, thank goodness. We've all been so worried about you." He looked up at the pristine spring sky, as if he was thanking God, and Meg had to hold back a snicker at his ridiculous antics.

They met a bit closer to the carriage house than the porch since she'd had a head start on him, and once he was before her, with his arms spread wide for an embrace, Meg wondered what she'd ever seen in him to begin with. He was quite handsome with his light blond hair and inquisitive eyes, but something about the way he held his mouth should've let her know that only lies would come out of it. He had the slack jaw of a deceiver.

He stood there with his hands spread wide, and Meg just looked at him for a moment, absently noticing scratches on the back of his hands and near his wrists, wondering how much work he'd been doing in the garden lately. "Please, don't call me that," she said, making no move toward his open arms. Eventually, he put his hands down. "I've only come to speak to you about Charlotte. I'm concerned for her well-being."

"I'm quite concerned for her as well," Ezra said, his head hanging low. He slipped his hands into the pockets of his trousers, ones Meg noted she had purchased for him. "I've told the police everything that I know."

"The police know that your story is a fabrication, you realize?" Meg asked as the breeze sent the loose strands of her hair flying about. "You told them I went with you and Charlotte when you left, but when you decided to come back, Charlotte stayed with me in the car. Obviously, they know that isn't true now. They know that you left before me, and that you took the car, the one they found wrecked and covered in blood."

Meg heard a noise behind her and turned to see Charlie standing on the porch, leaning against the brick enclosure that surrounded the perimeter. A sigh of relief escaped her lips before she even realized she'd been holding it in.

"Who is that?" Ezra asked, his voice changing just a bit. "Is that... Charlie?"

"I believe Mr. Ashton would be a more appropriate way for you to address him," Meg replied, her eyes cutting.

Ezra swallowed hard, as if he was just beginning to realize he might not be able to charm Meg in the same way he had before. "I told the police that my initial story was a fabrication I invented in order to keep your mother from worrying about your whereabouts. I gave them my adjusted story just a few days ago. I told them the truth this time, and I'm certain they are doing all they can to find Charlotte."

He looked sincere, and for a moment, Meg wanted to believe him. She didn't. "What is the truth, Ezra? Where is Charlotte?'

"I told you, I don't know. Meg, you must believe I didn't want to leave with her. I didn't have a choice."

"Am I to believe that Charlotte kidnapped you against your will?" she asked, the snicker back in her voice.

"No, of course not," he replied, withdrawing his hands from his pockets to rest them on his hips. "Meg, she came to me that morning, after you were back in your room, and she said she needed help. Once she told me what the problem was, I knew I had to help her."

That explanation made the rage well up inside her again. "She needed help—so you dropped everything to help her? Where were you when my uncle was carrying me up the stairs?" She was shouting now, and she glanced back at Charlie to see he'd taken a few steps in her direction. She shook her head at him to let him know she was all right.

"I tried to follow him, I really did," Ezra said, moving closer to her himself. "Your mother stopped me. She said... she said if I did anything to intervene, she'd let my father go. Meg, what was I to do? My father was so ill. He needed the money he earned here to pay for his medication. Now... he's on his deathbed, Meg. If I had tried to stop your uncle, my father would be out on the streets and likely dead." He had tears in his eyes; his voice was imploring. He looked the picture of a son in misery, unable to help his father.

"So you chose to leave him behind when you took off with Charlotte—and my money, and my uncle's auto—instead?" Meg questioned, clearly not buying his bleeding heart story.

"I told you, I didn't have a choice, Meg. Charlotte came to me in tears. She didn't know what to do." He took a step closer and lowered his voice. "She was pregnant Meg—she is pregnant, I mean."

Meg's eyebrows shot up at both his admission and the way he had originally made the statement. She decided to focus on the former for now. "Was this your doing?"

He ran a hand through his blond hair and took a step back, looking down. "I don't think so. We were always careful—I mean the one time that it happened, we were careful." Meg shot him a look of disgust that should've let him know she didn't believe his "one time" explanation, though his intellect was quickly falling into doubt now that he'd slipped up twice.

"Even one time wouldn't be all right, though, now would it, Ezra?

193

You and I had been pledging ourselves to each other for months by the time we decided to leave."

"I know, Meg, but I thought—as long as you were engaged to... him—what difference did it make if I was having a little fun with Charlotte?" He nodded in Charlie's direction, and even though Meg knew Charlie couldn't hear the comment from that distance, it made her stomach knot up. Perhaps Ezra had a valid argument.

Except that he didn't. "You, more than anyone, except for maybe Kelly, knew I had no plans to marry Charlie. You knew I was only writing to him, and that was only because my mother wanted his money. You cannot blame your lack of self-control on me, Ezra Bitterly."

"No, I'm not trying to, Meg, I promise you," Ezra replied, stepping toward her again. "But I didn't know if it was my child or not. There was a chance, a small chance, it was mine, but it could've also been your uncles, Meg."

Meg's eyebrows shot up again. "What do you mean? Was my uncle taking advantage of Charlotte as well?"

"No," Ezra said, dropping his eyes once more and pushing at the soft grass with the toe of his work boot. "She did it for other things—money, little trinkets, that sort of thing. She thought that as long as your uncle liked her, she'd be able to stay employed here and still have a bit of freedom. She wouldn't have to work so hard. Of course, your mother thought differently...."

"I don't really care how my mother felt about Charlotte, Ezra," Meg said, crossing her arms. She couldn't believe Charlotte had been prostituting herself out to her uncle. It made her detest the girl even more, though it didn't lessen her insistence on discovering what really happened to her.

"She knew if your mother found out she was carrying your uncle's child, she'd lose her mind. She'd likely kill Charlotte, the same way she killed...." He stopped talking, and Meg felt all the blood rush out of her face.

"The same way my mother killed... whom?"

His mouth was hanging open, and his eyes were wide. It took a long time for him to say anything at all, but when he did, he was shaking his head slowly from side to side. "No one."

"Ezra?" She took a slow step forward on an unsteady foot. "Whom do you say my mother killed?"

"No one," he repeated.

She stared at him, her eyes repeating the question, but even without an answer, she knew what he had meant to say. "What do you know?" she asked, quietly, her voice just a whisper.

Ezra cleared his throat. "I don't actually know anything, Meggy. I only know what I've heard, and what my father says he saw."

"And what's that?" Her voice was uneven, and she could feel her hands shaking where they were folded against her sides.

He licked his lips. "My father says, when we were younger, your mother used to take trips to the local druggist nearly every other week to procure arsenic. She used it on her face, like most women do, but she used... a lot of it. Then, my father said, after six months or so of that, your mother seemed to spend an inordinate amount of time pruning the oleanders."

Ezra's eyes darted over her shoulder and then returned to her face. Meg could feel large tears sliding over the wells of her eyes and bounding down her cheeks, but she didn't move to wipe them away.

"There was never any proof, no investigation. It could've been... someone else. There were other servants working here then. Kelly's mother. Your uncle even. My father didn't know for sure. He said he'd never accuse her because he didn't know. When the police questioned him that night, they only asked him if he saw anything suspicious, and they didn't pay him much mind, what with his thick accent and the fact that he was only a gardener."

She was still able to keep up with his words, but they'd begun to lose meaning. The feel of Charlie's hand on her shoulder gave her courage. "Your father believes that my mother poisoned my father?"

Ezra nodded once, sharply.

Charlie's grip tightened, and Meg pressed down hard on the lids of all of the boxes in her mind—including the one that held memories of her da. Thoughts of him pushing her on the swing, just under the tree there. The pram she'd pushed around the garden after he brought it back from his trip to New York. The lilacs he'd pick and tuck behind her ear, calling her his little flower when he did so. Without wiping the tears from her cheeks, Meg looked Ezra directly in the eyes and said, "What happened to Charlotte?"

"I don't know," Ezra mumbled, seemingly shocked that she'd reversed topics so quickly.

"What happened to her?" she asked again, more forcefully this time.

He took a full step back. "We... argued. She wanted me to take her to a physician in Essex. I didn't want to. If there was a chance the baby was mine, I wanted to keep it. She wanted to end the pregnancy. We drove into the night, and then, she... she was bleeding. I pulled over. I wanted to help her, but she didn't want my help. The arguing... it got worse. I finally got out of the car, Meg, and I began to walk. I thought, if she didn't want my help, she could take care of herself."

"You left her there, bleeding?"

"I didn't have any choice," he said, running his hand through his hair again. His sleeve slipped up a bit, and Meg noticed the scratches went even higher than she'd imagined. They looked old. She glanced around the yard to see if there'd been much pruning, but she didn't notice any. "She didn't want to listen to me. I thought it was better for me to leave than to stay there and continue to fight. I was hoping she'd make it to Essex. We were nearly there."

"Did Charlotte even know how to drive an automobile?" Meg asked.

"Yes. I showed her how." The comment caught Meg in the gut. Even though she no longer cared for Ezra, she did remember when he had taught her how to drive the same car. "She took off, and I caught a ride back here. I made up the story about you being with her because I didn't want your mother to worry, and I thought Charlotte would never return. I didn't think she'd want to face your uncle after she'd left, especially not if she thought I'd tell them she was expecting."

"Where did you get that bruise on your neck?" Charlie asked, his hand never leaving Meg's shoulder.

She hadn't notice it before, but when Charlie mentioned it, she could see a black and blue streak just peeking out from his shirt collar. It was yellowing at the edges, as if it was beginning to fade.

"A branch struck me when I was cutting back the trees," he said with a shrug. "Scratched my hands up right good, too," he said, bringing them out of his pockets.

"Why weren't you wearing gloves?" Charlie asked.

"I prefer not to wear gloves." He shrugged again. "Meg knows that."

She didn't remember whether or not he normally wore gloves, but she wasn't buying his story. "I believe Det. Weber would like to speak to you again."

Ezra looked over her shoulder, as if he thought the detective might be standing behind her. "I've already told them everything I just mentioned to you. I shouldn't mind speaking to them again, but I don't really see the point."

"I suppose they have their reasons," Meg said. She brushed her hands up and down her face, finally wiping away the tear streaks. She'd weigh out what he'd mentioned about her parents later. For now, she needed to make sure Det. Weber had an opportunity to thoroughly question Ezra one more time. She cleared her throat. "Ezra, I want to thank you," Meg began resting one hand on her hip.

"What's that?" he asked, looking from her face to Charlie's and then back again. "Thank me for what?"

"For leaving," she replied. "If you'd stayed, if you'd carried through with what we talked about, I would've run away with you. If I'd left with you the night of Alise's ball, or if you'd had the gumption to attempt to save me from my uncle and take me away the next morning, I would've missed out on my destiny. I never would've boarded *Titanic*. I never would've met Charlie. Thanks to your ineptitude, I will now leave here with the most wonderful man imaginable as my fiancé and return to a life in America with nothing but freedom and happiness on the horizon. So... as much as you hurt me, as horrible of a human being as I believe you to be, I at least must say thank you. I appreciate your cowardice more than you can possibly imagine."

Ezra's brow was furrowed and he stared at her in confusion.

"I concur," Charlie replied, slipping his hand down around Meg's waist. "Thank you very much for being the most pathetic bloke who has ever walked the earth."

The door opened behind them before Ezra could formulate a sentence, and Jonathan stepped out, followed by Det. Weber. "I hate to interrupt, but your mother has finished her statement. Det. Weber has more questions for Mr. Bitterly, and I believe Officer Brown is ready to speak to you as soon as you are ready, Miss Westmoreland."

Meg nodded at him, and then without even turning back to face the gardener, she said, "Goodbye, Ezra."

Charlie followed her up the steps as Det. Weber began his inquisition. "Are you going to speak to your mother about Ezra's accusation?"

"I suppose I have to," Meg said, her breath catching.

They began to make their way through the kitchen, and Meg noticed Tessa had moved on to some sort of baking. She offered a smile but said nothing as they passed through. Meg made a mental note to make sure that Tessa received enough money that she wouldn't have to work anymore. It was the least she could do for the woman who'd served her mother and put up with her uncle for so long.

Mildred was standing in the foyer speaking to an officer Meg didn't recognize. The other officers Det. Weber had mentioned must have arrived, because several men in uniforms stood both inside the entryway and on the porch. Officer Brown was speaking to the ones on the porch, and Meg decided to wait for him to notice her rather than announce her presence and be forced to get on with her report of what happened with her uncle any sooner than necessary.

"Mary Margaret," Mildred said, turning to face her daughter. "You've returned. Did you get everything taken care of with the Bitterly boy?"

Meg found it unamusing that her mother still addressed him that way after all of these years. "I did."

"Good. I had a feeling he wasn't telling the truth. And to think you nearly gave up everything for that wretched man." She looked at Charlie as she spoke and then back at Meg, a snide grin pulling at her thin lips.

The words stung worse than they should. "Yes, Mother, I suppose I nearly did. Would you happen to know anything about that, Mother? About making the wrong choice?'

"I don't know what you mean...."

"When you chose Bertram over Da. Did you ever regret that? Once his promises of making the company so grand and profitable fell through, when he buried himself in a bottle and embarrassed the hell out of us at social functions? Did you ever think perhaps you should've stayed loyal to Da?"

"Mary Margaret, your uncle and I have only ever been like brother and sister," Mildred said, her head shaking slightly as she said it.

"Please don't speak to me as if I am an idiot, Mother. Anyone could see that was obviously not the case. I just don't know when it all started. I'd always assumed you found solace in the arms of that vile creature after Da passed, but now, I'm not so sure."

Mildred looked at the officer she'd been speaking to, who was now at least a foot closer to the door, and at Charlie before she said quietly, "Mary Margaret, I'm not sure now is the time to discuss such matters."

"There will be no other time, Mother. Once I leave here today, you can rest assured I will never return."

The older woman took a deep breath in through her nostrils. "Perhaps we should retire to the parlor then...."

"No, Mother. That's not necessary. I see everything on your face. I had hoped that the information I just received concerning your... participation... in Da's death was simply rumor, but you really are capable of killing, aren't you, Mother?"

"Mary Margaret!" Mildred warned. The police officer looked much more interested in the conversation now. "I don't know what you're speaking of, but I assure you, I was just as shocked when your father passed away as anyone."

Meg couldn't say more, not right then anyway. She had secretly hoped for a confession, that her mother would admit what she had done, and while the answer was written all over her smug face, Meg realized she should've known better than to think Mildred would actually confess. She had always been about self-preservation. "You're right, Mother. Now is not the time."

Her mother nodded, and even though she was nearly four inches shorter than Meg, she still managed to look down her nose at her daughter. "I shall assume your accusation is due to your flustered state and shall let it go."

If she expected an apology, she wouldn't get one. Especially now that Meg realized what she'd done to her poor, trusting Da. The tears threatened to come again, and Meg crushed them with the weight of her hatred.

"Mrs. Westmoreland, we are ready to move forward with our investigation," Officer Brown was saying as he stepped back through the door. "We have enough information now to take him in."

Meg glanced out the door and saw Ezra being put in the back of one of the police vehicles. "Are you arresting Ezra?" she asked, stepping closer to the glass so she could see better.

"We are," Officer Brown nodded. "We believe he is responsible for the murder of Charlotte Ross."

"Dear God," Mildred mumbled, her hand flying to cover her mouth.

Meg felt her stomach lurch. If it hadn't been for Charlie's arm tight around her waist, she may have fallen forward.

"Have you a body then?" Charlie asked for all of them.

The officer nodded. "She was found yesterday in some brush near where the automobile was located."

"What was the cause of death?" Meg asked, her hands trembling.

"Strangulation," the officer replied, dropping his head. "That's all I can say at this time."

"Poor dear," Mildred said, casting her eyes at the ground. Then, raising them, she looked at her daughter. "That could've been you, Mary Margaret."

Meg didn't need her mother to say the words in order to know that. She said nothing, only stood on weak knees, thankful that Charlie had become a steady rock in a stream that was quickly breaking over its banks.

"We would like to collect your brother-in-law, Mrs. Westmoreland, if you don't mind." The voice belonged to Det. Weber, and Meg realized she hadn't even noticed him coming back in through the back door, Jonathan behind him. The politeness, she was sure, was just a formality.

"Of course I mind," Mildred replied. "But I suppose I have little say in the matter. Two arrests in one day," she mused. "Mr. Ashton, you aren't reconsidering your arrangement are you?"

He tightened his grip around Meg to the point she could hardly breathe. "Not in the least. Meg is certainly not a product of the evil that has gone on under this roof for far too long."

Mildred only raised her eyebrows. "I shall get him for you," she said, glancing at the detective before she turned to ascend the stairs. "It will give me the opportunity to say goodbye to him privately."

Meg was certain that last comment was a jab at her, but she ignored it. The emotions running through her mind were too much, even for her carefully guarded compartments, and she felt like she might begin to crumble at any moment.

"Miss Westmoreland, we are prepared to take your statement whenever you are ready," the detective said quietly.

"Give her a few moments, won't you?" Charlie said on her behalf, only lessening his grip a bit as he did so.

"Yes, of course," Det. Weber replied, taking a step backward into the parlor.

"Would you like some water, Meg?" Jonathan asked.

She turned to look at him and could see concern all over his face. She realized she must look a mess if he was worried about her. "I'm fine, thank you. Just shocked. I'll be all right once this is all over."

"The worst is past," Charlie assured her. She knew his words were meant as comfort, but that was only because he had no idea how difficult it would be for her to sit across from Det. Weber and tell him all of the things Bertram had done to her. She realized she didn't want to be standing there when he came down. She never wanted to see him again.

A scream broke through the silence in the house, making them all jump and look up at the second story as if they could see through the floorboards. "Dear God! Someone—help!"

It was her mother. As the shouting continued, the officers took off up the stairs, even some who had previously been standing outside, Jonathan joining in the pack. Charlie held Meg back. "Stay here."

"What... what do you think.... Why is she screaming?"

"I'm not sure, but I suppose we'll find out shortly."

Tessa came running in. "What's happening? Why is your mother shouting?"

"I don't know. But I want to go find out. Charlie, please?"

He released her. "All right, but I wish you wouldn't."

As soon as she gained her freedom, Meg began to climb the stairs on shaking legs. Here, where her Da had bounded up the steps to catch her in his strong arms upon returning from trips abroad, always with a gift in his hands. Here, where she'd scraped her knee, and Da had scooped her up to bandage it, singing a silly song about little girls who tumble down the steps as he did so. Here, where she'd stomped down the stairs to confront her mother when a servant had accidentally delivered a letter from Charlie. Here, where Tessa had saved her from her uncle—momentarily—when she'd fallen and he'd snatched her ankle. Here, where Bertram had carried her up the stairs—screaming—to her room to torture her. Here, these steps, the ones that led to the second story and her room, the one place she swore she'd never enter again. The hallway where he'd stood and shadowed her doorway time and again—lurking. The hall where her mother had screamed at her—barely conscious—as she lay in agony on her bed. This doorway, two past her own, where a flood of police officers stood staring up at the ceiling, her mother sobbed, and Jonathan waited for her in the threshold.

"I need to see," Meg said quietly, Charlie just behind her.

Jonathan nodded and crushed himself against the doorjamb so Meg could squeeze through.

The officers parted as she entered, as if they all knew the importance of closure.

Meg looked up. Her uncle dangled from a rafter, his face blue, his eyes bulging, the rope around his neck frayed and thin. A chair lay on its side beneath his dangling feet, one shoe sliding off at the heel. Her mother had called for help, as if there were a possibility of saving him, but he had been lost to humanity long ago. Meg nodded once and backed into Charlie, who escorted her out of the room.

The monster was gone forever. Suddenly, Meg could feel the air in her lungs in a way she'd never felt it before. Her shoulders fell back and her head tipped up as if they were free of the weight of years of distress.

"Are you all right?" Charlie asked as they continued down the hallway.

Meg didn't slow. She only said, "Yes," and proceeded toward the stairs. She'd still have to deal with the knowledge that her mother had killed her father, that Ezra had strangled Charlotte, and that the demons in the boxes may still try to get out from time to time, but for now, there was no reason to tell the officers what she'd endured. She could return to America, freer than she'd ever been before.

At the bottom of the stairs, she paused and imagined her Da coming through the door, a large grin on his face, his arms open. She imagined flinging her six-year-old body into his arms, giggling, the feeling of security enveloping her as he pulled her close to his heart. One last time, a tear slipped from her eye, and Meg let it fall. She closed her eyes tightly, and looking up at the heavens, she said, "Thank you, Da." She walked out of the door of the only home she'd ever known and kept right on walking, never looking back.

CHAPTER TWELVE

The First Class dining experience aboard the passenger liner they'd booked the next day to take them home was nothing compared to *Titanic,* and the ship was much smaller, which made the rocking more obvious, but as Meg sat next to Charlie at dinner, she was just happy to have him with her. She had been right in thinking he'd be more at ease on the way home.

They'd insisted on having Jonathan and Carrie accompany them, and no one had objected. Dr. Shaw belonged there with them as much as anyone else, but Meg enjoyed watching Carrie's face as others served her for a change, and Meg thought she looked lovely in one of her gowns.

They'd spoken at great length about all that had transpired, and yet, from time to time, someone would still muse aloud, bringing the most astounding topics back to the conversation. Meg hadn't allowed herself to shed a single tear for either Bertram or her mother, and she was hopeful that Ezra would get what he had coming to him, though he swore he was innocent.

Her uncle's suicide note had confessed to the poisoning of Henry Westmoreland nearly fifteen years prior, and he said he'd acted alone.

Meg pushed those thoughts aside and refused to take part in any discussion whenever it came up. She knew the truth—her mother had killed her father—and thanks to her uncle, she'd never pay for it. She liked to think Mildred would be tortured forever at the thought of what she'd done to her husband, but Meg knew her mother wasn't capable of feeling regret. If she were going to feel remorseful, she would've done so many years ago.

"I am so glad that you got the letters," Charlie was saying to Jonathan as the last course was presented before them. "Now, I know that they are under my control and I don't have to worry about some newspaper grabbing hold of them and publishing the drabble I wrote when I was ten."

"Your letters were always well-penned," Meg disagreed, coming back to the conversation. "If I'd known you were speaking from the heart, they would've been much more touching."

"How's that now?" Carrie asked, digging into her dessert. "You thought Mr. Ashton was being dishonest?"

"Not exactly," Meg replied, shrugging. "I suppose I just assumed he was being forced to write them and having them looked over before he sent them, just as I was."

"Unfortunately, I cannot blame any of my prose on anyone other than myself." Charlie took a drink of his chardonnay .

"Do you still have all of Miss Meg's letters?" Dr. Shaw asked, clearly amused at finding out such personal information about his clients.

"I do," Charlie nodded, "though they are not nearly as entertaining as mine, I assure you."

"My mother read every single one of them," Meg explained. "I had to be prim and proper. And discreet."

"And disinterested." He said it with a wink, but Meg felt a tinge of guilt just the same.

"I think it's wonderful," Carrie said, smiling.

"What, the letters or your cake?" Jonathan asked, with a cheeky smile.

"Both." Carrie daintily wiped at the corners of her mouth. "I imagine it will be something lovely to share with your children one day. You do plan to have children, don't you?"

"Yes, dozens," Charlie said nodding.

With a laugh, Meg said, "Probably not that many, but yes, we should like to have *some* children someday."

"I can hardly wait to see cute little Megs and Charlies running about the estate," Carrie said with a dreamy look on her face.

"While we can name all of our daughters Meg if my beloved likes, I think our first son shall be named Henry," Charlie said, catching Meg's eyes.

She felt her heart melt as a smile slowly crept across her face. "I'd like that very much."

Before they could say more, they were interrupted by a middle-aged man with wire-rimmed spectacles and patches of graying hair above his ears, the rest of his head reflecting the lights above them. He stopped next to Dr. Shaw's seat, a taller, thinner man standing behind him. "I thought that was you, Robert," he said, resting his hand on Dr. Shaw's shoulder. "How are you?"

The man was rather soft-spoken and had kind eyes, Meg noted. "Dr. Morgan!" Dr. Shaw said, grasping the other man's hand as he rose to greet him. "I had no idea you were aboard. I'm well. How are you?"

"Quite well, thank you," Dr. Morgan replied. "I'm just returning from a trip to visit my mother in Winchester. I tried to coax her into returning with me, but she says New York is not for the faint of heart."

They had a good chuckle, and the rest of the table joined in as well. "Dr. Laurie Morgan, let me introduce you to Charles Ashton and his wife-to-be, Mary Margaret Westmoreland."

"How do you do?" Charlie asked, shaking the man's hand.

"It's lovely to meet both of you," Dr. Morgan said, releasing Charlie's hand to take Meg's. She noticed his grip was rather slack and his voice gentle.

"It's nice to meet you as well," Meg said.

"This is my man Jonathan Lane, and Meg's lady Carrie...."

"Boxhall," Carrie supplied as the doctor shook her hand in turn. "How do you do?"

"This is my assistant Edward Dane," Dr. Morgan said, and everyone said hello to him as well, though with this greeting Meg noticed a glimmer of something pass between Jonathan and this Edward fellow as he looked at each of them and gave a soft hello.

"Dr. Morgan?" Charlie repeated. "You aren't perchance *the* Dr. Morgan? That is to say, Dr. Lawrence Morgan—the famed psychiatrist?"

The doctor's face turned a bit red. "I'm not sure that's quite the word I'd use," he said with a shrug.

"No, I've been reading some of your work recently on the human brain. I find it fascinating," Charlie continued. "Your research is compelling, particularly where it lies in contrast to the work of Freud and others."

"The human brain is quite complex," Dr. Morgan replied. "The way one brain responds to a particular stimulus can be quite different than another."

"Yes, I suppose that's true," Charlie nodded. "I'd love to talk to you more about your findings, if you don't mind. Do you have time?"

Dr. Morgan looked at Dr. Shaw and then back at Charlie. "Yes, of course, I don't mind at all. If you're sure you want to sit with a couple of doctors and listen to us ramble on in medical terminology."

Meg noticed a brightness in Charlie's face she hadn't seen since before the sinking, and she couldn't help but smile. She tried to catch Jonathan's eye to see if he'd also noticed, but he was... preoccupied.

"Is that all right with you, Meg?"

"Absolutely," she said quickly. "I think it's a wonderful idea." How lucky was she that her fiancé actually asked her permission to leave her side?

"Would you care to accompany us to the smoking lounge?" Charlie asked Dr. Morgan, who readily agreed. "Jonathan?"

It took a moment for Jonathan to realize Charlie was saying his name. "Oh, yes? What's that now?"

Charlie's eyebrows crinkled for a moment. "Would you mind escorting the ladies to their room?"

"I'm happy to," Jonathan replied, rising.

Meg tried to hide her amusement. She'd never seen him disheveled before. "It was lovely to meet you, Dr. Morgan," she said as she stood and offered her hand.

"You as well, Miss Westmoreland," the doctor replied with a kind smile.

A few moments later, Meg had her hand on Jonathan's arm, and he was leading her down the corridor toward her accommodations, Carrie behind them. Leaning in, she quietly asked, "Do you know him?"

Jonathan feigned innocence. "Know who?"

With a coy smile, Meg asked, "Edward, I believe he said his name was."

"Oh, no. I don't know him." Meg looked at him expectantly. Jonathan's gaze traveled from the floor in front of them to her face and then straight ahead before he added, "But I'd like to."

She giggled. "Well, then, go back to the smoking lounge once you've delivered us."

He shrugged. "I don't know about all that, Meg...."

"Jonathan!" she said, turning to face him. "Why ever not? He was looking at you, too."

His eyebrows raised. "Are you certain?"

"Quite."

He tipped his head to the side, as if he would consider it, and she began to walk again. They were almost at the room, and he said nothing else in response until after he'd unlocked the door, and the ladies were inside. "Do you require anything before I depart?"

With a broad smile, Meg replied. "Only that you have a nice time."

He blushed and said nothing more before shutting the door. Meg broke into a fit of giggles, and Carrie wrapped her arms around the blonde's shoulders, laughing right along. "It's just so nice to see him..."

"Flustered?" Carrie asked.

"I was going to say happy, but I suppose that's true as well."

Letting go, Carrie replied, "I agree. It is nice. Now, perhaps you could play matchmaker for me."

"Matchmaker?" Meg repeated, her eyebrows raised. "I'd hardly call myself that."

"I need all the help I can get," Carrie replied, attempting to drop onto the settee but struggling against the confines of Meg's gown. "It was nice to wear this lovely frock tonight and imagine, though. Perhaps I could meet a nice gentleman if I pretend to be important enough."

"You are important," Meg reminded her. "Besides, you don't have to wear a nice gown to meet a proper gentleman. I met Charlie wearing clothing I'd borrowed from my lady, you know?"

Carrie nodded. "I should only hope to be half as lucky as you've been when it comes to love."

Meg sat down across from her. "I have been lucky in that one area of my life, that's very true," she agreed. The shortcomings everywhere else seemed quite trivial when compared to meeting Charlie.

"THE BRAIN IS STILL QUITE A MYSTERY," Dr. Morgan was saying as he sat across from Charlie in a plush velvet chair, Dr. Shaw seated nearby. Circles of smoke lingered around them from the cigars of several dozen gentlemen seated in similar groupings, discussing business and other inconsequentialities. Jonathan and Edward were sitting across the room, and Charlie glanced in his friend's direction every once in a while, noting that he seemed unusually amused about something.

"I've been reading Freud's theories of psychoanalysis," Charlie said with a nod. "Do you think there's any truth to his findings? Particularly regarding the unconscious mind?"

Dr. Morgan nodded. "I can't say that I completely agree with all that Freud has to say, but I do with his theory that the unconscious mind plays a larger role in our actions than we previously understood."

"Do you believe memories can be trapped there and cause us to act in a particular fashion?" Charlie asked as a waiter brought him another drink.

"I certainly believe that is possible," Dr. Morgan said as he waved the servant away with a polite smile. "Tell me, Mr. Ashton, what do you remember from *Titanic*?"

Charlie cleared his throat. "Why, that's just it, doctor. I don't remember much of anything once Meg was safe on the lifeboat. There are flashes from time to time, and once in a while I feel as if I'm about to remember something, but then... it all fades away. I remember helping some of the Third Class passengers try to get up to the lifeboats, but there was so much confusion. I can see their faces in flickers before me, but they don't last. Sort of like the explosion from a flashbulb, if you will."

"Interesting," Dr. Shaw said, taking a puff from his cigar. "And you don't recall boarding *Carpathia* then?"

"No," Charlie shook his head. "In fact, I don't even remember disembarking *Carpathia*. But then, I may have been unconscious. Meg says they were giving me some pretty heavy sedatives. There were times I couldn't even place her." Turning back to Dr. Morgan, he said, "Do you think that's... normal, doctor?"

"I do," Dr. Morgan assured him. "If what the papers are saying is true, you expired for a bit aboard *Carpathia*. Do you think that's accurate?"

"Meg says I died," Charlie agreed. "I remember feeling as if I were floating away, then opening my eyes to see her there, and I remember fragments of the conversation we had after that, but then it all goes hazy again."

"I don't think this sort of reaction to such a traumatic experience is out of the ordinary," Dr. Morgan said, adjusting in his chair. "In fact, coupled with the medical issues you've also faced, I'm a bit surprised you recall anything at all."

"Is that so?" Charlie asked, feeling a bit relieved. "You think it's typical, then?"

"I do."

"What other sorts of reactions might be considered normal?" Charlie asked, not wanting to bring up the voices that were imploring him to help them, even as he sat in the safety of the ship.

Dr. Morgan shrugged. "If you've read my most recent theory, you'll understand that it could be unique to each individual's experience."

"I have read it," Charlie replied. "The theory of individual capability."

"Precisely," Dr. Morgan said with a small smile. "Your experience could be exactly the same as someone else's, and you could still walk away with a completely different memory, a completely different recount, of everything that happened. Even the other gentlemen who were in the water with you that night could have a wholly different recollection from you."

Once again, Charlie found himself nodding along. He had read Dr. Morgan's recently published work, and he had already come to that conclusion on his own. "And what of the memories I have that I cannot bring to the surface? I find it a bit ironic that Freud likened memory to an iceberg of all things."

Dr. Shaw snickered. "If he'd been aboard *Titanic*, he might have changed his theory."

"Indeed," Charlie said, trying not to roll his eyes. "Do you feel it's possible or even beneficial to try to recall them?"

"I believe so," Dr. Morgan said. "It's my opinion that remembering as much as possible about a traumatic event will allow you to deal with that experience and move on from it."

"Would accessing those memories be difficult?"

"It all depends on the patient," Dr. Morgan replied. "Some might be able to draw those memories out quickly, face their fears, and move on. For others, it might take months, years even."

"Charlie, perhaps Dr. Morgan could help you with some of the anxiety you are having as a result of the sinking. Are you seeing new patients, Dr. Morgan?" Dr. Shaw clearly had his patient's best interests in mind, but Charlie was hesitant to ask for help. He still wasn't convinced Meg would approve.

"I'm not taking new patients as a rule right now," Dr. Morgan said. "However, I'd be more than happy to make an exception for you, Charlie. I believe someone of your stature, who has been through the horrific events you've experienced, would be an interesting patient to assist, and I'd be honored to have the opportunity to work with you."

Charlie raised his eyebrows, unsure how to respond. The chance to receive professional assistance from someone as skilled as Dr. Morgan did seem tempting, especially since he was beginning to think the doctor could actually help him. "Thank you, Dr. Morgan," he began. "I would need to speak to Meg first."

"I find it... charming how you consistently take into account Miss Westmoreland's wishes," Dr. Shaw said, with a chuckle. "Will that be the way of it with you youngsters? Letting women have an equal say in all household operations?"

Though he wasn't offended, he didn't find it amusing, either, and Charlie said, "I can only speak for myself, but I plan to consult my wife whenever possible. For one thing, I value her opinion; she's much more intelligent than I am. Secondly, I should like to stay in her good graces. I've worked for years to get here, and I should hate to have to start all over again."

The other gentlemen laughed, and Charlie chuckled along with them out of politeness, but he'd meant every word he said.

"I hardly think Miss Westmoreland could be more intelligent than you, sir," Dr. Shaw said.

"You should try playing any sort of game with her then, particularly if trivia is involved. She's sharp as a tack, I assure you."

Dr. Shaw only guffawed, as if he thought it impossible that a woman could be smarter than any man, particularly one who had graduated from Cambridge.

"Once we reach New York, please telephone my office or come by," Dr. Morgan encouraged. "We'll be happy to see you, discreetly of course, Charlie. I do believe I can help you begin to feel like your former self."

Letting out a sigh of relief, Charlie, "Wonderful, Dr. Morgan. I do look forward to putting all of this behind me. Of course, this doesn't mean you'll be giving me any type of medication or sending me off to live in an asylum of any sort does it?"

Dr. Morgan laughed quietly. "No, of course not. I don't believe in medication, and the only way I'd send you away is if I thought you were a danger to yourself or others."

"Very good," Charlie replied with a nod.

"What of Miss Westmoreland?" Dr. Shaw asked, pausing to take a sip of his brandy. "How is she handling all of this?"

"Meg? She's fine," Charlie said with a shrug. "She's been through so much, and yet it doesn't seem to trouble her one bit. She tried to explain to me once the system she has, mentally, of dealing with all that she's had to go through in her life, but I'm not sure I quite understand."

"That's good to hear," Dr. Morgan said. "Of course, should the need arise, I'm happy to see her as well."

"Thank you," Charlie said with a smile, though he knew there was likely no chance he'd ever get Meg to see a psychiatrist after the conversation they'd had regarding him seeing one himself. She'd just keep shoving her memories down inside those boxes in her mind until they were so deep, she'd forget the boxes even existed. Either that, or she and her boxes would simply come unhinged. He hoped for the former.

CHAPTER THIRTEEN

Meg sat on a plush sofa in Maurice's shop near Columbus Circle. From here, she could see the people outside bustling by on a warm June day, and she wondered where they were going and if any of them would mind if she went along. She'd rather be just about anywhere else.

"I like the taffeta," Grace was saying, "though with that tulle underneath, it seems a bit too... poofy, don't you think?"

It wasn't Meg she was speaking to, so she remained silent, watching a plump, older woman proceed down the sidewalk with a little boy who she believed might be the woman's grandson. He seemed reluctant to walk, and Meg imagined they must have had a disagreement. Perhaps he wanted a snack from one of the many street vendors, and Grandmother had said no....

"Meg? Are you listening?"

She turned her head to see Pamela addressing her. "I'm sorry— were you speaking to me?"

Pamela let out a soft giggle as if she wanted to be angry at Meg for being distracted but couldn't because the girl was just too pathetic. "Yes, darling. I was saying this chiffon would look lovely with your complexion, don't you think?"

Meg looked from the fabric Pamela was holding out toward her to the bolt Grace was holding. While Meg had worn her fair share of just about every popular fabric in creation, she'd never really bothered with learning the differences. They were both ivory, she knew that much. They looked quite similar. "I like it," Meg said, forcing a smile. "I defer to your expertise."

Pamela's smile broadened. "Darling, don't you want to pick your dress? I know we've done most of the choosing for you, but surely you have something in mind for your wedding gown?"

Meg thought about a portrait that used to sit in her mother's parlor, one that had been gone for quite some time. It had been of her parents on their wedding day. Her mother had looked stunning in a fitted white gown with a high neckline, a lacy veil over the back of her head. Despite desperately wanting to marry Charlie, she hadn't put much thought into the wedding itself, thinking it would be a bit of an olive branch to allow his sister her say as much as possible, under Pamela's guidance. Now, since they were asking, she found she did have an opinion after all.

"I think I should like a full skirt, one that does have a bit of—what did you say, Grace? Poof? Yes, I think I should like that. And I would like the neckline to be lower—not scandalously low, but not choking either. As to the fabric, anything but lace."

Pamela and Grace exchanged looks. "Very well, then. I think we can accomplish that," Pamela said, still smiling. They went on about their conversation, Pamela occasionally asking Meg if she agreed and Grace periodically shooting daggers across the room. Eventually, they settled on the chiffon with a tulle under-layer, and Pamela went out to find Maurice to let him know of the decision.

Grace set the bolt of fabric they had chosen against the sofa where Meg had been sitting for nearly an hour now and stretched her back. "It's a pity your friend couldn't come. What's her name? Kitty?"

"Kelly," Meg replied, knowing Grace was likely aware of her

friend's name. If Kelly had been there, it may have been a more hostile situation. Meg had wanted to ask her but decided against it. This was a day to be endured, and she would gladly do so if it took her one step closer to being Charlie's wife.

Sitting down several feet away from her, Grace said, "I imagine you're quite pleased you won't have to wait until the fall to make sure Charlie can't change his mind."

Meg's eyebrows shot up. "I wasn't aware that was a possibility," she said with a shrug. "I'm fairly certain I could wait a few hundred years and he wouldn't change his mind—though I'll be the first to admit it is surprising."

Grace looked at her curiously. "You believe so?"

"Yes, of course." Meg straightened her back. "I'm fully aware that I don't deserve your brother."

One perfectly formed eyebrow arched above a brown eye. "You are?"

"How could I not be? He's nearly perfect, you know. I don't suppose any woman truly deserves him. I certainly don't. I'm aware of all the mistakes I've made over the years, Grace. We've discussed them, I've apologized and explained, and he has forgiven me. Perhaps you might consider doing so yourself one day."

Grace continued to stare at her as if she didn't understand the language Meg was speaking. After a few moments, she settled back into the sofa and turned her attention toward the large window in front of them. "It isn't that I don't forgive you, Mary Margaret. It's only... I was afraid you might want him for other reasons. That you might be more concerned with becoming an Ashton than becoming Charlie's wife."

"I can understand that," Meg nodded. "But that isn't the case. I tried very hard not to become an Ashton, but it wouldn't take."

She turned her head to look at Meg and a bit of a smile began to creep into the corners of her mouth. Grace shut it down. "Do you have something against the family name?"

"Not at all," Meg replied, smiling. "I've only heard pleasant things about your family. Your parents' generosity is well known. They were certainly loyal friends to my father."

"Then why wouldn't you want to marry into the family?"

Meg took a deep breath and scooted a bit toward Grace, who didn't move away. "I wanted to choose, Grace. I wanted the capability of standing in front of a man and saying, 'Yes, you're the one.' I wanted that for Charlie as well. While I knew in my heart my father would always have my best interests in mind, I also knew my mother didn't, and I wasn't quite sure whose request I would be fulfilling if I went along with this. But then I realized my da had chosen Charlie purposefully, and I couldn't have made a better selection if I'd been given all the men in the world to go through."

"But Charlie deserves a choice, too," Grace interjected, spinning around to face her. "That has always been my contention. Peter might not be perfect, but I chose him. Charlie didn't get that opportunity."

"Oh, but he did," Meg assured her with a nod. "He chose me more than once when I didn't think he would. I gave him every opportunity to leave me and go on about his life, but he wouldn't do it, so here we are."

"No, Charlie would never go against father's wishes and let you go when he knew how much the arrangement with Mr. Westmoreland meant."

"He easily could've if Mary Margaret Westmoreland was missing in England or had died aboard *Titanic*. Both of those things could've happened." Meg dropped her eyes to the floor and added quietly, "Both of those things did happen." She raised her eyes to Grace. "For whatever reason, I cannot say, but believe me when I say your brother has chosen me. And if I am lucky, he will continue to choose me every day for the rest of my life. Don't be cross at me because you believe I am unaware that I am unworthy. I'm quite aware of that fact, and that's just one of the reasons why I thank God every day for knowing what was best for me when I had absolutely no idea."

With a sigh, Grace blinked back tears and slowly wrapped her arms around Meg. Neither of them said anything, and when Pamela came into the room, Maurice on her heels, Meg heard her let out a slow gasp. Meg couldn't help but think Mr. and Mrs. Ashton had chosen the correct name for their daughter after all.

DR. MORGAN's office was on the third floor of a five story building, nestled between two similar looking offices, and Charlie attempted to be discreet as he slipped inside for the first time. He knew that the field of psychiatry was growing in acceptance, yet he didn't necessarily want to make an announcement to the world that he needed help. However, the accompanying chorus of voices that stepped off of the elevator with him was a reminder that he hadn't been capable of getting better on his own.

The receptionist was an older woman with a nice smile. She asked Charlie to wait one moment while she informed Dr. Morgan that he was there, and though there were a few leather bound chairs to choose from, Charlie chose to stand instead. He peeked beneath the curtains at the few autos and pedestrians traveling about below and wondered if any of those people belonged in here as much as he did.

"Mr. Ashton!" Dr. Morgan said, his quiet voice still showing excitement. "Nice to see you again."

Charlie turned to grasp his outstretched hand. "You as well, doctor. Please, call me Charlie," he reminded the psychiatrist

"Won't you come in?"

The doctor led him into a cozy office with more leather furniture and a dark desk and bookshelf, almost black. The smell of leather and a faint whiff of cigar smoke filled his nostrils, and he absently thought one of the doctor's previous patients must be a smoker since, as far as he knew, Dr. Morgan was not.

"Would you care to have a seat there, on the lounger?" Dr.

Morgan asked, sitting in a chair across from it. "You can sit or recline. It's up to you."

Charlie chose to sit and settled himself in the corner. Dr. Morgan held a pad of paper and a pen but said nothing as Charlie took in the rest of the room. The paintings were what one might expect; hunting scenes, a picnic, the seaside, all in darker hues. On a small table next to the doctor sat a lamp with a white fabric shade, a picture of Dr. Morgan and a woman about his age in a golden frame underneath.

"Is that Mrs. Morgan?" Charlie asked, nodding in the direction of the photograph.

Dr. Morgan tipped his head down and looked at the portrait next to his elbow, as if he'd forgotten it was there. "It is."

"She's lovely," Charlie said politely, though there wasn't anything particularly striking about her.

"Thank you."

"Have you any children?"

"We have. Two boys and a girl. All in various levels of study at universities here in the city."

Charlie nodded. Ordinarily, he might ask more questions about Dr. Morgan's family, but he knew this was not a conversation. This was about him.

Dr. Morgan offered, "My wife, Rachael, decided not to travel with me to visit my mother after having had a premonition of a ship sinking. After *Titanic*, all she could say was, 'I told you so.'"

Charlie raised both eyebrows. "You don't say? Do you think there's anything to it?"

"Possibly," Dr. Morgan shrugged. "It's difficult to say. I suppose we'll know someday exactly what the human mind is capable of, though we don't know for now."

Charlie nodded again and cleared his throat. He was out of objects to stare at. He looked at his hands, folded in his lap.

"Tell me about your family, Charlie. How are your relationships with your mother and father?"

"Wonderful," he replied, no thought needed. "I've always gotten along quite well with them. My father is very nurturing. He's allowed me the opportunity to learn the business on my own, under his guidance. My mother is quite loving. She has become a bit more involved with the social scene these past few years, but I think that's more my sister's influence than anything else."

"And you get along well with your sister?'

"Oh, yes. Grace is a wonderful older sister. She's a bit overprotective from time to time, but nothing outrageous. She and her husband Peter live in Buffalo."

"No nieces and nephews?"

"Not yet. Although, Meg's friend—who is really more like a sister to her—she has two little girls. Ruth and Lizzie. They are like my nieces."

"Is that so?"

"Oh, yes. Precious little girls those two. Ruth is a bit of a troublemaker, I suppose. But I love them. Getting to see them... lightens the load, I guess. It makes me feel like all of my worries are gone, at least for a bit."

Dr. Morgan nodded. "Sounds lovely. Tell me about Meg."

Charlie knew he was grinning like a school boy with a crush, but he didn't care. "Meg is... perfect. I've always known she'd be my wife, but I had no idea we would love each other so completely. It really is quite a relief to know that I will spend the rest of my life with such an incredible woman."

"It doesn't bother you at all to know you had little say in who you would wed?"

"No, not anymore. Oh, there were times when it did, I suppose. As a matter of fact, I know that there were. But that was before I knew her. Now that I have Meg in my life, I can't imagine living without her."

"How wonderful," Dr. Morgan offered with a small smile.

"It is. It really is," Charlie nodded, still grinning ear to ear at the thought of her.

"And the wedding is soon?"

"Yes, in two weeks. You must come. I'll make sure my mother gets you an invitation."

"I don't typically attend events held by my patients...."

"Dr. Morgan, if my mother and sister get their way, everyone in town will be talking about this wedding for years to come. You simply must be there."

Letting out a low chuckle, Dr. Morgan said, "I suppose Rachael will have my head if I say no."

"Likely," Charlie agreed. "Bring your man. Edward, is it?"

"That's him," Dr. Morgan nodded. They shared a knowing smile but said nothing more on the topic they both had in mind. "Now, Charlie, what is it exactly you'd like for me to help you with?" Dr. Morgan asked, setting his notepad aside.

Charlie swallowed a lump in his throat. "I should like to get back to my former self. I feel that, ever since *Titanic* sank, part of me is missing. As if it were dragged down beneath the sea, and I can't get it back. It's been replaced with... thoughts of despair and distress. I don't like feeling that way, Dr. Morgan. I don't like jumping at loud noises or feeling as if I'm about to cry—or shout at someone—for no apparent reason."

Dr. Morgan was slowly nodding, his hands bridged in front of his face. "All of that is normal, Charlie."

"Is it? I mean... Meg's been through so much more than I have, and she seems just fine. Jonathan has gone on about his life, as have Kelly and Daniel. Other people from the ship are making the papers, going on like nothing has ever happened. And I'm... a puddle of emotions."

Dr. Morgan straightened his glasses. "I am aware that some of the other survivors are also having a hard time, Charlie. You are not the only First Class passenger seeking psychiatric help. I have heard that one of the other gentlemen has already turned a pistol on himself, ending his life. There are others who may never recover, Charlie. You were wise to ask for help. It will do your friends good for you to keep an eye on them."

While he was glad to know he wasn't alone, the stories were tragic. "I'm very sorry to hear that, Dr. Morgan."

"Why don't we start at the beginning, Charlie. Why don't you tell me about what it was like to board *Titanic*? Slowly, over the course of the next few weeks—months if necessary—we'll get to the dismal part, the part of the story you're trying so hard not to remember. I believe, if we go slowly and truly work through all that has happened, we will restore you to your former self. What do you think?"

"I like that idea very much," Charlie nodded, relieved that they would take it slow and that he wouldn't have to try to remember the worst of it right from the beginning.

"Very well, then. Charlie, tell me about how you arrived on *Titanic*."

With a deep breath, Charlie thought about the beginning of the story and replied, "I boarded *Titanic* at the last moment in an attempt to change my fate. I had no idea I was really walking into the hands of destiny. It's funny how we think we can control our lives, but honestly, *Titanic* has taught me that we are all part of a much bigger picture, and while we may have a bit of influence on our circumstances, there's no avoiding the inevitable." He set his hat next to him on the sofa and ran his hand through his hair. "Do you believe in fate, Dr. Morgan?"

"I'm not sure, Charlie. Do you?"

"Yes," he said without a moment's thought. "And fate had decided I was going to wed Mary Margaret Westmoreland or die in the process. As a matter of fact, I did die—and even that wasn't enough. Thankfully, my fate is one I no longer wish to escape."

Dr. Morgan smiled. "Tell me about that first day—when you came aboard."

Charlie closed his eyes and remembered that morning, only a few months ago. He could smell the sea air, feel the breeze on his face. He was standing on the deck, looking down. A crowd stood on the pier waving, shouting goodbye. The vast ocean spread out all around them. And there, below him, looking around at the crowd as if she was missing someone, was the most beautiful blonde woman he'd ever seen. He'd had no idea the person she was looking for was him.

Sitting next to Meg alone in the overly opulent dining room, Charlie couldn't help but smile. Even though the voices still clung to him, he had a feeling Dr. Morgan could actually help. For the first time since he'd arrived back in New York City, he felt hopeful that he could return to his former self.

"You look awfully chipper this evening," Meg said, as she took a sip of her soup. "I suppose that means Dr. Morgan was helpful?"

"It does," Charlie admitted, noting how lovely she looked in the light blue gown she wore. It made her eyes sparkle. "He really does know precisely what to ask and how to ask it."

"Are you studying him as much as he's studying you?" she asked, amusement pulling at the corners of her exquisite lips.

He looked at her for a moment, his head tipped to the side a bit, seeing if she would break into a giggle. She did. "And what if I am?"

"No, that's fine," she replied. "So long as you feel he's helping you."

"I *feel* he's helping me or he is actually helping me?"

"Either." She shrugged and carefully raised a spoonful of broth to her mouth. "Wouldn't he argue that perception is reality?"

"I believe you're mistaking him for a philosopher," Charlie noted.

"Two very similar fields."

"I suppose so, but I'm not sure Dr. Morgan would agree that thinking one is being helped is the same as actually being helped. And I'm sure he would say he is actually capable of helping me."

Meg nodded, though Charlie didn't know if that meant she was truly convinced. "I hope so. I'd love to see you jovial all the time, the way that you used to be."

"That was you, Meg. Believe me, I didn't walk around the streets of New York City with a sappy grin on my face all of the time before we met."

She raised an eyebrow. "Does that mean I don't make you happy anymore?"

"Of course not," he said with a sly smile. "It only means that I've lost a bit of myself. Now that I'm seeing Dr. Morgan, I think he shall help me find it."

She wiped the corners of her mouth with a napkin. "I hope so."

"You know, I'm sure he could help you, too. If you'd let him."

Setting the napkin back on her lap, she asked, "What is it, exactly, that you feel I need help with?"

"You've been through quite a bit, Meg. Perhaps it isn't healthy to push everything down inside." He knew he was walking a thin line between offering a suggestion and upsetting her, so he attempted to be nonchalant.

"I'm fine, Charlie. In fact, knowing that my uncle is gone for good has renewed my energy. I feel much more content than I have in years."

He nodded, not sure he believed her but certain she believed herself. "That's wonderful to hear."

"With the wedding approaching, and the knowledge that we will soon be man and wife, I haven't the time to be upset about anything. I'm just fine, Charlie. I assure you."

"I'm glad, Meg," he said, deciding to let it go. Perhaps it was true. Perhaps she had found a way to deal with all of the horrific experiences of her short life. "Tell me how it went today. Did you decide on a pattern for your dress?"

"I did," she said, her face lighting up. "More importantly, Grace and I have reached an understanding."

"Really?" Charlie asked, perking up a bit. "That's great."

"Yes, she cares so much for you. It's no surprise she wanted to protect you."

"And control everything," Charlie muttered, returning his attention to the bowl in front of him.

"That may be true," Meg shrugged, "but I don't mind. I've never been one for throwing parties or events. I'm certain the wedding ceremony will be lovely."

"And you're sure you don't mind postponing the honeymoon?" She'd already agreed the first time he'd mentioned it, on their way back from Southampton, but he felt guilty asking her to put it off.

"Not at all," she replied. "In fact, I'm relieved that I'll have the chance to move in here and get settled into the role of being your wife straight away."

Charlie smiled and let go of a deep breath. "Good. I feel I must return to work and get things straightened out with the textile factory as well."

"It will be nice to see Westmoreland Textiles up and running properly again," Meg noted.

"And once we are ready, I shall take you wherever you'd like to go. France, Egypt, China—anywhere."

A grin broke out on Meg's face. "I think I should like to see America," she replied.

Charlie raised an eyebrow. "America? Why is that?"

"Why not? I've always dreamt of visiting, and now here I am. When you first awoke, you asked if we could take a slow train. Let's do that instead. Let's go to St. Louis, and then on to the Grand Canyon. We'll go to California and see the Pacific Ocean. We'll stick our toes in the water but won't get in. What do you think?"

"I think...that sounds lovely," Charlie replied, smiling widely at her. "As long as you are there, I'm sure it will be wonderful."

"You know I'll be there, Charlie. You can't get away from me. Surely you must know that by now."

"Luckily, I don't want to," Charlie said with a wink, and he wished the next two weeks would fly by so he could finally make Meg his wife at long last.

CHAPTER FOURTEEN

Meg stood in a room crowded with over four hundred people, approximately a dozen of whom she knew, and that was being generous with the definition of the word "knew." Wearing her long white gown, which poofed out around her in just the fashion that would've made her absent mother beside herself, she shook hands with faceless, nameless well-wishers and smiled until her cheeks began to ache.

Charlie seemed every bit the carefree soul he'd been the night they'd fallen in love at the Third Class dance. That was the Charlie she pictured most times when she thought of the man she loved. He'd been there, too, at dinner that night in the First Class dining hall—at least until she'd shouted at Mrs. Appleton and run out, leading Madeline Astor to reveal Meg's true identity.

But that Charlie was here now, or at least he appeared to be, though she thought his expression showed from time to time that he was still battling the voices. Perhaps Dr. Morgan's tactics were helping him win the fight.

Ruth looked adorable in her pink dress, which hung to the floor, nearly tripping her as she danced around her parents. Kelly had stood beside Meg, along with Grace, and Charlie had been proud to have both Walter—who turned out to be every bit as silly as Charlie had described—and Quincy by his side.

Now, it was all over, except for the reception. Then, Meg would return to Charlie's house—the house they would share together—and embark on a new adventure, that of being Mrs. Charles Ashton.

"Meg Ashton," she said aloud, once the last of the well-wishers had moved along. "What do you think?"

Charlie was already grinning from ear to ear, but his face brightened even more. "I think it sounds remarkable."

"That's my name now, you know? Meg Ashton."

"What about Mary Margaret Ashton?" he asked, leaning close to her ear.

"Heaven's no. That's such an awful name anyway. Mary Margaret. There's way too many Mars."

He laughed so loudly a few people standing nearby turned to look. "Are you going to give up Westmoreland forever? It was your father's name."

"That's the only reason I can tolerate it at all," she admitted. "Perhaps Meg Westmoreland Ashton, though that's very complicated. Meg Ashton is nice and crisp."

He bent down and kissed her temple near the veil that hung over the back of her head. It was made of tulle, an idea her mother-in-law had come up with after she insisted the veil have no lace, and it had been fastened over the back of her hair the entire ceremony, with only one thin layer needing to be flipped back once she was standing in front of the altar—on Jonathan's arm. She couldn't think of another soul worthy of giving her away in lieu of her father.

"Do you know all of these people?" she whispered while he was so close to her.

"No, only about half. Possibly," he admitted.

Meg giggled, glad she wasn't the only one who felt like she didn't quite belong. "Grace has planned for us to cut that enormous wedding cake and then everyone shall have a slice."

"Cut the cake? You and me? How interesting."

"Well, I think only one piece. She is a bit of a trendsetter, that sister of yours."

"She's yours now, too," Charlie reminded her.

"She suggested I smear some all over your face. She thought it would be a lark."

His eyebrows raised. "And did you agree to this prank?"

Meg grinned at him slyly. "I suppose you'll have to wait and see." She had no intention of playing the joke, though she thought it might be fun to see him squirm a bit between now and then, unsure of what she might do.

"It would be a shame to get cake all over that dress, but if I'm forced to defend myself...."

It was her turn to raise an eyebrow. He began to laugh, and she resisted the urge to elbow him in the ribs, since his mother had asked that they please attempt to be as serious as possible when standing at the head of the room.

Grace walked in front of them, looking as though she was on her way to direct the Master of Ceremonies to get on with it, her pink gown nearly dragging on the floor as she went. Once she'd passed through her line of vision, Meg's eyes fell on another somewhat familiar face. Stella.

"Well, Mrs. Cartwright doesn't disappoint does she?" she asked, turning her face so that she was practically speaking into Charlie's shoulder.

"What's that?" he asked, turning to look. She pulled him back around.

"She looks as if she'd like to have my head on a platter."

He laughed. "She just doesn't like to be proven wrong, that's all."

Meg took another glance in her direction. Stella was still stabbing Meg with her cold eyes. "Perhaps I should say something to her."

"What? Why?" Charlie asked, taking his new bride by the shoulders. "Meg, she doesn't matter. We'll hardly ever see her. She's jealous, and that's all right. She'll get over it. Just let her be."

"But... I hate that she's so angry."

"Meg, you can't make everyone happy all the time," he reminded her. "There are plenty of other people who are very happy for us. Let's concentrate on them, shall we?"

Just as he finished the sentence, one last guest they hadn't yet seen stopped behind Meg and said, "Well, if it isn't the prettiest little miss this side of the Atlantic!"

Before she even turned around, Meg recognized the voice. "Molly!" she shouted, wrapping her arms around Mrs. Molly Brown. "I had heard you were out of town."

"I wouldn't have missed this for the world!" She let go of Meg and turned to Charlie. "You look so handsome, Charlie!"

"Lovely to see you, Molly," he said, embracing her. "If it weren't for you, this day may never have happened."

"Nonsense," she replied, waving him off. "All I did was keep you kids pointed in the right direction. Anyhow, I just wanted to tell you congratulations."

"You're staying aren't you?" Meg asked, hopeful she'd have the opportunity to talk to the eccentric millionaire again before the affair was over.

"Yes, of course," Molly assured them. "But it looks like Mr. Big Britches over there is about to make an announcement." She was gesturing at the Master of Ceremonies who was doing his best to get everyone's attention without using any loud noisemakers, as Charlie and Meg had requested.

Eventually, the tall, thin man Meg had learned was called Mr. Rudolph announced it was time for the first dance and he went about organizing partners, quite a feat in such a crowded room.

"Meg Ashton," Charlie said, bowing low, "would you do me the honor of dancing our first dance together as man and wife?"

She took his outstretched hand. "Yes, Charles Ashton. It would be my pleasure." He led her to the dance floor, and she wondered what might have happened if she'd gone to Alise's ball. They would've shared their first dance that day instead of on *Titanic*. Would everything have turned out the same? Would they still have sailed on *Titanic*?

The song was a lively one, and Meg lost herself as Charlie twirled her around the dance floor. As she spun and whirled, she completely forgot the hundreds of eyes fixated on her and focused only on Charlie's smile. His eyes twinkled, and she could hear him laughing over the sound of the music. Despite all that they'd been through, she was his wife at last. Nothing would ever change that.

SHE'D BEEN in Charlie's bedroom a few times before, but this time was certainly different. Butterflies fluttered around her stomach, some of the nervous variety, but most of them fueled by excitement.

They were sitting on the edge of his bed, the door closed and locked, the drapes pulled tightly. She knew that there were a few servants elsewhere in the house, but they would leave the couple undisturbed at least until mid-morning. Glancing up at him, she could see that he felt much the same way that she did.

"It turned out quite well, don't you think?" Charlie asked, clearly meaning the wedding.

"Yes," Meg nodded.

"Even though a few guests certainly had too much to drink."

She giggled, thinking of one older gentleman who had made quite a spectacle of himself trying to climb atop one of the tables to dance. He had been escorted out, but Meg was thankful for the diversion. For once, everyone wasn't staring at her.

The veil was gone, but she still wore her gown, a thousand pins keeping her hair up. Charlie had on his suit pants and shirt, his tie loosened, his jacket long discarded. The room was lit by a few candles, but she could still see him well enough, particularly the twinkle in his eyes.

He slipped his hand onto the back of her gown, making her catch her breath. "There must be... a million buttons back here."

"One for each dollar your sister spent on the wedding," Meg joked. He laughed. "I wanted a zipper, but your sister said that was 'too modern.'"

"Rather too practical," he noted. She felt his fingers on the back of her head. "And is there a hairpin for every button?"

"It simply wouldn't do for them not to match," Meg shrugged.

Once again, the sound of Charlie's laughter filled the room. He removed his hand from behind her and took her hand in his. "Meg, I must admit... I'm a bit frightened."

She glanced up at him, her eyebrows raised. "Why is that?"

"I'm afraid I might hurt you. Or scare you. Or break you."

She tightened the grip on his hand. "You won't, Charlie."

"No?"

"No." She pulled the skirt of her gown around so that she could face him. "Charlie, you really needn't worry about any of that. There's a distinct difference between the things that were done to me and the loving touch of my husband who I give myself to freely."

His eyebrows arched, and Meg thought she saw tears in his eyes. "You know I would never do anything to hurt your or make you uncomfortable, don't you?"

"Yes, of course."

"At any time, if you feel you can't continue, please let me know. I do love you, Meg, more than anything. I can't take back what's happened to you, but I can promise you, it will never happen again."

Tears were streaming down her cheeks now, but she didn't feel the need to hide them or force them to stop. Never showing weakness or vulnerability had been her battle cry for so long, but with Charlie, she knew she was perfectly safe to show her true self. The monster was gone, forever. There was no need to push him down inside the box in the back of her mind because the box was empty.

Meg slowly leaned forward and slid her hands up the side of

Charlie's face. "I love you. Thank you for fighting for me, even when I was the one you were fighting against."

"Thank you for bringing me back from the dead." His lips found hers, and any fears or hesitations were all gone as Meg surrendered herself fully to the man fate had chosen for her such a very long time ago.

EPILOGUE

April 15, 1913

C harlie paced the hallway outside his own bedroom, unable to sit for more than a few moments at a time. Jonathan sat watching him, an amused expression on his face, as he wandered from one end of the hall, turned sharply on his heel, and headed back.

"You are going to wear the carpet out," Mr. Ashton mused, also watching his son.

"Perhaps if this wasn't taking so long, it wouldn't be necessary," Charlie replied curtly.

"As excruciating as it is for you, imagine how Meg feels," Jonathan reminded him.

He had a point. She'd been in the bedroom with Dr. Shaw, Kelly, and his mother for over four hours now. Every once in a while, he'd hear a small whimper, but for the most part, she was silent. He imagined that had more to do with her mettle than a lack of pain.

"It shouldn't be too much longer now," his father assured him.

"I should hope not," Charlie muttered, turning and heading back the opposite direction. Looking down, he thought to himself, *"We can always purchase new carpet."*

His own thoughts were not alone in his head, however, and even though he'd been seeing Dr. Morgan for over nine months, from time to time, he'd still hear the voices. Now, they were more like background noise, like something one might overhear in a restaurant. The violent thrashing sounds had all but faded, the flickers of faces saving themselves for times when he was most stressed or anxious. Right now, he was both, and the other passengers in the water seemed set on reminding him that he did not wait alone.

Almost another hour went by before his mother came to the bedroom door. "It shouldn't be long now," she said, stepping out into the hallway. "We can see the baby's head."

"Oh, he's crowning!" Mr. Ashton explained, seeming proud to have known the medical term.

"Yes, and Meg is doing splendidly. She'll start pushing, and soon you'll be a father, Charlie."

The words were said with such pride, Charlie almost smiled, but concern for his wife and their child prevented him from doing so. "I wish I could come in."

"Don't be silly, Charlie," Pamela said with a laugh. "A father in the birthing room." She shook her head as if it was the most ridiculous notion she'd ever heard. "I shall let you know when we have a baby, though I think you might hear for yourself."

Charlie nodded his thanks and went back about his pacing.

"I have cigars all ready," Mr. Ashton said. "It's a tradition, you know?"

Charlie didn't answer. A few moments later, Meg's whimpers turned into grunts punctuated with sharp screams, and he wanted desperately to enter the bedroom to make sure she was all right. He could hear Dr. Shaw's reassuring voice letting her know she was doing just fine and reminding her to bear down and push, but it wasn't quite enough. Just when Charlie was about to throw tradition aside and let himself in, a new sound filled his ears.

It started off as a shrill screech, but within a second or two, it morphed into the most beautiful sound he'd ever heard. Turning to face his father, he asked, "Is that my baby? Is that the sound of my baby crying?"

Mr. Ashton was on his feet, clapping Charlie on the back. "I believe it is, my boy," he replied. "Congratulations."

While Charlie accepted the hugs and handshakes from his father and Jonathan, he anxiously awaited his mother's return to the door. It couldn't have been more than five minutes, but it felt like an hour.

With a flourish, Pamela opened the double doors. "The baby is here! And Meg is doing just fine."

"Let me in," Charlie insisted, nearly pushing past her.

"Dr. Shaw isn't quite finished cleaning up," his mother cautioned.

"I don't care," Charlie replied, waiting for her to move her arm, which she did with a smile.

He paid no mind to Dr. Shaw still seated at the end of the bed doing something under the sheet Charlie probably didn't want to know about. Meg's face was beaming, lighting the entire room. Kelly was next to her, but she moved aside as Charlie entered.

He approached cautiously, but even from across the room, he could see the tiny bundle she held to her chest. Tears of joy slipped from his eyes and he let them run. "Hi, Da," Meg said, in a soft voice, turning the baby as if the voice came from the tiniest lips Charlie had ever seen.

"My God, what a beautiful face," Charlie said, bending to kiss Meg on the forehead. She tilted her head so that he found her lips, instead. Turning his attention back to the baby, he continued to stare into a pair of blue eyes that seemed to match Meg's almost perfectly.

"This is Henry," Meg said, as Charlie sat down on the bed next to her. "And he has ten fingers and ten toes. He's absolutely flawless."

"Henry," Charlie repeated. "I have a son?"

"You do. A perfect baby boy," Meg assured him. "Would you like to hold him?"

"More than anything," Charlie replied. Carefully, he took the baby from Meg's arms and held him nestled against his chest. Henry made a small gurgling noise, and looking into his eyes, Charlie saw nothing but happiness—a new beginning, a new chance to start life afresh with every opportunity before them. Any doubts he'd ever had about the existence of God were washed away as he marveled at the amazing being before him. "You did an excellent job, Meg. He really is perfect."

"Why thank you," she giggled as Dr. Shaw assured her everything was just fine. "You may have had something to do with it."

"No, all of the credit must go to you, my love." As much as he wanted to hold his son forever, he realized Meg wanted him, so he carefully handed him over, staying right there beside her, his arm around her shoulders.

"I've always wanted a little boy," Meg mused. "And now I have one. A perfect one." She looked tired, and Charlie thought she might fall asleep.

Others seemed to notice as well. "We'll give you a few moments," Dr. Shaw said. "I'll return in a bit to check on you."

Pamela and Kelly both smiled reassuringly at the happy family before they made their way out of the room.

Meg tilted her head into Charlie's shoulder. Looking down, he could see that Henry was dozing off. The room was silent, and he held his wife and gazed upon his son's face in pure wonder and joy. Then, it occurred to him that the room truly was completely silent. Not a whisper, not a shout, not a thrash, nothing. The only sound he could hear were the breaths of his wife and son and his own heartbeat pounding in his chest. For the first time since *Titanic*, Charlie enjoyed the sound of silence. Gazing down at the face of his son, he reveled in the thought that life did go on after all, and the morbid remembrances he had from that night were drowned out once and for all by the love he felt for his family and this new beginning.

The End

A NOTE FROM THE AUTHOR

Thank you so much for reading *Residuum*. I hope that you've enjoyed Meg and Charlie's story. When I first wrote *Titanic*, I didn't know for sure how it would be received, but I'm so happy to see how well-loved these characters have become. Can you believe that I originally wrote *Titanic* in three days? Only one scene was later revised before the editing process.

If you enjoyed *Residuum*, please consider leaving a review on Amazon, as well as Bookbub and/or Goodreads. Reviews help other people know whether or not they will enjoy the books. They also help me decide what type of stories to write next. If readers hadn't let me know they loved *Titanic*, I may never have written *Prelude* or Residuum

Let's stay in touch! You can download *Leaving Ginny*, another historical romance, based on my full-length novel, *Beneath the Inconstant Moon*, for free when you sign up for my newsletter. You can find it here, on Instafreebie:

https://claims.instafreebie.com/free/Eypqj

You can find my other books in the "Also by ID Johnson" section. Thank you again for your support!

ALSO BY ID JOHNSON

Stand Alone Titles

Deck of Cards

(*steamy romance*)

Cordia's Will: A Civil War Story of Love and Loss

(*clean romance/historical*)

The Doll Maker's Daughter at Christmas

(*clean romance/historical*)

Beneath the Inconstant Moon

(*literary fiction/historical psychological thriller*)

Pretty Little Monster

(*young adult/suspense*)

The Journey to Normal: Our Family's Life with Autism (*nonfiction*)

The Clandestine Saga series

(*paranormal romance*)

Transformation

Resurrection

Repercussion

Absolution

Illumination

Destruction

A Vampire Hunter's Tale (based on The Clandestine Saga)

(paranormal/alternate history)

Aaron

Jamie

Elliott

The Chronicles of Cassidy (based on The Clandestine Saga)

(young adult paranormal)

So You Think Your Sister's a Vampire Hunter?

Who Wants to Be a Vampire Hunter?

How Not to Be a Vampire Hunter

My Life As a Teenage Vampire Hunter

Ghosts of Southampton series

(historical romance)

Prelude

Titanic

Residuum

Heartwarming Holidays Sweet Romance series

(Christian/clean romance)

Melody's Christmas

Christmas Cocoa

Winter Woods

Waiting On Love

Shamrock Hearts

A Blossoming Spring Romance

Firecracker!

Falling in Love

Thankful for You

Melody's Christmas Wedding

The New Year's Date

Reaper's Hollow

(paranormal/urban fantasy)

Ruin's Lot

Ruin's Promise

Ruin's Legacy

Collections

Ghosts of Southampton Books 0-2

Reaper's Hollow Books 1-3

The Clandestine Saga Books 1-3

For updates, visit www.authoridjohnson.blogspot.com

Follow on Twitter @authoridjohnson

Find me on Facebook at www.facebook.com/IDJohnsonAuthor

Instagram: @authoridjohnson

Amazon: ID Johnson